Become

Freyja Wolfe

Always follow your heart!
xo

LISA MERRAI

ISBN: 978-1-66780-739-3 (print)
ISBN: 978-1-66780-740-9 (eBook)

CHAPTER ONE

THE SIGNAL IS GETTING WEAKER

She walked into the building as though it was a surreal painting. The old school structure dripped and drooped, bending towards her melancholy mood as she plodded up the main steps. The interior white walls rippled like rain puddles as she passed by. The fluorescent hall lights flickered and roiled across dark skies above a tumultuous tiled sea. Freyja made her way into the illusionary headwinds, heaving her weight into the exit door. The brisk morning air swirled around her. She patted and whisked the dread from her clothes as she made her way towards the outbuilding and code-compliant ramp. She resisted the urge to run the other way, resigned to the walls that held an eternity of minutes and hours between her and freedom.

Freyja opened the door to a crackling voice, "Welcome to the real world . . ."

In classroom 101, students didn't try to pretend they could escape their box, their track through the system. They didn't imagine themselves as president, famous athletes, or admired celebrities. The stark honesty of their frailty, profound limitations, and deep appreciation for the simplest pleasures gave Freyja the courage to leave her fears and prejudices at the door. On her difficult days as the student aide, their courage was an antidote to her self-pitying. How bad could her life even be? At some point, she had choices they would likely never have. She had no idea that she would be crossing such a broad threshold between two worlds. She never imagined her life would be forever altered in that room.

The back door rattled loudly with the brisk autumn air blowing across the ramp as Freyja stepped over the threshold. Ben, holding court in the room, leaned into his dictation microphone and began narrating things that occupied his mind, most often his favorite lines from movies.

"Do not try to bend the spoon. That's impossible. Instead, only try to realize the truth," Ben whispered loudly to no one in particular.

"Hey, Spoon Boy, how ya doing?" Freyja asked.

"I'm trying to free your mind, Neo. But I can only show you the door," Ben replied.

Freyja chuckled at Ben's repartee and dropped her backpack next to the door. The day's agenda lay on top of a nearby table. She murmured out loud to no one in particular, "Ben has a math check. Ally has reading. Greg has speech therapy."

A stack of student folders sat untouched from the previous afternoon. Freyja realized that the teacher, Mr. Berg, was snoring loudly in the big chair. The stout, balding man often snuck in an afternoon nap, but this was a bit early.

She tapped him on the shoulder. "Hey, Mr. Berg, I'm here."

Mr. Berg mumbled and whisked her hand away with an awkward swipe, "Okay, just a second . . ." he slurred. A faint cloud of alcohol lingered around him.

"Seriously?" Freyja said a little too loudly.

Greg stuttered and parroted her, "Seriously . . . seriously."

Ben's voice cracked as he began coughing and gasping for air, slamming his fist suddenly on his desk.

"Hey, Ben, you okay?" Freyja took note of his posture and demeanor. He was prone to outbursts, like yelling random words or phrases, but sometimes they preceded a partial or petite mal seizure. She had learned to sense the difference as she had gotten to know him and because she had seizures as a child. She knew well what it was like to feel frozen in time, suspended outside of your own body. Medication controlled hers now, but Ben's were more delicate and complicated. He had a VNS, or a vagal nerve stimulator, implant to help with the worst attacks. So far, she had only seen the magnet used once.

Ben's lips turned faintly blue as he slapped himself in the face.

Freyja moved quickly to touch the back of Ben's chair. She had been trained not to handle him directly. She had learned this the hard way on her first day when he went into a fit of screaming after she innocently squeezed his arm. His autism made him extremely sensitive to touch and sound. Not many students wanted to be special needs aides, but Freyja fell in love with these students. For years, they were the only people in the world who were truly happy to see her. Most days, when she arrived in class, they would clap or cheer her arrival. But, today, something was off.

Ben jerked his chair back and forth and started flapping his hands frantically. His gesticulations grew wilder, and he slapped himself again, hard.

"Mr. Berg! Ben needs help!" She sensed that Ben might be having a seizure.

Mr. Berg roused to the commotion and Freyja's urgent tone. He swiveled in his chair and fumbled to his feet. "Oh . . . oh! Hey, what's going on, buddy? Let's see. Yes. Something is happening. Let's find your box. Where's your little magnet thing?" Disoriented, Mr. Berg hunted the desk for Ben's equipment.

"It's okay, Ben. I'm here." Freyja patted Ben's chair, hoping she could keep him focused on her.

Ben grunted and moaned woefully. His glasses slipped off his face and hit the floor. His dark hair buffered his headbutting as Freyja tried to grab his sleeves and gently move his clawing hands from his face and eyes to the desk.

"Eeeeeeeeee," Ally, a newer part-time student with cerebral palsy, squealed nervously from her wheelchair in the corner. Her right hand twitched as she reached for the controller to turn her chair away from the excitement.

"Ben, listen. Look at me." Freyja tapped his sleeve.

He dropped his head onto the desk in a loud bang.

Greg, a student with Down's syndrome, wandered over to Ben's side and repeated what Freyja had just said, "Ben, listen. Ben, listen." He paced next to Ben, reaching out his hand to touch Ben's thick mop of hair, but recoiled his hand as if he had touched a flame. Greg took another anxious track around the room. As he paced, he hummed. Ben rolled his head on the desk and moaned. Ally whimpered. Freyja held her breath as Mr. Berg continued to rummage through the drawers of his desk, searching for the VNS magnet.

"It's here. It's just . . . somewhere . . . here," Berg mumbled to himself.

The wall placard on Room 101 sloped to the right so that "Ed" was hidden behind a flier and read only "Special." If you were quite literal, it said, "Special Room." A room tethered to the world of normalcy by ramps and laws granting free and adequate access to education. Though the state provided supports in the form of teachers, aides, and educational plans as required by law, resources were always lacking, and the potential of their lives remained a roll of the dice. Though any student's actual potential in Roosevelt High School was a Venn diagram of effort and talent, these students floated in the space of hollow platitudes and earnest hopes.

"Progress, not perfection," Mr. Berg often mumbled the mantra that was more like a pep talk to himself.

When Freyja started as a freshman, she absently selected student aide as her first elective. She hoped to be stamping tardy slips, not helping student peers eat snacks, get to the bathroom, and access assistive technology.

Freyja learned long ago to avoid emotions and drama. As a child, her father deeply discouraged any kind of outbursts, calling edicts to run laps or work for hours doing farm chores "inner discipline." Freyja held memories of hiding in closets from his anger like abandoned boxes she never cared to excavate. In Room 101, her extraordinary sensitivity was like a stethoscope for wordless whispers. The messages between scripts and moans and mumblings had meaning to her. Alone and afraid was a familiar place and one she was able to escape by holding a light for others. The students appreciated her. She had their trust, and they had her heart.

Just then, Ben's agitation escalated. Bent forward, he began whacking his head repeatedly on his desk.

Freyja grabbed his crumpled sweatshirt on the floor and placed it as a cushion between his head and the desk. "Ben, I'm here! Let me help you."

Then he stopped. His head flopped over to the side, and his eyes rolled up into his head. Freyja glanced at the big digital clock hanging on the wall next to the door: 10:10:10. Berg hovered over his desk, still scratching his head in confusion. Freyja's heart began to pound—Ben was having a seizure.

The teachers kept Ben's seizure magnet activator for emergencies in a box on his desk with a laminated instruction sheet. The magnet was sometimes implanted in the chest next to the vagus nerve to interrupt seizures faster in severe cases.

"There you are!" Mr. Berg exclaimed upon discovering the device under some papers.

Ben's body quaked. His breath was erratic. Mr. Berg pried his arm up enough to trace the magnet line from his left armpit across to the center of his chest, following the basic instructions diagramed on the laminated sheet. Ben's body slumped in an instant.

Suddenly, the classroom phone rang. Freyja eyed the ivory phone sitting on the edge of Mr. Berg's desk as it rang once more before going silent.

"Uh, should we call 911 or Ben's parents?" she asked.

Mr. Berg slowly collected himself. "Call the office. Have them follow protocol. Tell them it's an emergency."

"Greg, stay right here, okay?"

Greg hovered over them anxiously. "Stay right here . . . Stay right here."

Freyja rushed to the phone and picked up the receiver. *How do I call the office?* She hit a few different buttons as the labels and numbers were unclear. Then, Freyja received a painful, forceful blow to the back of her head. Her vision went black, and she crumpled to the ground. She was aware enough to instinctively protect her head with her arms. She rolled slightly to spy Ben's vacant eyes gazing down at her. He turned and picked up a chair and lifted it high over his head.

"Ben! *No!*"

Freyja scrambled back away from him on her palms and heels, but he kept coming towards her with the chair.

"I'm trying to free your mind, Neo," he said with an eerie calmness, "but I can only show you the door."

Ben's pupils engulfed his icy blue eyes, making his expression deadly and haunting. His six-foot frame towered menacingly over her. He kept repeating lines from *The Matrix* as he advanced on Freyja, who frantically searched for a way out.

Ben froze like a robotic statue as Mr. Berg tried to grab the chair from his hands. Freyja seized the chance and sprang over to try to protect the others. Greg was behind Ben. Ben gave up the chair, but continued to move forward threateningly.

"Ben, wake up! You're okay now. You are safe! It's over."

Freyja grabbed the back of another chair and shoved it between them as Ben lunged at her once again.

"You must see it for yourself," Ben spoke in a lucid monotone.

He ripped the chair away from her with alarming force and thrust it across the room. Freyja raced to the opposite side of the room to draw him away from the other students, while Mr. Berg wobbled, grasping at Ben, who continued to evade his grip. Mr. Berg finally grabbed ahold of Ben's wrists and wrangled his arms up around him in kind of a pretzel hold, called a "safety hug."

"Shhhh. Ben, you are safe. Calm. Calm…" Mr. Berg whispered into his ear in between heavy breaths, trying to soothe him and hold him at the same time. "Ben, listen to me. Please."

Ben writhed and kicked, and then just stopped. Mr. Berg winced as he held Ben tightly to his chest.

Freyja gasped. Ben's big eyes appeared sad and scared, a tiny bead of sweat trickling down his cheek. Freyja reached out to just lightly wipe the sweat away, to reassure him that she wasn't angry with him, and he was going to be okay. In a flash, he bit her hand, deep into her palm. The pain it caused shot through her like lightning.

"Ow! Ben!"

She yanked away in horror at the blood streaming from her hand. It was a deep scarlet like thick wine.

Ally was now shrieking from her chair, "No-no! No-no! No-no!"

"Are you okay, Freyja?" asked Mr. Berg.

"Are you okay?" repeated Greg, whose face was pale with concern. "Greg, not okay."

"I . . . don't . . . know . . ." Freyja whimpered.

"Freyja, I'm so sorry. You need to go to the nurse now. I've got Ben. Tell Principal Stein's office to send someone." Mr. Berg chanted some soothing words into Ben's ear. Then, as Ben began to relax, Mr. Berg turned to Freyja, "Go, go now."

"Okay. Are you sure? I mean. If you are sure . . ." The pain in her hand was sharp and pulsing as she squeezed the wound with her right hand.

"I'm sorry. Ben's never been violent like this before. You didn't do anything wrong," Mr. Berg said soberly.

Ben, now slumped like a rag doll in Mr. Berg's arms, turned his head towards Freyja and said, "Wake up . . ."

Freyja didn't understand his words nor what possessed him to attack her. She folded her injured hand in her shirt and headed towards the main building.

Freyja found the bathroom just inside the doors. The dim fluorescent lights cast a sickly pall over the chipped tile, the dilapidated metal dividers, and the porcelain commodes. Freyja went straight to the closest sink and turned on the faucet to rinse her bloody hand beneath ice-cold water. She pulled off the rings from her inflamed and numb hand. The sensation was like a burning fire as the water flowed over and into her wound. She grimaced hard.

Then, she felt something else in there—deep and sharp. On close inspection, her breath stopped. There *was* something in there! It was a small clear bloodied cylinder. It was smaller than a sliver, and it poked out of her flesh like a thorn. Freyja's mind numbed. After a minute of hesitating to get help, she took a deep breath, gritted her teeth from the oncoming pain, and then pinched the tiny object to slowly pull it out.

"What the hell . . .?" she muttered to herself, holding it up and narrowing her view of it. It was a tiny chip, or maybe a piece of cartilage, except it wasn't a natural thing. Instead, it was sleek and smooth and had small hairlike wires protruding from one end. She inspected it closer; inside the translucent tubelike body was a faint glowing light.

Suddenly, vertigo washed over her, while a tremendous gong barreled through her head like church bells. She gripped the sink in front of her, dropping the device into it while clinging on to steady herself. The bathroom walls and ceiling reverberated with warping light waves as though everything around her was rocking on the high seas. She gripped the sink and tried to connect to her reflection in the mirror. Her façade rippled beyond recognition.

There was a cacophony of voices as though every conversation in the school was streaming into her head. Chills and heat alternated in radiating goosebumps across her skin. A pungent smell of roses overpowered the bathroom bleach odors. Her senses were overrun entirely, as her mind felt squeezed through an impossible vortex, like being reborn into the stark light of a hospital labor room. She screamed as her body heat up like a furnace.

To her great surprise, the old scars on her right arm began to glisten and glow. They slowly lit up like a firefly's belly. "What . . . the . . .?"

Then a single voice said, "Hurry up. The signal is getting weaker . . ."

Freyja searched around the bathroom for the voice, as she grew desperate to hang on.

"Who said that?" she mumbled, and she then finally passed out.

CHAPTER TWO

GROWING PAINS

Freyja's body crumpled in a ball as she recovered her senses. The icy tiles brought her back to the high school. She was still here, though her head and hand throbbed terribly. As she slowly sat herself up, Freyja remembered the creaky wooden floor in her aunt's kitchen when she was a child. Her aunt Lucy called them spells. She would bring her a blanket and glass of water, allowing her time to come around.

"Darling, are you alright?" Aunt Lucy's face and big almond eyes played like an old film in Freyja's memory.

A few years ago, after Freyja was sent to live with the Rahumans, her foster family, a new doctor had called her spells petit mal or absence seizures. He said she would outgrow them and prescribed some medications that she had to take daily to keep them at bay. She hadn't had one in so long that she forgot what it was like to suddenly go black. She sometimes imagined a puppet master holding the strings to her body and brain, pulling her this way and that, testing her will against theirs.

Freyja sat up, orienting herself to what had just happened. Her ears were ringing faintly. This time something changed. There was blood still dripping from her hand.

What happened to that strange implanted device? Where did it go?

Her hand ached. A translucent light emanated from her arm. "What?" she gasped. Her scars began to shimmer ever so faintly. Then, one by one, the jagged lines and swirls appeared to turn on and somehow tune as though they were dials on a machine.

Freyja caught her breath. *My lightning.*

She had been struck by lightning as a girl, around five. The scars appeared because of the intense energy that had ripped through her body. If you survive a lightning strike, there are often fractal-shaped scars left somewhere on the body. The way Aunt Lucy told the story, Freyja was chosen by the Gods of Light, and someday their gifts would be revealed. Her parents told her she was fortunate to be alive. Lighting storms were quite common in the mountains where she grew up. A tree in their yard had been struck several times before, but never a person. She was forbidden from playing next to that tree after that.

Now, in the Roosevelt High bathroom, her scars were aglow and faintly warming too. Freyja gasped, wondering if perhaps her aunt's tales were not so made up.

She steadied herself next to the bloodied sink, spying her ghastly appearance in the mirror. Ambered roots peeked out from her blackened crown. Freyja had carefully assembled a moody introvert uniform, black kohl eyeliner, a collection of symbolic rings, and a black suede choker. The choker was the only thing that visually camouflaged the few scars on her neck. She preferred not to have to explain what all the faint spots were.

Freyja lifted her flannel shirt off her right shoulder to inspect her shoulder and arm. Her severe scars were all softly lit, like sunlight refracting on water. They mapped her shoulder and arm like rivers falling down the mountainside, cutting through muscle ridges, swirling into eddies of flesh, hugging the shoreline of her veins before tapering off the edge of a joint. Some of the scars were in distinct shapes and patterns, like an ancient map of a hidden treasure or a coded language she was to decipher.

The first day of school while in foster care had been a lesson in covering up. A kid had pointed to her arm and said she had cooties. A girl named Marley told him to shut up and that they were a secret language that only brilliant people could decode. Freyja and Marley became friends for a while. And then one day, Marley just turned on her for no reason, and they acted like strangers. After that, Freyja wore long sleeves and never spoke about scars or lightning or a secret language again.

The scars began vibrating, almost aching, which was a very strange sensation. Freyja quickly pulled her shirt back up and rolled her sleeves down, hugging her arm and rubbing it self-consciously. She ran her wounded hand under the cool tap water. Wincing at the pain, her mind raced with questions.

The class bell rang, and Freyja decided it was best to move on and get through the day. She grabbed some toilet paper from the stall behind her and wrapped her hand in a makeshift bandage. Still dazed, she staggered out of the bathroom and headed towards her locker.

"Hey!" shouted a familiar voice.

Freyja paused. She pushed ahead through the sea of faces, confident that he'd catch up.

"Wait for me!" he yelled. Nash tapped her shoulder as he plowed through the crowds. Black unruly hair, ice-blue eyes, and a devilish smile, Nash was her first real friend. In middle school, he gave her his only pencil and sat with her at the lunch table. "Hey, you! Where ya been?"

Freyja quickly whisked her injured arm into her shirt. "Hey . . ."

"What happened to you?" Nash asked.

"Uh . . . yeah . . . Ben bit me."

"Ben?"

"Yeah, he went nuts today. I don't know what hap—" Freyja slammed hard into someone passing by in the hall.

An imposing, athletic girl swung her thick mane like a whip. "Watch it!" growled Marley.

Freyja rolled her eyes. "Really?"

A posse of aggressive girls flanking Marley turned to glare at Freyja.

"You should watch where you are going!" growled Marley.

"Hey now, Marls, this is a public hallway," Nash chuckled. He put his fist up and slowly raised his middle finger at Marley. Then he winked.

Freyja pushed through the lineup. She had no interest in engaging with Marley.

Marley's snarl vanished as she flirted openly with Nash, touching her finger to her lips and sending him an air kiss.

"You are quite the viper, aren't you?" asked Nash, staring her down. Nash could charm a snake out of its venom. Although he made little effort, he was widely liked by everyone at Roosevelt.

"Whatever," Marley snapped. "Nathaniel, why do you let *her* drag you down? We are so much more fun!"

"Hey now, stay safe in these dangerous halls, okay?" Nash gave her a peace sign as he dashed off.

He raced through the crowds of students rushing towards the next period. "She's a piece of work," he said as he came alongside Freyja.

Nash was always the diplomat, neutralizing conflict everywhere he went. Freyja wasn't sure she would have any friends without him. He didn't seem to be bothered by her weird anti-social tendencies. She thought maybe he liked her precisely because she *wasn't* part of any cliques or groups, like an island with no wi-fi. He could pretend to be an outsider with another outsider. It was far easier to have one friend with few expectations than many with complex rules and obligations.

The hallway began to thin out as students reached their classes for the next period. As they walked past her science classroom, Mr. Franklin caught her eye. She would not be able to ditch that class now.

"Ugh. I hate this class," Freyja said.

"Good luck with that," said Nash as he sailed down the hall, whistling a tune to a song he was working on for his band.

Freyja swiveled back into Mr. Franklin's biology classroom, and took her seat.

"Let's get started," Mr. Franklin ordered, scooping a few strands of hair over his creeping bald spot. After more than thirty years at Roosevelt High, he was on the verge of either retirement or burnout. "So . . . cells. Let's begin with cells. How does a human grow from a single fertilized cell into an individual containing billions and trillions of cells?"

Danny, Mr. All-star, raised his hand, "Very *carefully*?"

The class snickered.

"Yes, Mr. Runyon. It is an exact dance. Remember we talked about the parent cell, the one your parents made when they made you, dividing into daughter cells?"

The class snickered again as Danny feigned offense at having girl genes.

"In about ten seconds, those daughter cells each split into another set of cells. In another ten seconds, those new four cells split into eight new cells. In less than two minutes, there are now nearly four thousand new cells. What can you do in two minutes, Mr. Runyon?"

The class jeered, and his buddies poked him.

Danny sat back, grinning, and said, "Winning shot from the free-throw line last Friday night, Mr. Franklin."

The class roared.

"Shhhh. Alright, alright. Seriously, can anyone tell me what happens when our cells multiply too quickly?" Mr. Franklin glanced around the classroom, hands on hips. He spied Freyja in the back avoiding eye contact. She knew the answer, but she hated speaking up. "Freyja, what do you say?"

Freyja shifted uncomfortably in her seat as every eye turned towards her. For most of her life, her school had been at her family's farm. Her teacher, her own aunt Lucy, had conducted a curriculum of interdisciplinary excellence worthy of any college in the state. The only other classmate was her pet lynx, Keyo. Any review of the literature would require learning about the country and culture from which it came. Likewise, any science study would need experiments and philosophy to understand the theory being tested. Her Aunt ended every lesson with, "And that is what we've been told."

Freyja missed her aunt. She really missed her mom and dad, what she could remember of them. She missed her pet lynx Keyo, the farm, the miles and miles of fields, and the magical woods, her home filled with curios and artifacts her parents brought from their travels. The day they took her aunt away was a nightmare that woke her nearly every night. The images pulsed with anxiety and confusion:

The panic in her aunt's eyes as they race down a fire road in the old beat-up wagon. The police sirens lighting up the forest highway's shadows as several cars force them off the road. Her aunt getting pulled out of the car by a uniformed officer.

She turns to Freyja and says, "Watch the skies, my love. Never forget who you are."

Despair washes over Freyja as she is led to the back of another police car. Keyo, her brown-spotted lynx, watches from the trees. Freyja sobs, reaching for her wild pet, for her aunt, for her freedom.

"What happens when cells multiply too quickly?" Mr. Franklin asked, drawing Freyja out of her dreaming.

"Cancer," she said.

"Very good," Mr. Franklin said with a wink. Then, he began to outline an experiment they would all conduct in pairs to better understand cell division and how it worked.

But Freyja was distracted. For as Mr. Franklin did this, a strange sensation rose in her chest. "Whoa!" she said, jumping. Her heart thumped, and she tried to shift the discomforting sensation away. "Ow!" Freyja jerked back again as an electric shock zinged through her fingers resting on her spiral notebook.

The pain stunned her. She gasped loud enough to attract quizzical looks from the students sitting beside her. Freyja grimaced and buried her face in her notebook, staring at her hands, wondering if she had a pin or needle jammed somewhere.

"Ms. Wolfe, perhaps you need to excuse yourself?" said Mr. Franklin, brow furrowed with concern.

The class laughed as Freyja grabbed the hall pass and quickly left the room. As she walked down the hallway, there was a current still running through her fingers. She lifted her hand. A luminescent wisp of energy fluttered between her fingers like a tangle of fine hair stuck to a sleeve. She tried to flick it off, and it vanished like mist and then returned as soon as she opened her fist to check. Her eyes grew wide.

What's happening to me? she thought.

Panicking, Freyja sprinted down the hallway to find her locker. Once there, she struggled with the combination. She had to use one hand, and it took her more than a minute to finally unlatch the metal door. She drew from it her notebook on the top shelf, and then paused at her reflection in the little mirror on the door. To her astonishment, her eyes were blazing with blinding fire. Her naturally blue-green eyes were consumed like embers by a smoldering swirl of reddish-orange and yellow flames, beaming out from an inner furnace. She blinked hard, and the sight vanished.

Slamming the door shut, Freyja tossed her skateboard along the floor, jumped on, and then kicked off as quickly as she could along the hallway and towards the west wing doors.

"Ms. Wolfe." Principal Stein rounded the corner from the entry hall where her office and the theatre were. Unfortunately, Stein had less humor than a British palace guard, and even less amusement for students out of class.

"Oh. Sorry," Freyja said weakly, and then hopped off the board, kicking it up into her hand. "I was late for class."

Stein cleared her throat and stepped back a bit to appraise her. "Where are you supposed to be?"

"Uh, biology. But... um... I actually need to go to the nurse." Freyja lifted her hand up to the principal, whose eyes widened at the sight of the reddening toilet paper bandage. One end of it was coming loose, adding to her desperate story. She grimaced to appear even more haggard.

"Goodness. What happened?" Stein asked, taking a step forward.

Freyja, shadowing her movement, took a step back and then quickly explained the events that had taken place in Room 101: Ben, his attack, the bite . . .

Principal Stein's countenance shifted from natural alarm to odd disinterest as she robotically directed Freyja to the wing where the nurse's office was. "Watch yourself, Ms. Wolfe. You seem to attract trouble."

Freyja moved quickly past Stein, curious about her off demeanor and comment. A strange dark mist seemed to rise off the principal's pantsuit. It floated around, but also clung to her.

"Ms. Wolfe, what are you waiting for?" came the principal's stern voice. "Move along."

"Oh, yes, Principal Stein," Freyja sputtered.

Stein was an imposing figure of authority with her dark hair, snappy suits, and stiff lips.

Freyja moved along, and Principal Stein followed her with narrowed eyes. Freyja took a few more steps, evading her glare. She glanced over her shoulder to study the strange hanging miasma once more. Principal Stein was walking away down the corridor, yet the mist still clung to her. It was some sort of translucent netting. It was not misting as such, as Freyja had earlier thought; it was too dense for that. It was more like a web, delicate and silky, with tendrils draped all over Stein, but moving and shifting like flags undulating in a breeze. They were long and hypnotizing as they stroked the floors, the walls, and the ceiling. Not only that, but they were moving *her*. Principal Stein was nothing more than a puppet on a string.

I've gotta get outta here, Freyja thought. Her heart was thumping harder than ever. What was happening? What were these things? She pressed her hands to her temples. *I'm going mad. I'm . . . I'm going mad!* her mind screamed.

A group of leadership council students swarmed up the hall, forcing Freyja to press her back against the lockers to avoid them. She had to escape them, for the dreadful web clung to them too. One of the tendrils suddenly whipped out from one of the girls' legs as she went past. Freyja couldn't avoid it as it slid over her fingers, which numbed instantly.

Freyja screamed as the cold sensation began crawling up her arm. The students stopped and turned towards her. She dropped her arm and patted it down like it was on fire.

Freyja's head swam. In near terror, she sprinted down the hall, hoping to escape everything connected to the black web. It was like a tumor, fast growing, crawling like ivy over every wall and floor and ceiling. The school exit door was so thickly draped there was no sunlight through it at all, and she was reasonably sure it was still daylight.

The door to the theatre, slightly ajar, was oddly free of the web. Freyja ran through it and closed the door behind her. When she turned, a spotlight illuminated a narrow space on the stage. There was a small table and two chairs just off to the right. Freyja edged her way down the right aisle in the theater, in between many rows of chairs. She scanned the room for that deathly black web, but she couldn't make any out. Beyond the small space lit up on the stage, it was too dark in the theatre.

Like a moth, Freyja approached the light. Halfway down the aisle, groping in the darkness so as not to trip up over any chair legs, she heard a gentle voice call out,

"Hello, my dear."

Startled, Freyja gave a small squeak in shock. But the origin of the voice was not startling at all for it came from an older woman, full and round, striding gracefully from the wings towards the edge of the spotlight. Her sparkling eyes lit up an otherwise serene face. The woman's black hair was pulled back into a beautiful collection of braided dreadlocks that nearly reached the floor. And she stood barefoot, dressed in a white flowing tunic and a long turquoise necklace. She spun around as if to introduce herself.

"I've been waiting for you," the woman said without moving her mouth.

"Me?"

"You don't yet remember, but you will," she said.

Freyja's heartbeat quickened.

"Yes, those are my thoughts you hear," she said, smiling at Freyja.

The woman turned to the small table set with a pot of tea and two floral teacups. She waved her hand to invite Freyja to join her as she poured the steaming tea, and then sat down. Freyja proceeded cautiously up the wooden steps. Finally, she sat down, facing the woman.

"I am called Sarana. And you are Freyja."

Freyja, dumfounded, reached down and held her cup.

"Go ahead. It will help."

Freyja sipped the sweet and earthy tea, and set the cup down. Sarana reached out for her injured hand. Hesitating, Freyja then offered it to her, and Sarana folded it into both of hers. The contact didn't hurt. Then, a kaleidoscope of images flashed before Freyja's eyes like a picture reel: lightning storms, dense forests full of creatures and round thatched-roof buildings, rolling seas, horses galloping with magnificent glowing riders dressed in strange attire, meteor showers blazing through the atmosphere, and repeatedly an image of an old key with brilliant stones embedded in it. Freyja held the key, standing in the middle of a crumbling ruin. Rain lashed as a violent storm was beating all around her. She knelt to insert the key into a stone door. Then, blinded by a bright pulsing light, she ripped her hand away from the woman.

"It's a lot to take in, I know," Sarana said.

"Who are you? What does this all mean? Are you connected to that creepy black web outside? Am I dreaming or something?"

"You are dreaming. You are also now awake."

With that, Sarana's body vanished with a thin wisp of smoke left in her place.

Freyja pushed back, falling out of her chair, staring at the stage in disbelief. She scrambled to her feet. The table with the pot of tea was also gone. And her hand . . . The paper bandage had come completely undone, and the wound . . . it had healed.

"What the hell?" Freyja raced out of the theatre as quickly as she could. The corridor was no longer sick with the black web. "I really am going mad," she muttered to herself. Then she snatched up her skateboard and bolted out of the front doors.

* * *

18

Principal Stein moved swiftly down the hall to administration, past the front desk, and into her office in the back. She closed the tall door and locked it. Her office had a generous modern desk with stacks of folders, a phone, and a reading lamp. Next to a framed Dali print of melting clocks was a narrow window facing the courtyard and fields of Roosevelt High School.

Stein picked up the phone, dialed, and slid into an oversized cobalt swivel chair behind the desk.

"Yes?" asked a voice.

"10203," she said.

"What's your message?"

"Adept Wolfe is awake."

CHAPTER THREE

EVERYTHING IS CONNECTED

The control room flickered and hummed with large panels of data and images flowing across the thirty-foot wall. Along the floor were a dozen stations with curiously uniformed men and women, each of them seated in large cockpit-style seats, like pilots in a small data stream. They wore sophisticated helmets that covered everything except their mouths, and appeared to be typing and waving in a virtual space in front of them with sleek metallic gloved hands. Each of the data pilots was processing information for the center, reflected on the screens around the room.

"Sir, we have another Adept off-grid," the lieutenant spoke into her headset. "Agent 10203 confirmed." She tapped notes into the air in front of her as she waited for a response.

A low hoarse voice asked, "When?"

"Sir, just now," the lieutenant said. "That's the second event this week."

"Hmmm." The man with the hoarse voice appeared at the railing overlooking the control room.

Many of the screens along the walls hung like giant windows out to the world. They showed satellite or drone images across different landscapes of Earth. Photos cycled automatically, as if they were searching for something. There were urban centers and streets, rural highways and truck stops, shipyards and jungles. Above these searching screens was an extended rectangular monitor with a series of numbers counting down.

Under a projector in the ceiling, in the middle of the room, was a holographic image of Earth, spinning very slowly. A translucent grid overlay enveloped it. There were blue, green, and red dots lit around the grid, primarily across the landmasses. Green dots clustered in the cities, with a few in rural or unpopulated areas. There were also isolated blue dots, and these were mostly in populated urban areas, but very few. Then there were the red dots. They were few, but they had photos linked to each of them. Another holographic window hung adjacent to the spinning planet and showed a stack of faces with laser tethers to each red dot. Some of the red dots vanished and reappeared as though the signal was being dropped and picked up again.

"Send me that file. And get Mackay," said the man with the hoarse voice. He stood staring intently at a photo of a young woman in the holographic window of red dots.

"Yes, Director Drake," confirmed the lieutenant.

In a moment, an alert sounded. Drake touched a button on a screen to enlarge a photo and other documents. He flipped through the digital stack quickly. The first one showed an image of Freyja. It had her name, date of birth, and details about her parents and her aunt. A medical file showed what appeared to be DNA markings, and several of them highlighted in neon colors.

Drake grabbed the DNA model from the file and put it into a holographic stand on one side of the desk. The helix moved as he studied it, touching different parts that sent details to his screen for further reading. He hit a button on the stand, and the helix disappeared.

Drake paced around his desk, moving towards the massive windows facing east over the Potomac. He rubbed his face and sighed. Drake reached into his pocket and retrieved a bent and worn playing card, an ace of spades. He flipped it methodically between his fingers like a master magician.

"The doctor is online," the lieutenant's voice echoed in the room.

He walked to his desk and touched a button. "Another implant failed," Drake said.

"Okay." Dr. Mackay sounded annoyed.

"Coincidence?" Drake asked.

"How would I know?" she said.

"Why don't you guess, Deborah? That's always fun."

"You think this is a game?" she said.

"What I think is that, if we keep losing these kids, we're going to have a real mess to clean up. And you know how I hate messes."

"You look cute in an apron." She laughed.

"What's the status of Arktik?" he asked.

"Still in testing."

"Is it stable?"

"Listen, I understand the pressure you're under, but I can't deliver something that isn't ready. The Nine aren't going to be happy when one of these kids implodes, and the whole world starts to ask questions." Dr. Mackay's voice was tired.

"What they've specifically said is that everyone is expendable . . . everyone, and that includes you and me. We can't afford to lose these kids," Drake barked.

Drake was not about to throw away twenty years of research and the program's success to pander to the esoteric whims of a bunch of ideologues, no matter who they were. Their last advisor to the Council of Nine had been found dead in his bathtub, officially a suicide. That did not inspire confidence. Who else was after this research? He could no longer trust the agreement with the Nine, an organization so secret no one was certain who controlled it. If he were going to survive this, he would have to create a fortress, assemble alliances, and play their game better than they did.

Drake's program was elegant and peerless. The data he had now was more advanced than any other in the world. It only got more reliable with genetic testing to identify those carrying the genes and those likely to become activated. People were now voluntarily sending in their gene code. There was no need to do covert collection. And with every passing day, they understood more about the secrets hiding in so-called junk DNA. Hiding these findings from their competitors and the world was a full-time job, one that he did with pride. But he wasn't anyone's lap dog. The program was his, and no one was going to threaten that.

Malcolm Drake was on the cutting edge of controlling human potential. He was not going to take a seat in the stands. The Nine were indeed correct about one thing—humanity was not ready for the truth, not even close.

Dr. Mackay's Arktik program was the last resort, to be sure. The technology allowed for a seamless genetic interface with the host, rather than just GPS tracking of the physical body. There was potential to tap into other hosts' consciousness layers and processing, like a layer of artificial intelligence combined with a remote operating system. But the device had proven extremely volatile. Most early subjects had expired and, in a few notable cases, very traumatically.

"Please, tell me when it's ready. We'll send Freyja to you," he said.

Dr. Mackay sighed, "Fine. We'll be waiting."

Drake stood up and stretched his shoulders back. Gray streaks painted his dark black hair like an owl's feathers, making him appear older than he was. Flipping the playing card between his fingers, he hit the call button on his desk.

"Lieutenant, alert the Trackers. Let me know as soon as they have Ms. Wolfe in custody."

"Yes, sir."

CHAPTER FOUR

OPEN THE DOOR TO YOUR MIND

Freyja sprinted down the road between the high school and the field, past the small gas station and the run-down bungalows fronting the quiet residential burrow behind it. It was a good mile to the Rahumans' home, but with all the adrenaline pumping, it felt like a few hundred feet. She slowed her pace at the empty lot next door to the Rahumans' house. It was a wild pocket of grasses, trees, and creatures frolicking just below the suburbia's manicured fences. She missed the wilds desperately.

She rounded the corner to find her neighbor, Mrs. Simpson, standing on her front porch in a very confused state. She had furrowed brows, hands on hips.

"I can't seem to find the letter from my Harold," she said.

"It should be here tomorrow," Freyja yelled at her.

"Huh?" Mrs. Simpson narrowed her eyes and cocked a hand at her ear. "Oh, hello, dear!" Mrs. Simpson was hard of hearing. She always put on her bright red lipstick to open the door, but couldn't remember that her husband had passed away. She wore large smock-style gowns she had sewn herself, with an apron tied around so she could keep her reading glasses and a crossword puzzle handy. "He mailed it last week. It shouldn't take that long, should it?" Mr. Simpson asked.

"No, it shouldn't. Can I bring in the garbage can for you?" Freyja asked.

"Oh, thank you, dear. Can you be sure to close the garage door right now? The wind bangs it like the dickens."

Maple Street contained a well-established neighborhood. Green elms and oaks overhung neat rows of Craftsman bungalow homes and manicured lawns. The average length of time people lived on Maple Street, the assigned quarters for working middle class and their tenants, was twenty years, enough for babies to be born and raised. In some cases, the homes passed to heirs, but most of them sold for cash so the owners could move to a retirement condo on a beach.

The Rahumans had taken Freyja in five years ago. The middle-aged couple dressed in matching khakis and tidy haircuts had stood on the front porch, overly excited to greet her, as she was escorted up the walkway by a uniformed officer. Despite the confusion and terror of being ripped inexplicably from her home and only remaining family, Freyja remembered this moment as an odd omen of an ill-fitting reality. Mrs. Rahuman smelled of sticky sweet sauce and cleaning supplies. Mr. Rahuman was strangely curious about her appearance, asking how she had grown into such a beautiful young girl. But the strangest thing about them was how they spoke in riddles, never really answering her questions.

"Why am I in foster care?" she had asked them.

"Honey, you know that is a question for your caseworker. We are just here to support you and keep you safe," they said.

"Where are my parents?"

"Again, we don't know these things. But we do know that if they were able to, they would find you. Absolutely," they said.

"Where did they take my aunt?"

"Honey, your aunt was not well. We are sure that she is in a better place," they said.

What they meant was that Aunt Lucy was not well in the head. Freyja remembered her frequent bouts of anxiety, where they would roll in and consume her for days. But it wasn't like a criminal offense. Freyja never had a care in the world, other than missing her parents after their disappearance. She remembered that her mother smelled like roses and would dig in the garden with her. Her father would read bedtime stories and bring her interesting gadgets from his trips away. And then one day, they didn't return, from somewhere. Aunt Lucy seemed very afraid that whatever had happened to her parents might happen to them.

"Freyja, you must always be watchful," Aunt Lucy would say, peering out the windows, scanning the horizon for something. Then, she would grab Freyja by the chin, gazing deep into her eyes, and say, "I don't know if I can keep you safe. Do you trust me?"

"Yes, of course, I trust you, Auntie," Freyja would reply, wondering why her aunt kept asking her. "But what are you afraid of?"

"In time, you will understand."

The Rahumans had given Freyja a tiny violet bedroom in the back of their small but comfortable home. A twin bed with a green and purple floral comforter and a couple of matching pillows became her hideout from the world. Next to the bed was a short chest of drawers with a small reading lamp and an alarm clock. There was a fan on the ceiling that spun with incessant clicking due to imbalanced blades. The percussive serenade was preferable to the humid air blanket, often trapped in these dense overbuilt walls. The window hid behind a blacked-out shade that she rarely lifted. She preferred not to think about how far away the farm had gone. These walls were like a cell, and her awareness of that served to fuel her determination to flee them eventually.

Freyja was saving every cent she earned babysitting and running errands for Mrs. Simpson so that she could move out as soon as legally possible. She had researched emancipation, though she didn't feel completely ready. The Rahumans were generous and told her she could stay if she needed to. She had started hiding extra money in a cut-out inside a book, her copy of Tolstoy's *War and Peace*, a year ago. She had so many questions about who she was. What happened to her parents? She wanted to find her aunt, get answers, return home in some way, even if the truth was hard.

Freyja tip-toed into the Rahumans' home, and slipped past the living room and kitchen to the back hallway. She closed her bedroom door as quietly as she possibly could. With great relief, she collapsed on her bed and closed her eyes.

Slowly, she let go and went to sleep.

* * *

"Freyda … Fredo … Freydidley-doo …" chimed a small voice.

Sammy poked Freyja on the toe with a long stick. He was hiding at the foot of the bed, a young cinnamon cherub of a child, with dark sparkling eyes and an unruly mop of hair. When Sammy arrived at the Rahumans, she fell in love with him. They found him abandoned in a box outside the city hospital. Many nights, when everyone would go to sleep, Freyja would sneak into his room and pull him out of the crib to hold him. She would sing old lullabies and bury her nose into his curls and kiss his chubby fingers. His little warm body gave her solace, and she hoped that the nagging loneliness might release her.

"Stop." She grunted, rolling over into her pillow.

"But I found something," he said brightly.

Freyja opened one eye and peered at him. He was holding up something dark and black high above his head, an object she couldn't make out.

Then Freyja realized what it was and gasped, "Where did you get that?"

She sat up straight to grab it, but Sammy pulled it away from her, and then squealed with delight and raced out the door. Freyja's heart thumped inside her chest. Was this the key from the vision she had at school?

"Sammy! Wait!"

Freyja jumped out of bed and dashed down the narrow hallway after him, passing Anna Beth in the living room plodding along on the treadmill. Anna Beth had arrived at the Rahumans' first, maybe a year before Freyja did. She was a few years younger than Freyja and a lot shorter, but she had the loudest mouth to go with her mad bushy brows and gold-flecked hazel eyes. She was a hurricane force to steer clear of whenever possible. Freyja had given up asking about her story long ago. It always changed. What was true was that she had no father, and rumor was that her mother was a drug addict who had abused her. Ultimately, Anna Beth was an arrogant, petulant girl, and Freyja despised her.

"Where's the fire?" Anna Beth yelled.

The television droned in the background as the scent of burnt popcorn emanated from the kitchen. Freyja ignored her and headed towards the front door.

Crash!

"Darn it!" Mrs. Rahuman dropped a hot pan of flaming kernels into the sink. Cursing under her breath, she came out of the kitchen, disheveled and exasperated, and saw Freyja sneaking out the door. "Freyja, darling, school called . . ." Her voice more serious than usual.

Mrs. Rahuman was a typical middle-aged mom kind of woman. She wore basic jeans and collared shirts most of the time. Her hair was a short length to make it easier to get up and go. She walked every other morning around the track at school with one of the front office ladies. She and Mr. Rahuman worked as "consultants" for NuTech, though only she could work from home. She liked to take a lot of mediocre photos of flowers.

Mr. Rahuman could have been an accountant with his khaki pants and white shirts, but apparently, he was an engineer. He left before dawn every day except Sunday. He usually came home with pizza takeout or frozen lasagna from the deli down the street. He liked to read the *Wall Street Journal* and make fly fishing hooks. Neither of them had biological children, though they had three children they said God gave them.

Freyja darted out the front door chasing Sammy. She ran straight out past the yard, hedges, and lawn to the sidewalk curb, with a long view in either direction of Maple Street. The Rahumans' home sat back a dozen feet more than most of the other houses, making room for a large hedge across the front, functioning as a natural fence between the street and the front porch. The border had grown thick and dense over the years, making a green fortress around the property's corner. All the foster kids had tunneled through the hedge, bending and breaking a few branches here and there to create little forts inside to imagine faraway places and adventures.

Anna Beth had told Freyja about the legend of a hidden treasure, left by a former foster kid. No one had found it yet, but everyone had their theories about where it was and what was inside. Most kids imagined an old map, rubies, gold coins, or stolen jewelry, but Freyja's favorite was always the rumor that it contained keys to a safe-deposit box, where a small fortune was awaiting the boy when he reached adulthood. However, the story went that the kid had forgotten where it was, and that one day, in a mad rage to find it, he dug up the whole yard until there was not a square inch of turf left. The Rahumans said it wasn't real and that there was no buried box, but Freyja wondered whether the Rahumans had found it and kept it.

"In here!" Sammy squealed. His giggles came from a spot inside the hedge between their house and the next. Freyja followed the sound, and spied his bare foot peeking out from a bush. She pushed aside the branches to a sizeable hollowed-out area amid the hedge and, behind that, a big cardboard box. It was Sammy's fort. There were odd toys, sticks, a dirty cop, and a beat-up tackle box inside.

Freyja took a deep breath. She realized that Sammy was thrilled to play hide-and-seek. He could probably do it all day long. She thought about taking a different tact to slow him down. "What a cool fort you have!" She crawled in and sat in front of the grinning three-year-old. "Is this your special place?"

"Yep. It is my house. See?" He swung his arms around him, grinning at the magnificent green hideout.

"Well, I love it … Where did you find that?" she asked, pointing at the key.

"I dunno."

"Can I see it?"

"Okay, but you hafa give it back, okay?" he said, sternly crossing his chubby arms.

"Oh, of course. It's just so pretty." She held it carefully, its familiar weight in her hand. It was now that she realized she had seen it before in her dreams, and then today, on the stage with Sarana at school.

Are my dreams memories? she thought.

Freyja folded her hands around the key instinctively. It was unexpectedly heavy, made from some dark metal or heavy stone. It was warm to the touch, not cold. There were three spirals in the handle, with three empty, hollow indentions. Freyja mused on this, wondering if they used to hold some jewels or decorative bits. The key, which just fit in her hand, would not turn the lock of any door Freyja had ever seen. Mrs. Rahuman had a collection of antiques in the storage shed. Then Freyja remembered how Sammy liked to rummage in there.

Perhaps this is just some old key from there; maybe it just looks like the one from my vision?

"Sammy, did you get this from the shed? I think Mrs. Rahuman will want this back, don't you?" Freyja said.

"No! I found it!"

"Where? And why did you show it to me?"

"She told me to."

Freyja's heart thumped.

"Who? Who told you to show it to me, Sammy?"

"The lady," he whispered.

"What lady? Where is she?"

"I dunno . . . Over there," he pointed to the street. "I like her."

Freyja turned, her eyes following the direction of his little extended finger. The only presence was the wind rustling through the trees. Freyja's spine tingled.

Sarana?

Sammy turned to play with his toys and began digging in the dirt. Freyja put the key in the pocket of her hoodie and kissed Sammy on the head.

"It's going to be dinner soon. Let's get washed up."

"In a minute," he said, a phrase repeated incessantly, each day, by all the older people in his life. He quickly forgot about the key as he dug into his play.

CHAPTER FIVE

SOME KIND OF MADNESS

The sun rose, and with it came the roar of a rebellious rock band from the radio alarm on the bedside table. A long pale arm reached out from under the duvet and hit the snooze button. After a minute or two, Freyja slowly hoisted herself up and squinted at the morning light streaming through the misaligned shades. Climbing out of bed, she found some clothes on the floor. She pulled her Nine Inch Nails t-shirt over her head and wrestled her legs into her jeans.

"Freyja, breakfast," came Mrs. Rahuman's voice, accompanied by an abrupt knock on the door.

"Coming," she mumbled.

First, she went to the bathroom. Foaming toothpaste dripped into the sink as Freyja reflected on her appearance. She inspected her shoulder and arm. They were lighter, more translucent than before, and most importantly, not glowing. Maybe she just imagined it all.

Then her ears began to ring loudly. She quickly covered her ears, but it made no difference. Low whispering voices haunted her mind like a radio left on in another room. She couldn't make out what they said. She shook her head instinctively to dampen the sound. She took a deep breath and headed into the kitchen.

"She's aliiiiive . . ." said Anna Beth before shoveling a spoonful of cereal into her mouth.

Mrs. Rahuman glanced at Freyja. "What would you like, dear?"

"Um . . ."

"Ma'am, I wanna scramble eggs," chirped Sammy, pushing away his bowl of cereal.

Mrs. Rahuman patted Sammy on the head. "No time, honey. Here's your lunch box. Gotta go to daycare today. Who needs a ride to school?"

"I'll just skate," mumbled Freyja, grabbing a piece of toast.

"Freyja, honey . . ." Mrs. Rahuman started.

"Yeah?"

"Dr. Mackay called. She needs to rerun your labs."

Freyja screwed up her face. "Why?"

"Well, you know how careful she is. Think about if you have any new symptoms or changes you would like to discuss with her. You know, she needs to hear it all. Right? We can stop by after school today or tomorrow."

Freyja shrugged. She had been visiting Dr. Mackay since she arrived at the Rahumans, getting all kinds of lab work and shots. They said that her aunt hadn't gotten her proper medical care before, so she had to get caught up like all the other kids. She hadn't had any seizures with the new medicine, but she still had to have all these check-ups just in case. Freyja didn't care for Dr. Mackay, but she was used to it by now. She wasn't sure she wanted to tell anyone about the voices or music in her head and, indeed, not her radioactive scars.

"So, what happened at school yesterday?" asked Mrs. Rahuman. Her voice was forthright, studying Freyja's reaction.

"Nothing. Just a weird day."

"Principal Stein called and said you were injured?"

"Oh, that. One of the students in Room 101 went a little crazy, but I'm okay. Just kind of shook me up, you know?"

"You're good with them. You should think about going into teaching maybe. Remember, your mom and your aunt were teachers. That may be why it comes so naturally for you," said Mrs. Rahuman.

"Yeah." Freyja moved swiftly towards the door, evading eye contact, and hoping to lose the conversation as well.

"Listen, I'm going to call Dr. Mackay…"

Freyja slid the door closed behind her as Mrs. Rahuman continued talking. She didn't want to talk or even think about what had happened. A terrifying thought that maybe she was crazy like her aunt was nagging at her.

Freyja lay down her skateboard and kicked the ground hard. The wind caught her hair as she cruised along with the cookie-cutter neighborhood, past piles of autumn leaves and customized mailboxes. Freyja hit the cracks and curbs like a dolphin riding the waves. She charged at the barking dogs who ran out to the edge of their lawns to warn off intruders.

The road to Roosevelt High was her road and her game. She claimed every stride as her beat for surviving the day. If she could coast most of the way without needing to pump the board, it would be an easy day. If she had to stop and start too many times, that meant she'd be counting down the minutes on the clock by the end of the day.

Despite being a bit late, today, she was drawn to a stop at an empty lot near the Rahumans' home. It was a wild, unruly field. The leaves rustled with brilliant fall colors, dancing across the dry grasses. A "For Sale" sign, which had been there for a while, had a new sticker on it. She didn't want anyone to buy this land and build another stupid house. She had the habit of tearing the sticker with the agent's number so no one would be able to call and inquire. She grabbed the corner, ripping the last two numbers away.

On the far side of the field, backed into a forested glen, there was a small roof peeking through the tree line. All the hours spent in this field, running, hiking, exploring, and she had never seen houses on the other side. There was a little puff of smoke drifting into the sky above. Did someone live there? She would have to check it out another time.

"Wait up!" came a voice suddenly.

Freyja glanced over her shoulder to find Nash skating up next to her, huffing and puffing.

"You might go faster if you just ran." Freyja smiled mischievously.

Nash was not very athletically inclined. "You're gonna be late," he said, teasing as he started to overtake her.

"Yeah, but so are you!" Freyja bumped her board into his, causing him to lose his balance and wobble off. He grasped her as he fell and pulled her onto the ground with him. They landed in a hard tumble of knees and elbows.

"You jerk!" He laughed.

"Ha ha." She leaned her fists into his chest and hoisted herself up, pleased that she had caught him off guard again. It wasn't hard.

Nash sat on the ground, hesitating. "Hey, um, what do you think about the spring fling?"

"I think it's a lame, socially contrived ritual to encourage teenagers to dress like goons and act like dilettantes," Freyja replied, giving him a hand to pull up. She realized that he was earnest and wondered what was going on. "Why, don't you?"

Nash grimaced, "Well, yeah, maybe . . . but Mom is on the planning committee. She's trying to get me to play with the band there. She thinks I should go and make her look good. You know, obedient son."

"You should do it. You're one of the best. And your mom doesn't need you to look good. She's the coolest mom in town."

"Ha. Maybe so," said Nash.

Freyja loved Nash's whole family, especially his mom. She wanted to be adopted by them. Freyja kept an overnight bag stashed at their house for all the marathon movie and game nights she spent there.

Nash's mom was a freelance artist and often volunteered for school stuff. She told incredibly vibrant and dramatic tales at dinner, though sometimes her intensity disturbed Nash. She had a turbulent childhood growing up with "poor hillbillies" deep in the woods. He would try to cut her off a lot. "Yeah, Mom, you told us this one last time. Remember?" He was embarrassed by her honesty.

His dad was a music teacher at the university and played in a rock band on the weekends. Nash had inherited his talents and was quickly surpassing them. His dad often pulled out multiple instruments after dinners to do jam sessions, giving a pair of cymbals to Freyja so she could join in. Nash could play piano, guitar, drums, and saxophone; pretty much any instrument was easy to figure out.

He was always humming a tune or taping out the beats to some song he was learning, though lately, there was a heaviness in his music. Nash said his dad was putting on pressure to apply to the best music schools for college.

"Well, you should go. I mean, it might be good for some laughs."

"Yeah. Maybe." Nash chuckled unconvinced.

"Race?" Freyja pushed Nash over and jumped on her board to get a head start.

"Oh no, you don't!"

Nash pushed ahead furiously, determined to catch her. He had upgraded his ride with some better bearings, so he caught up quickly. They swerved in and out, moving faster and faster down the sidewalk as they hit clear blocks with no cars or people. He wobbled awkwardly as he pushed his limits. Just a few yards ahead, Roosevelt was in sight, and Nash pulled off near the gate and sprinted to the parking lot, throwing down his board.

"Ha ha! Beat you!" he yelled, sailing around to the back door as the first-period bell rang.

Freyja smiled and waved back, heading to the opposite wing of the school. She didn't have time to stow her board, so she slid it behind the boxes of books lining the wall near the door of Ms. Argot's English class. One of her more comfortable subjects, English was a class she could almost literally sleep through and still ace the exams.

"Nice that you could join us, Ms. Wolfe. We are reading from Chapter 19," said Ms. Argot. She tucked her sandy brown hair behind her ear, staring intently at the book in her hand. "Brice, could you begin, please?" Ms. Argot pointed her claw-like nail at a gangly boy in a Knicks tee shirt and giant white basketball shoes.

Freyja slunk down in her chair, flipping open her copy of *A Tale of Two Cities* to Chapter 19.

Brice began reading: "Worn out by anxious watching, Mr. Lorry fell asleep at his post. On the tenth morning of his suspense, he was startled by the sun's shining into the room where a heavy slumber had overtaken him when it was dark night..."

Brice's voice droned on, but Freyja's thoughts wandered back to all the strange events since yesterday: Ben's outburst, the bite, the implant or device, the black web, Sarana, the key, her scars. She glanced down at her arm and then gingerly opened her hand to see what would happen.

Brice's voice grew louder: "Even when he had satisfied himself that he was awake, Mr. Lorry felt giddily uncertain for some few moments whether the late shoemaking might not be a disturbed dream of his own . . ."

A warm heat was rising in her chest and face. It was like yesterday. Her hands were shaking, but there was no electricity, no illumination. There was just intense pressure. Her head started to pound. A bead of sweat now rolled down her cheek. Ms. Argot caught her eye, obviously concerned. She was aware of Freyja's health history and waved her out of the room. Most of the teachers understood that Freyja didn't want to make a scene, and they would give her generous leeway with the hall passes.

Freyja propped herself up and, as quickly as she possibly could, made her way to the front of the class and out of the room. As soon as she reached the doorway, everything around her began to shift like a funhouse mirror. The ceiling lights, the walls, the floor were all bending and moving in slow motion. Freyja reached frantically for the door, and let herself out into the hallway. She tripped over Marley, leaning against the door, picking at her nails, her leg extended just outside the door.

"Oh! Sorrrrrry," said Marley.

Freyja landed hard on the ground. A cold heat washed over her in a swirl of vertigo. A puddle of water drenched her clothes where the water fountain next to the door had been leaking on to the floor. Confused and angry, she wanted to reach up and strangle Marley, but her body betrayed her. Ever since middle school, this girl had made it her mission to bully and humiliate her. Marley stood overhead and dealt her a pernicious grin. Freyja felt a surge of fury rise from the tips of her toes to the ends of her hair. She managed to push herself upright.

"What is your problem?" she seethed.

"Me?" Marley said with feigned shock, before her lips spread once more into a wide sneer. "You're the one groveling on the ground. Oh, and just so you know, Nathaniel said he would come with *me* to the spring fling dance next week." Marley paused to allow the arrow to find its mark before adding, "So, I guess he's not your boyfriend after all."

Freyja's teeth clenched. He wasn't her boyfriend, and yet, Marley taunted her over it anyway.

Before that thought could torment her further, a jolt of nausea overcame her. Her hands clutched at her stomach, which was now tossing and turning like a stormy sea. Pushing Marley out of the way, she stumbled across the hall and into the bathroom. Once inside, she hoped to regain composure in her own reflection in the mirror. Her face was flushed like she had a fever. She had an odd tingling sensation and immediately thought of the scars. She pulled her right arm out of her sweatshirt. Her skin was mottled and hot like lava in between the spots that now glowed faintly. Freyja narrowed her eyes and studied them. This time they formed distinct shapes, more than before. Were they patterns or symbols? The swirls alternated in contrast and depth, and although they weren't moving, this effect made it appear as if they were dancing, like a mirage in the desert.

"What the . . . ?"

Freyja stretched out her arm and twisted her shoulder to study the patterns more closely, heart thumping. What was going on? Her mind raced. It was almost as if the symbols depicted an ancient script or language. They reminded her of runes or Sanskrit symbols. And they were glowing, then fading, burning, hen fading, hot and then cold. Her eyes flickered wildly; her head was shaking.

What's going on? she asked herself.

Tears rolled down her cheeks. With an anguished cry, she pulled her sweatshirt back on, fell to her knees, and hugged herself.

Moments later, the bell rang. Freyja thought about heading home, but art class was next. Outside of Room 101, art was her refuge from everything. She was able to stretch and explore and get lost in the safety of her imagination. Seeking any kind of familiar sanity was the next best thing to do.

At the end of a large open room, Freyja scurried to a desk in the back row. She grabbed the seat like a life preserver, sliding onto it and taking several deep breaths. The heat had begun fading, so she thought maybe distracting herself further might help. Freyja picked up her charcoal pencils and started sketching on the blank parchment clipped to the easel in front of her.

"You know, you have several pieces that you ought to submit to the state competition," came the voice of Mr. Martinez, who was peeking at Freyja from behind her easel. In his forties, Mr. Martinez still carried himself like a young surfer, with a handful of art pens in his back jeans pocket and a flop of thick black hair he reflexively combed back with his fingers. Moving around the easel, he nudged his glasses down the bridge of his nose and examined the drawing. After a few moments, the young teacher made a few noises of satisfaction before saying, "So, what do you think?"

"Yeah, I don't know," Freyja replied. The idea of having her work analyzed by some state suits made her anxious.

"It would be good for you," he scolded. "To test your talent."

"Maybe," she said quickly. Then, to change the subject, she said, "Hey, what causes static electricity? I got a horrible shock in class yesterday."

"Static electricity, huh? I think it's when there is a build-up of a positive or negative charge, like when you encounter an opposite ground or conductive object, like through metal or something. Maybe it's that grumpy attitude biting you back!" He chuckled.

Freyja laughed. Mr. Martinez was cool. Unlike most teachers, he considered the students to be real people with brains in their heads. She mused at her sketch. Suddenly she realized that, in her trance, she had drawn the key. The sketch filled her with anxiety.

Maybe I ought to just head home, wait for my appointment with Dr. Mackay, and try to figure out what is happening to me, Freyja thought.

After the bell rang, Freyja waited for Nash at their usual spot near the stairs, but he did not show. Meandering back to the lockers, she saw he was smiling and laughing with Marley. Flirting mercilessly, Marley leaned into Nash's shoulder and whispered something. Freyja hung around, wanting to avoid the whole scene but dying to know what was happening. Her heart ached for her friend. He could do what he wanted, but why with *her*? This was a betrayal she hadn't experienced before.

As her emotions roiled, the room spun, and the walls came alive with dark shadows and pulsing lines. Freyja's heart thumped harder. Her pinned eyes traced a translucent miasma woven from floor to ceiling, connected in some way to every single person who moved through the hall. Some of the threads glistened like tiny beads of light, while others were very dark and oily. Something in her wanted to touch them as students walked past. These strands were quite fragile, drifting off in wisps. Some were thicker and clingy. Most would instantly rebuild themselves. She couldn't help noticing how dull and draining to the touch they were, like a wire sapping a battery.

Freyja's heart pounded as she studied the threads dancing around Marley and Nash. Marley appeared to be wrapping heavy cords all around Nash like a noose with every swoosh of her hair. Even the air coming out of her lungs encased him in a dark bubble. Every motion in his direction lassoed him tighter into her. He was oblivious as her threads coiled around his body, some of them burrowing into his body, disappearing. It was like witnessing a microscopic world under a giant telescope.

Freyja closed her eyes. What was happening? She tried to suppress the jealously and confusion that was turning her insides out. After a few moments, she opened her eyes to Marley, eyes narrowed, lips pressed together, poking her in the chest and mouthing, "See, I told you."

A black fog descended upon Freyja like a terrible immobilizing chill. She thrashed, trying to move out from under Marley's baleful energy. The force was too intense. Heat and rage gathered in Freyja's body as she screamed, "Get off me!"

As Freyja pushed Marley away, something erupted from her hands in a flash of bright light, propelling Marley across the hall and into the wall. Freyja's hands and body trembled. Marley lay dazed on the floor, hair swept around her sleeping head like a storm. Teachers and students ran out of classrooms to investigate. Time slowed as they all turned towards the scene. Shocked and frightened, Freyja ran blindly down the hall, trying to get away. The web pulsed and shifted as though messages were being telegraphed somewhere down the line. They shuddered and turned, but not smoothly. It was like a matrix glitch. Tears streamed down Freyja's face as she raced towards the main doors.

"Hey, girl," Mr. Martinez called after Freyja, who was running frantically down the hall. He stepped into her path. "You okay?" he said, louder this time.

Freyja didn't stop. Face strained, tear-dashed, she collapsed straight into his arms.

"Freyja! What's wrong?" Mr. Martinez bent low as his arms absorbed her weight. She was like a doll, limbs like spaghetti, unable to hold herself up. She sobbed through the string of events that could not have made any sense to him.

In between his gentle words, footsteps came heavy and slow from behind. When she turned her head and opened her eyes, Principal Stein was marching grimly towards them.

CHAPTER SIX

THE FIRE THAT STITCHED HER SOUL TO HER SKIN

Freyja waited for Mrs. Rahuman outside Principal Stein's office. She sat dumbfounded in one of the plastic office chairs lined up next to the front desk. An ambulance had arrived to take Marley to the local hospital to get checked out. She wore singed clothes; the hem of her skirt and the cuffs of her preppy shirt were all frayed and blackened. She lay on a gurney with instructions to hold an ice pack to her head. As the gurney rolled by the office, through the open door, Marley's face contorted with fear and rage. Slowly, she raised a trembling hand and pointed at Freyja.

"Freak! You freak!" she screamed, her voice high and hysterical.

The paramedics managed to calm her, but they appeared wary of the girl staring back from inside the office.

Freyja just glared back at Marley, unsure what else to do. Marley deserved more than that for all the bullying over the years. She didn't regret anything, though she didn't mean to launch her across the hall. More than that, she didn't know *how* she had done it.

"Beverly, you know we can't have this," Stein's voice was low and barely discernible.

"We will take care of it," Mrs. Rahuman said.

Ten minutes later, Mrs. Rahuman pulled the door shut behind her as they left the principal's office, staring intently at Freyja. They stood out in the corridor.

In contrast to earlier, it was so eerily quiet and still. "Can you tell me what happened?"

"I don't know." What could she possibly say? She was angry and confused, and very freaked out. It was all very surreal and yet somehow made sense. They walked to the car in silence. Mrs. Rahuman's phone beeped. She read a message and sighed. "I need to finish up some things for work, and then we can head over to Dr. Mackay's office."

Dark clouds gathered over the valley, occasionally lit by sharp flashes of lightning. Freyja recalled her aunt's words. "Watch the skies."

Freyja had been watching for as long as she could remember: at the farm, when she lay in the grasses at dusk, when she studied the stars overhead with Keyo, the wild lynx that befriended her. Sometimes, with the telescope her parents gave her, she focused it on the moon, studying its craters and valleys. Other times she observed the storms that rolled in from the west, the way they injected life into the woods and streams with furious renewal.

She had always thought it spoke a strangely familiar language. Lightning gnashed at the boundary between Freyja and something far beyond her. The galloping forces of destiny raced in her veins, vibrating, humming, nudging her as though she could not turn back. Storms carried the bearings of unresolved conflicts, building up in intensity and ferocity, as if to let off steam or pressure, to balance things between heaven and earth.

"Looks like a storm," she said almost to herself.

"Yeah, it does. You love storms, don't you?" replied Mrs. Rahuman.

"Sometimes . . ." Freyja murmured. She studied the skyline through the window in Mrs. Rahuman's car. "You can time how far away it is."

"How far away what is?"

"The lightning . . . You start counting as soon as you see the flash. Each second between the flash and when you hear the thunder is about half a mile."

It was the lightning she connected with the most, the fire that had stitched her soul to her skin.

"How do you know so much about lightning, dear?"

"My aunt . . ." Freyja's voice trailed off as memories flashed in her mind.

Aunt Lucy had taught her all about lightning, especially after Freyja's experience as a young girl. She remembered the day like it was yesterday.

Freyja was sitting near the tree out behind the farmhouse. The clouds had gathered rapidly and violently above her. Keyo paced oddly next to her, mewing and growling in such an unusual way. A fiery hand reached down and snatched her into the sky. It didn't hurt until the fire let go and left her flesh riddled with wounds. Her mother ran screaming towards her, grabbing for her feet. Her father was there and caught her when the fire dropped her. They rushed her into the house. She had bandages head to toe for at least a month.

Aunt Lucy had taught her that positive and negative charges build up within the clouds and below it, creating leaders that stream out in search of their opposite. When we see lightning, we see it reaching up from the ground and meeting another leader from the clouds.

Freyja smiled at Mrs. Rahuman. "I grew up with a lot of lighting."

"That's nice, dear. It is good to be interested in things," Mrs. Rahuman said, glancing at her phone that was buzzing wildly in her purse.

When Freyja had first arrived at the Rahumans, she didn't watch television or even her computer. Instead, she took to just watching the skies out of her window or the forests behind the house. The Rahumans thought it odd, of course, but Freyja was too preoccupied with the storm to care. When the clouds rolled in, their atmosphere weighed on her body and pressed into her mind. The pulsation radiated through her veins. She would run to the bathroom and gaze at her reflection in the mirror. Her hair swelled with static, lifting all around her.

And now, yesterday, for reasons she had yet to figure, her lightning scars were lighting up. Why? She rolled back a sleeve and studied her right arm. She grabbed it with her left hand; it was hot to the touch. What else was going to start happening to her? And why?

Mrs. Rahuman slammed the breaks of her car, pounding on her horn. "Are you kidding me?" she yelled at the pileup of cars in front of them.

Another driver had apparently run a red light, clipped one car, and slammed head-on into another, causing a fiery accident that blocked the traffic route. A couple of witnesses ran to the blazing mess and pulled the drivers out to safety. Others got out to ogle the spectacle or call for emergency services.

"Unbelievable!" Mrs. Rahuman peered around the headrest, hoping for a way out of the mess. But they were blocked in, surrounded by other cars. She huffed and sighed. "This is going to take a while."

Mrs. Rahuman got out and slammed the door. She stood with her hands on her hips, and then she reached into her pocket, pulled out her phone, and made a call. She paced outside the car. Mrs. Rahuman was one of the calmest people, so Freyja assumed the accident was upsetting her. Freyja lowered her seat to recline and closed her eyes.

A loud boom of thunder rocked overhead. Freyja imagined the startling drumming as a warning from the Gods, or God, depending on what you believe.

"We are coming."

She peered out the window, towards the skies. Dark clouds rolled over them. "Are you talking to me?" Freyja said. The storm was communicating something beyond "Raindrops are coming."

Just then, she remembered what Mr. Franklin, Freyja's science teacher, had once said: "If a tree falls in the forest, and there is no one around to hear, does it make a sound?" He loved to pose riddles to stump the class.

"Of course, if it falls, it makes a sound!" someone always answered.

"How do you know?" asked Mr. Franklin. "There is no way to prove it. The only way is to listen with your ears or through a device that transmits the sounds elsewhere. Without a way to receive the sound, there is no way to know if it exists on its own."

Freyja remembered her answer to the riddle, one that went against Mr. Franklin's argument: But even if you turn off all the televisions, devices, radios, and mechanical noises, there are millions of natural sounds and vibrations that we can sense beyond the range of our ears. Like the wind kissing tender cheeks, footsteps shaking windowpanes, the distant propulsion of vehicles, the insect with tiny tapping whiskers, the entire Earth's playlist of sounds is layered in a catalog of memory that most of us hear the moment we are born. Even those who cannot hear properly may still feel the sound in their ears' skin and bones. Hearing is not all about the amplification of a sound. Sound rides vibratory waves, feeding the subtle senses whether we perceive it or not.

Of course, that's what Freyja would have said if she had been brave enough. Instead, she just sat there, wondering why she couldn't stomach the nerve to say something.

Mrs. Rahuman still paced intensely while on her cell phone. Freyja could not hear the words exactly, but the energy of them. The fire's energy and police cars rolling into the intersection weighed like massive tons of steel on her arms, as if she were holding them.

Freyja closed her eyes and remembered sitting next to a tree as a young girl. She would listen to her heartbeat. She imagined it was the pulse of the tree, or perhaps the earth.

In one of her history lessons with Aunt Lucy, Freyja had learned that Joan of Arc might have received her advanced warning of the invading English by sitting in a tree. There, propped comfortably between the boughs, she might have listened to the wind. It shook the leaves, and, from their vibrations, she might have understood the warning. This communication was part of the ancient arbor network.

Fascinated, Freyja was hungry to learn more. She read and read, inhaling books on botany like air. She read how the world's oldest interweb, the fungal network, connects root systems worldwide. She discovered that trees talk to each other, and so do the tiniest life forms, everything from the ant to the butterfly. In her reading, Freyja wondered if humans were able to do the same. Perhaps they could, and had just forgotten?

She remembered a story about Native American scouts and how they used their long hair to pick up signals about invading tribes as they slept on the ground.

That makes sense, she thought.

Bats and dolphins use sonar to navigate their worlds. Dogs can hear things people cannot. Who has not heard stories of dogs pacing and barking hours before an unexpected return?

Surely humans can do the same, she repeated to herself.

Her aunt had once suggested that our senses' limit might be our beliefs about what we can perceive with them. One of her aunt's heroes was a philosopher called George Berkeley, the man University in California, Berkeley, was named after. He had argued in the 1700s that nothing exists until it is perceived. Unlike the famous Shakespeare quote, "To be or not to be," Berkeley said, "To be is to be perceived."

Perhaps that is why being ostracized is so painful for human beings? Freya thought.

If your family or tribe refuses to accept you, to recognize you, then do you cease to be? Are our senses merely tools of our imaginations or ideas? And where does the information that is our imagination come from, if not our body-sensory minds? These big questions fascinated Freyja, even if she could not answer them.

A cloud suddenly burst over the intersection. The police had cleared out and rerouted dozens of cars. Everyone was running for cover as the fire trucks pulled out and tow trucks pulled in.

Mrs. Rahuman climbed back in the car, escaping the downpour. "Oh my! What a mess."

"Hmmm . . ." Freyja mused.

"You are looking so pale, dear. Are you taking those vitamins Dr. Mackay gave you?"

"They hurt my stomach."

"I know, but food today is just not what it used to be. You need to take those vitamins." Mrs. Rahuman continued with a mini lecture about nutrition as the traffic cleared and the police directing the traffic waved her on.

Freyja sighed, turning towards the passing street life outside her window.

Mrs. Rahuman pulled the gray Subaru into the garage. "Go rest for a bit," she said. "I'll find you when it's time to go."

Freyja slung her backpack around her and trudged slowly to her room. She swung the door closed and collapsed on her bed. The fan spun in a hypnotic elliptical motion, speeding up slightly as the blade passed the mobile hanging near the window.

The image of Marley flying suddenly struck Freyja. She sat up and rolled through her memories of the past two days: the little object she had pulled out of her hand, the strange woman in the theater, the key, the electrical shocks, her buzzing scars, and then the unknown force that came from her. What was going on? She struggled to find any reasonable explanation.

Freyja was frightened.

For the next five minutes, she sobbed uncontrollably. She hunched into a ball, cradling her knees over the longing ache in her heart. She missed her family, Keyo her pet lynx, the forest, the farm, her home. She just wanted to go back to where she belonged.

Suddenly, someone or something was behind her, touching her shoulder. Startled, she bolted upright and spun around onto her butt, using her heels and palms to recoil back from the strange presence. Peering into the dark, there was nothing. Yet the essence of something remained. What was that?

"Go away!" she screamed, crawling backward until her back hit the headboard. The sound of her voice shocked her. It lingered in the air. Something was there, listening. "God," she gasped, "who is there? Who are you? I can't take this anymore!" She whimpered, "Help me! God, if you *are* there, help me right now! I'm going crazy. I'm going to kill myself. I mean it!"

She held her breath for as long as she could to demonstrate her conviction. Taking deeper and deeper breaths, she puckered her cheeks until she could not resist the exhale. "Stop making me breathe!" she demanded.

In a sudden bout of rage, she pounded her fists into the pillows. Then she buried her face into them, screaming, pushing the bulk into her nose and mouth, trying to suffocate herself.

Aaaaahhhhhhh!

And then, ever so suddenly, a warm energy pierced the stiffness of the bedroom walls and radiated around the room. It entered Freyja's cells too, like the heat of a warm bath. Slowly, she lifted her head. Her entire body tingled. Her skin prickled with a spooky sensation that wasn't scary or painful, but curiously soothing.

It was . . . love—pure, unconditional, abundant love.

With only indirect comparisons, she imagined that love was something warm, oozy, and yummy. She lingered in it. Her body vibrated as if energized joy could be bundled in a cozy blanket. She closed her eyes and imagined she might be floating there on top of her bed.

The warmth soon dissipated like steam evaporating in the morning sun. She landed once again in the chilly room, aware of her surroundings and the return of her normal senses. But the experience left a delightful desire for more. An unseen world was just out there, grazing her fingertips. She wondered if the presence had been one of her parents, a ghost visiting her. Or perhaps it was God, right there, drifting into her bedroom, the big man himself.

As swiftly as it had left, melancholy returned to her immediate space, sinking back into the drawers, behind the closet, under the dusty lampshades—all the strange events of the past day. A final tear ran down Freyja's face as she realized that she could no longer stay here, not in that bedroom, not in that house. Something was urging her to leave. It was impulsive, this desire to just take off, possibly irresponsible. She decided not to dwell on whether it made any sense.

Freyja left a note on the bed for Mrs. Rahuman, telling her she would be back soon. She grabbed a few belongings and her skateboard, and dashed out the back door. She sprinted through the neighbor's yard and down the street.

Freyja rode until she reached the field. The sun expanded overhead as the wildflowers swayed rhythmically. A small hawk circled and screeched. Freyja closed her eyes to absorb the warmth. Her pulse slowed, and her breath relaxed.

Whoosh!

Before Freyja could react, a van pulled up next to her, and its side door was thrown open. Two large men jumped out and grabbed her. Freyja screamed as a cover was pulled over her head, and her shriek drowned into a muffle. Covered in darkness, pain jolted through her back, legs, and body as she was slammed onto a hard floor. No one spoke, but there was a slamming of doors and revving of engines. Her stomach twisted in the accelerating motion of the vehicle in which she found herself. Freyja screamed again. This time, it was loud. She prayed that someone outside would hear her. It was loud enough—that was for sure—high and piercing. She kicked her legs too, so hard they could have broken bones. But then something sharp jabbed her neck. She grew dull and numb. In a few moments, she couldn't move or shout or do anything.

Everything went black.

CHAPTER SEVEN

IN BETWEEN WORLDS

The van pulled into a large complex outside of town. The long driveway was heavily guarded as they rolled alongside a tall security fence lining the considerable acreage along an airfield. The driver showed his ID to a uniformed military guard at the gate. Once inside, they proceeded to a large garage door leading underground. The tunnel led deep into the base, winding for at least a mile until they reached a loading dock. More armed guards greeted the van with their guns aimed at its rear doors. When they swung open, a plain-clothed man jumped out. He helped to pull down a gurney with a girl's body strapped to it.

"Target delivery," said the driver, greeting a man in a suit walking towards them with a scanner device in hand.

The man in the suit nodded and moved closer to the gurney, staring down at Freyja. He held the scanner over her body. It made a soft beeping noise. "No trace of the device?"

"No, sir. No exit wound either."

The man in the suit gestured to the guards to take the girl into another building. He touched the lapel on his jacket and spoke into a microphone. "Adept en route."

* * *

Freyja stirred. The sensations arose once again, with the squeak of what sounded like wheels in her ears. She carefully peeked out through her lashes to a blur of black overhead. She was lying down; that much was clear. She tried to lift her arms, but only the tips of her fingers moved. As she struggled to focus her sight, she could make out that black figures were looming above her. An entourage of guards at the four corners of the gurney that she was riding pushed through the doors and entered a brightly lit examination room. The oppressive white of the room was blinding. She tried to twist her neck to shield her eyes, but it wasn't easy. She could barely move a muscle. She stopped trying, and instead focused on the surroundings. It was a kind of hospital. There were faint noises. There was a foreign torrent of low humming punctuated by guttural pops, and then, male voices pierced the thrum. Who were they? Panic flooded her mind like poison. She was trapped.

Where am I?

Freyja fought against the drugs they had injected into her, drugs that wanted to pull her back into oblivion. She tried to spring up and run and run and run, anywhere. Run as fast as she could. But she couldn't; restraints held her down to the table.

A chilly draft crept over her legs and torso as someone draped a white sheet over her body.

Beep, beep, beep. The heart rate monitor echoed in the room.

There was a cool prick as a needle entered her arm.

Noooooo, she screamed inwardly.

The sensation made her want to be sick. It was a violation.

A few moments went by, and the effects were quick to work. Soon Freyja was drifting in and out of consciousness: black then white, black then white. The only good thing was that whatever they had injected her with had kindled some life back into her muscles.

Freyja gritted her teeth. Once she could cling onto that strange, sterile space of the white room, and not the oblivion of the drugs, she used every ounce of effort to speak. Lips parted, she asked, "Who are you?"

The voices stopped, but only for a moment. There was a faint whir of some machine near her head. She focused all her strength on moving something, anything. Her heart pounded fiercely in her chest. She pushed against the restraints holding her arms and legs to the table, but they were too strong. Freyja squinted under the harsh light, trying to get sight of her abductors, the room, anything. To her right was a dark wall with machines affixed to it, filling the gloom.

Through her blurred vision, she could make out a figure in white standing next to her.

"The device is gone," said the figure. It was a female's voice. Freyja focused harder. She could make out blonde hair, goggles, and a face mask. Something about that voice was familiar.

"Has it been traced?" another voice, which was more warbled than the woman's, followed it. It came from a speaker.

By now, Freyja's sight was clearing of the blonde-haired woman peering down at a clipboard and shaking her head. The white coat was an obvious cue that she was some sort of doctor, though the goggles were creepy. What kind of doctor wears goggles? The doctor put down the clipboard, sighed, and flipped through some more data on a screen that was running diagnostics on Freyja's body.

"Yes. Somewhere in the school," the doctor finally answered.

"How did it get removed?" asked the voice, a deep male voice.

"That is what I'm trying to find out. Why don't you and your goons go fetch the device before someone else does?" the doctor snapped. She turned away from the data screen and disappeared through a side door.

Freyja realized she was alone. She raised her head as much as she could. She was in a cavernous room of some kind. It was silent, but for the faint hum of a row of massive processing machines lining the wall. Yet, at the same time, this place was strangely familiar. Flashbacks wrestled with the numbing effects of the drugs, the room, the doctor, the men in jumpsuits standing guard, all of it. Freyja struggled to hold on to the memory, and then the doctor's voice returned.

"Hello," she said, standing over Freyja.

"Where am I?" Freyja asked. Her throat was drier than sandpaper.

"Relax. There is no need to worry. Everything is going to be fine," said the doctor as soothingly as she could. But there is only so much compassion a person in a face mask can offer.

Freyja's mind spun like a whirling top. And then it clicked. She knew who it was and where she was. "Dr. Mackay?" she asked.

The doctor ignored her.

It *was* her. The brows, the eyes, all those visits to the office, another place, not this one, the blood draws and shots—what had they been doing to her? Freyja was too weak to argue or insist. Bursts of pain pulsed in her head. Her ears rang, and her stomach lurched. Then, faintly, three words echoed from the radio static.

"Unstable gene sequence."

"What was that?" Freyja stuttered through her numb lips. Her heart rate accelerated.

"This will be much easier if you remain calm," said the doctor.

More sensations returned, but Freyja tried to contain it all. She decided to play dead out of fear, praying for escape.

"Activation has begun."

Activation? Who was talking? The words flickered in her mind more than her ears. Something was vibrating or charging within her, like a ripple under her skin. A wave of warmth, or flush of panic—it was impossible to tell. It was all very kinetic. Something deep in her blood was fierce, powerful, impenetrable, like the source of a tsunami gathering speed and mass as it approached.

"Terminate."

"Wait, what?" Freyja panicked.

Whose voice was that? Was it in her head? Were they talking about her? There was a horrible whirring sound in the background, like a drill.

I won't stay here, she told herself.

As fear surged in and filled her chest like smoke, an ice-cold hand touched her on the arm. "Overriding..." said the doctor. "Implanting Arktik ... Begin ..."

The speaker system crackled back to life as the man's voice returned, "Is it stable?"

"Presumably," said the doctor.

"Can she handle it?" the voice sounded concerned.

"We are about to find out," the doctor replied, more measured.

"What if she—"

The doctor hit a button on the screen and returned to Freyja's side.

The effect was instantaneous: Freyja became wild.

"*Let me go*!" she screamed, finding her voice at last. Rage coursed through her veins, and a cracking light blazed from her hands. It burst out, snapping the restraints as if they were just string.

The doctor fell back. The light spiraling up from Freyja's fists filled the doctor's goggles as she scrambled back against the wall, all legs and arms, mouth gasping. Freyja sat bolt upright on the table, just staring at her with an intensely new sensation—courage.

Freyja began to survey every detail in the room as quickly as she could, trying to figure out where she was. There was a sizeable black screening window, concealing something behind it. Perhaps a viewing room? She *was* on a table after all, and the spacious room appeared to be some sort of an operating theatre or observation room. Maybe there were people in there, watching. The thought made her sick. Her eyes returned to the room around her. It was full of machines of more types than she had ever seen or could even begin to describe. Her hands tingled and burned from the blast. The ceiling above was severely damaged in the explosion, with a hole right through to some steel beams, knocking a row of high-tech lights off their hinges. The ruptured metal was twisted and gnarled.

Suddenly there were screams and shouts, and in amongst them, orders bellowed out. A moment later, a squad of men in matching black uniforms came rushing through the doors and tackled her to the bed.

They held her firmly. Then one of them took out a needle, lowered it, and another prick of ice flowed into her veins, dousing her fire. She screamed and thrashed, but they were all too strong. Then the effects of the drugs hit her, and Freyja became limp. She tried to fight it, to stay in control, but slowly she drifted back into the haze.

CHAPTER EIGHT

A PRIMORDIAL EARTH

Freyja lay in a dark limbo for what felt to be an eternity. Her slumber was broken by a soft grandmotherly voice like honey on the lips after a warm cup of tea.

"Get up. Get up."

Freyja floated in a dreamy space, unsure of how to respond with her body. No longer could she sense the restraints wrapped tightly to her wrists and ankles, but still, she couldn't move.

Freyja opened her eyes. There were people in the room. The guards, those who had tackled her, were injured and exhausted, some of them with nasty burns to their arms, chests, cheeks, and legs. Freyja couldn't hear their words, but could understand the pained way they spoke. There was the woman in the white lab coat, her back to Freyja, staring at a wall of screens and knobs and images like an X-ray and CAT scan.

Freyja willed herself to move, and began to float like a boat without a rudder all around the room. Her heart raced as she realized she was floating above while her body was pinned below a machine.

Why is my body down there?

The menacing machine had tubes and wires reaching out like the tentacles of an octopus. They all clung to other devices, while the central crown, from which wires hung down and were attached to Freyja's temples, was its great head.

Freyja gasped at the frightening image. This metal octopus was clinging to her body.

"Come now." There it was again, that soft voice.

Yet there was no one there.

Am I going mad? she thought. *What is going on?*

Freyja wondered if this was one of those out-of-body, near-death experiences. Was she supposed to go into the light now?

"Am I dead?" she asked aloud.

"Come." There it was again.

Freyja closed her eyes and listened carefully to the voice, trying to figure out its location. It had a vibrational outline, like a signature in the air, a light trail leading out of the room. She surveyed her own body. Hovering, she reached her arms out and analyzed them. They were wispy like plumes of smoke or tendrils of blazing gold. She looked right, then left, and then at her legs. Her whole form was ghostly, translucent, buoyant, an ember outline peeling away from the bed.

Is this my spirit body? she wondered. It was featherlight, and it could dance and move freely in the air like butterflies on the breeze. "What the . . ." she whispered.

Freyja became confused. She was dead, but not dead. Was this purgatory? Would she be trapped here forever, this half world where she would move like a ghost between walls? She didn't want this. It frightened her, and she tried to climb back into her body. But suddenly, a luminous ball of light hovered in the hallway like a tiny condensed star. She moved towards it. The star thing shimmered in response to her gaze, beckoning her to follow it.

It led them both through the door and down an eternally long corridor, and then through several walls. They sped up and out of a small hatch that opened to a very long shaft, leading straight up for thousands of feet. They were traveling up and out of the compound.

Once at the top, they hovered under the moonlight on a dark rocky hillside.

"Hello," said the star.

"Are you a ghost?" Freyja whispered. "What's happening?" She tried to lace her words with authority, to demand to know what was going on. But they sputtered out of her etheric mass in garbled sparks of notes like pounding on a piano or blowing clumsy sounds out of a trumpet. In this world, words did not come from vocalizations but another way of communicating. The etheric spirit body she now occupied did not function like her skin-and-bones body. She was frustrated and unsure of what to do.

The star danced and shimmied in front of Freyja, like an animated crystal ball filled with spiraling colors.

What are you trying to tell me? Freyja thought.

"Remember."

"Remember? What? You? I doubt I would ever forget someone, or something, like you."

"Remember."

Freyja realized that the star was hearing her thoughts. "Okay. Um, am I dead?"

"No."

"Uhhhhh. Who—or what are you?" Freyja pointed her thoughts as forcefully as she could with this awkward mode of communicating.

"Ursa."

She understood the answer, but marveled at the process. "Ursa?" Freyja repeated. When she did so, there was a wave of energy touching every particle of her astral body. She lit up brighter, like a flare on the sun. It was an energetic yes. "Whoa," she whispered.

"Remember."

Freyja wasn't sure what she was supposed to remember. And then something flickered across Ursa's surface and rose inside her mind. "Uh? Is that—are those . . . mine or yours?"

Images appeared in front of her like a projector on a screen. Ursa's iridescent surface reflected whatever Freyja thought about, like a smart screen.

"Nash?" An image of Nash stood in front of her. He started to play air piano or something, and she could hear an incredibly haunting melody growing up around her. Then the lab and crazy doctors popped up on her mind screen. Freyja cringed and shook herself to move away from those memories.

"Go further. Let go."

Then she let her mind loose with a quickening speed and fluidity of space. The wildlands around her childhood home appeared. Her mind touched down, and then flew farther into a spiraling vortex. She cut through an ocean of time like a torpedo, seeking islands of moments through lifetimes and epochs and, suddenly, a very different image of her planet.

Primordial Earth.

Freyja gasped as the image came out of her conscious memory, as clear as something from yesterday. "Uh, I don't get it. Have I been there?"

Ursa vibrated and hummed in affirmation. *"First Earth."*

Ursa's orb body reflected a world that was shockingly familiar to her, but how? These were humans. They were robustly healthy and happy. They were gathering, working, playing, building peacefully. She felt in her blood the energies of this time and place as though she had also lived it. The sensory memory of vibrancy, love, joy, and safety filled her awareness.

She soared like an eagle over the forests, lakes, lush gardens, dense jungles, sighting settlements all over this version of planet earth. Along the coastal regions were large highly technically advanced ships that appeared to be hovering. The people communicated in mental visions, the same way she was doing with Ursa now. *Telepathically*—that was the term, which she instantly recalled and understood as these memories arrived at her present moment observations. The thoughts were friendly and open. Schools were teaching Earth alchemy, plant healing, and arts. People moved and shaped elements with their own hands. Stones and metals were like putty. Homes were very modest and arranged in an organic geometric alignment. There were pyramidal structures in the center of every settlement.

A lake caught her attention, and she moved in for a closer view. There was a beautiful older woman, cinnamon honey skin, black and gray hair braided in long delicate interwoven pieces, and a splendid gauzy dress. The woman sang a seductive melody. Her words were foreign to Freyja, but she understood the meaning.

Great Mother, we honor you.

Bless our bodies.

Bless our homes.

Bless this land and sea.

She then placed a glowing crystal into the water's edge. The water immediately sparkled more brightly.

"What did she do?"

"Healing."

"Like medicine?"

"Yes."

"Who are they?"

"Humans."

"When was this?"

"Before…"

"Before?" Freyja realized that something awful was about to happen. An ominous horror rose into her being.

The skies above the people suddenly darkened. An armada crashed through the atmosphere across the planet. At first, it appeared to be an advanced alien attack. But these were meteors and fragments from a colliding star system—two worlds merging. The seers had tried to warn the others. A bewildering force of giant meteors bombarded the planet with the impact of hundreds of nuclear bombs.

"Why didn't they listen?" asked Freyja.

Ursa sent a comforting wave and nudged Freyja to continue.

The initial impact and aftershocks wiped out every village on Earth. The stream of space rock ripped open the mountains and displaced the seas. Fires and floods consumed nearly every inch of land. Many of these rocks from space carried foreign microbes and elements; these injected the planet's body with fiery force. Without their communities, shelters, clean water, or air, the humans were sick and dying.

The tired woman with the long braids went from shelter to shelter, attempting to bolster the survivors and animals with her medicines. There were massive piles of bodies on makeshift pyres and mourners everywhere.

The woman seemed familiar. "I know her . . ."

"Remember."

Freyja refocused on the moment, despite the trauma of seeing it all. Survivors were despondent, scared, and angry. Everything was destroyed, including their connection to each other. Some claimed the meteors were a weapon sent by an alien race desiring Earth for themselves. Others said the space rocks had infected people with mania and paranoia. There was an invasion of sorts. Fear now ruled every thought and every decision.

"So, were they invaded by aliens?" Freyja asked.

Ursa rippled and urged her to keep seeing.

The vulnerable survivors were frightened and sought reassurance, answers, guidance. The story of their peaceful garden had a tragic end. Everyone left behind their old lives to find a new way of being on this dangerously altered planet.

Once reasonable men developed iron fists to beat back the unknown and unknowable that paralyzed their efforts to rebuild. Without strong and clear leadership, fledgling communities were vulnerable to all manner of abuse, degradation, theft, and betrayal. The higher powers and abilities that once used to thrive and create beauty were now used to hoard, control, and concentrate power to the few. The pattern was foreign, but quickly adopted. Tribalism threatened to destroy First Earth. The advanced knowledge of human abilities and technologies was rapidly escalating into a dark weapon.

The survivors of the council of elders called a meeting. No one could leave until they had a solution to save Earth and humanity from this bitter, ugly spiral. The elders met for days and then weeks. They soon realized that the only way to stop the trajectory was to cut it off. They decided to wipe memories of this knowledge from nearly all the survivors and the unborn until humanity matured enough to handle these powerful tools.

"Wow. How did the elders decide who to keep the knowledge and who to erase?"

Ursa buzzed. *"The Nine."*

"The Nine? What's that?"

They were like ancient librarians or knights protecting the way: this self-selected group created nine books of knowledge and elected one individual to collect, update, and guard this knowledge before passing it on to a specially chosen successor. These books appeared like giant encyclopedias in her mind, full of ancient scripts, sketches, and calculations.

A DNA helix spun in space, like the models in her science class. The DNA helix was a model of all the genes that coded life. It was the ingredient list and included many mysterious parts that science was actively seeking to understand.

The Council of Nine watched as one of their groups manipulated DNA strands in some quasi-secret lab in the now primitive environment of Earth.

"What did they do?" Freyja's eyes widened as parts of the human genome turned black. "Did they just turn off genes for humanity?"

"Yes."

To protect their knowledge indefinitely, the Nine created a genetic treatment that turned off the genes with any memory of these abilities or their history. No future born children would be able to access this knowledge accidentally.

Then, one of the council members spoke: *"This knowledge is forbidden to all but those with this sacred covenant."*

The other council members all nodded in agreement.

"Wow," Freyja gasped. She realized instantly how the Nine must have created the myths around the world to caution humans away from the forbidden knowledge. It was necessary to prevent humanity from using this power before it was ready.

"Oh my God. All our myths! The garden of Eden, the folly of seeking or gaining God-like power, Prometheus, Icarus, Frankenstein, even the Manhattan Project—story after story, warning humanity against getting too close to insight or understanding."

"Yes."

"So, like the Gods were just humans who didn't forget? Zeus, Athena, or Thor, all those guys?"

"Yes."

"The Nine were like Gods after this?"

Ursa flickered yes.

Freyja was overwhelmed. What was she supposed to do with all this? This vision or dream was a helluva trip.

"Remember . . ." Ursa reached out with a small tendril of energy and touched what would be Freyja's forehead. She placed something into her etheric body. It merged into her being, like an inoculation of sorts. *"Remember."*

"Remember? Remember what?" Freyja asked. "That I've gone insane, and so has the world?" She was tired of being confused and angry. She was exhausted from asking question after question. What did any of this mean anyway? Was it even real?

Then, with the most delicate sigh, like a sweet exhale, Ursa faded from view.

Freyja's spirit grew heavy, and, like falling over a cliff, tumbled back into her body.

CHAPTER NINE

OUTSIDE LOOKING IN

The blonde woman in the goggles sighed deeply. The IV was half empty. She jiggled the bag of liquid. "Return her first thing in the morning."

"Yes, ma'am," answered one of the men in uniform.

The guards moved Freyja's body off the exam room table and back onto the gurney she came in on. The bandage on her neck, just under her left ear, was gently removed by a man in a white medical suit. There was a very tiny red dot that looked more like an acne scar than anything else. He dabbed it with a swab and nodded at the guard.

The woman removed her goggles and sighed. She had never intended to get emotionally involved with these kids. It should have been purely about the science. But it was hard not to worry. Something wasn't right, and she wasn't sure she could keep her safe anymore.

Dr. Deborah Mackay was recruited straight out of her PhD program at Cornell to continue her epigenetics work. Her specialty was controlling gene expression and, more particularly, how to turn it on or off. This work was highly controversial and challenging to prove, and because of it, she was coveted by every significant genomic biotech company out there.

When Drake had first approached her, his offer was as lucrative as it was intriguing. She was discovering how wireless signals could control genes, for example, how to turn off the cancer gene with one switch, or turn it on. If found, it would be the world's most potent bioweapon. Dr. Mackay had been excited about the prospects and the power this technology proposed.

This technology could cripple rogue nations in an instant if they failed to comply with peace treaties, for example. Rulers and despots committing genocide against their country could be stopped in seconds. Those who had this technology would hold the fate of the world in their hands.

Unfortunately, the science continued to elude NuTech. Animal experiments were somewhat encouraging, but the human trial results did not prove as successful. It was reasonably easy to turn cancer genes on, but far more difficult to turn them off. Too many variables in the environment were complicating their analysis. Her pilot program, Arktik, had killed nearly every animal and compromised every human subject to date. The most recent trials had been encouraging, but nowhere near the level of control necessary to use in the field.

Spontaneous combustion, a possible result of hyper-electrical concentrations being absorbed atmospherically in the body, left far too many corpses, and raised too many questions. The last incident had involved a young man in Paris, who took out an entire wing of a hotel when he imploded. The investigators found tiny pieces of the device in the debris and part of a code that could potentially lead to NuTech. France was raising a stink even though this was beyond national politics.

Deborah rubbed her temples as the guards hauled Freyja and the gurney out the door. She glanced up at the hole in the ceiling and sighed. Freyja's reaction was one of the more explosive activations she'd seen. It was probably the worst idea ever to give Freyja this remote genetic operating system, Arktik. But it was that or termination. An active Adept was very difficult to control and even harder to track without aid, like a shark in the Atlantic. They had to track where she was always and monitor her development.

The wild mutations were the most fascinating as they still had no idea what triggered their ancient genes to come online. Like a wild animal, these kids had to be tagged and kept under close surveillance. As risky as Arktik was, it bought them all time to see what Freyja could do.

CHAPTER TEN

IN THE MIDDLE OF NOWHERE

The chilly autumn air grasped fleeting fingers across her face as the sun's rays burned through the fog and forest around her. The warmth and light stirred her faster than the iPod alarm clock ever did. Bolting upright, Freyja woke up ready to run.

Where am I?

Her skateboard was resting upside down against the curb of the nearby street, on the edge of the field. She was sitting up in the grass, a dozen feet away, covered in dew.

"Wow, I must have wiped out pretty bad," she said, rubbing her head and glancing once more at the skateboard. Some seizures were worse than others, but this must have been a bad one, for her body felt wrecked.

Freyja held out her hands in the air and inspected her arms and legs—nothing permanent. Her head was pounding, but otherwise, she appeared unscathed. "Great."

Hoisting herself up, Freyja staggered over to the board, and wearily hopped on and skated home. The whole way home, she imagined excuses she could give the Rahumans for being gone so long and obviously after dark. They must be worried.

She arrived at the house and opened the door; inside was very quiet. Anna Beth and Sammy must not have been up yet. She roamed in, and found Mr. and Mrs. Rahuman at the kitchen table.

Mrs. Rahuman put down the phone exasperated. "Where have you been all night? I've been calling around everywhere."

"Um, I think I wiped out, or maybe I had a seizure. I'm not sure. I woke up in the field. Sorry." Freyja rubbed her head again, and then pulled out a chair at the table to sit down.

Mrs. Rahuman sighed. "You've been suspended from school."

"Oh."

"We wanted to talk to you about this . . ." Mrs. Rahuman pushed a brochure for a Southern Oregon school towards Freyja. The brochure appeared to be for a boarding school of some kind.

"I don't understand."

"We think that, perhaps, given everything you've been through, that maybe it would best for you to be in a place where they can support you."

Freyja shifted in her seat. She wanted to just run out the door, but was unable to move. Her hands started to tingle. She glanced down to check the scars on her arm, but they were unremarkable. Then, like a burning, stabbing pain, the ache pierced her head. "Ow!"

"Are you okay, honey?" asked Mrs. Rahuman.

"I'm fine."

They sat silently. Mr. And Mrs. Rahuman studied Freyja sternly.

"They have a place for you now. We can leave in the morning."

"Um. Yeah. Okay." Freyja was disoriented and confused. "I'll go pack."

Freyja stood up and smiled meekly. She tried to walk to her room, as though being thrown out to some boarding school was no big deal, but her stomach was tied in anxious knots. Like a leaf cast upon a rapidly moving river, all she could do was keep floating, keep breathing, and survive.

She sat on the edge of her bed, head in hands, trying to sort out the intense litany of thoughts and memories flooding her mind, like pulling that weird thing out of her hand at school just days earlier. What was that? How did it get into her hand in the first place? She returned to a vision of nightmarish black webs unfurling themselves upon people, her scars mysteriously lighting up like a Christmas tree, and she somehow hurling her mortal enemy, Marley, into a wall with just the tips of her fingers.

Swimming in confusion and anger, Freyja wondered if maybe she was going insane. Her scars were not glowing now. She scanned her room, but found nothing black or spooky. And far from having the power to assault people telekinetically, instead, she had suffered a seizure at a suburban field. No, she just felt dead and nothing more. Not powerful. Not special. Just numb.

"What the . . ." she muttered to herself. "I don't want to go away. These people can't help me. They'll lock me up like Aunt Lucy."

She sat in silence before grabbing her backpack, stuffing it with some clothes, her book with the money stash, the key that Sammy had given her, and her seizure medication. School would be starting soon, so she wiggled out the old window and jumped out onto the flower bed. Once out of the garden, Freyja jogged down the street to Nash's house. She had to say goodbye to him before she left, even if he would try to talk her out of running away.

Freyja knocked on the back door of his home.

"Hey, whassup?" said Nash, swinging it open. He was eating a piece of toast heaped with some green jelly. "Want one?" he asked with his mouth full.

"Uh, no. I got suspended," Freyja said, averting her eyes, embarrassed.

Nash stopped chewing. "Figured," he finally said. "You kinda went Hulk Hogan yesterday."

"Yeah, well, anyway. They're sending me away."

"What do you mean? Where?"

"I don't know . . . Somewhere down South."

"What? Why?"

"They think I need special help, I guess."

"Help? For what? Kids get in fights. You are a model student."

"I know. That's why I'm leaving," Freyja said.

"What do you mean?"

"I'm going *home*."

Nash hesitated. "Home? Like, your old home? To the farm in Hood River?"

"Yeah, I'm going back." Freyja peered at him sideways to see his reaction. She almost didn't believe herself, either. But as soon as she said it, it felt right.

Freyja turned to go. She wanted to run hard, but didn't want to look like an idiot either. She smiled and waved, thinking about her next move.

"Wait. It's not *that* far. I can be back before dinner." Nash ducked inside, bumping around his porch and the kitchen where he stashed all his gear.

"What?" She didn't expect that response.

"I'll go with you!" he hollered. In another moment, he popped out the door with his backpack and his skateboard. "Let's go."

Freyja drowned the urge to wrap her arms around his neck and squeal with joy. "Really? But school? Your parents?"

"Nah, it's cool. My parents don't care. Today is an easy day. I'm not missing much."

They skated to the MAX light rail station, and caught the first train to the bus station across town. Navigating the city was not hard, as pavements and tracks connected everything. They skated a few blocks to the Greyhound bus depot, a run-down glass and metal hub that reeked of oil and cigarettes. Hood River was an hour east, and buses left frequently to the rural towns no longer connected by passenger train.

Freyja pulled the money book out of her pack and set it on the counter. "One one-way and one two-way, please," she said to the dark-haired woman swiveling in her chair behind a desk.

"You want what, darlin'?" she hollered as though shocked by the configuration.

"Just *one* one-way, and *one* round trip to Hood River."

"So, one single and one return. Gotcha." She stood up and wiped potato chip crumbs off her blue polyester blouse. "Gimme one sec," she added, and then lifted a clipboard from another desk and flipped a few pages before pressing a stubby finger against the last page. "That would be the Gorge line."

Nash fished in his pocket for some cash. "Here. I just got paid. You save that," he said with a smile.

Freyja blushed. A rush of overwhelming big-fat emotion softened her heart towards him. She quickly squelched it, afraid to allow any vulnerability or weirdness between them—just friends. Best friends. Good. "Thanks."

Nash smiled. "No prob . . ."

The attendant gave her their tickets and smiled. "Good luck, dear."

Freyja nodded, and then paused confused. Why did she wish her luck? The woman stuffed another handful of chips into her mouth and returned to her seat at the desk.

The bus station had several rows of 1960s style bucket seats strung together on loose metal posts. The cool fluorescent lights flickered sickly so that everyone looked like cancer patients or zombies.

"So, what do you think you're gonna find in Hood River?" Nash finally asked as they waited for the bus.

"I don't know. Maybe my aunt is there?" She shrugged.

"What if she's not?"

"Then, maybe I can find her. I . . . I don't know. I can't stay here."

"Yeah, I get it."

Just then, a large aging bus rolled into a parking bay ahead of the bench where they were waiting. The sign on the front slowly flipped one letter at a time. It read: "THE DALLES."

"That's us." Freyja stood and stretched, and then swung her backpack over one shoulder and grabbed Nash by the sleeve. "Let's go!"

They hopped onto the bus and found seats near the back. The bus was dank and worn. Bits were peeling off the walls. Seats had holes in the cushions. The grimy windows had fingered words and smiley faces traced into the dust.

Hunkered down and anxious about the journey ahead, Freyja distracted herself by studying each of the colorful personalities who climbed aboard. There was a silver-haired woman in her fifties, wearing an ill-fitting sweatshirt that said "HE IS RISEN" on the front. Then a younger man with a wide belly, a beanie cap, and oversized headphones clamored down the aisle. After him came a haggard young woman, pale, with dark eyes, followed by a small girl dressed in pink with matted hair. The woman yanked the girl and steered her into a window seat with the other hand as she heaved their frayed duffle bag into the overhead rack. The little girl studied Freyja as she climbed into her seat a couple of rows in front of them.

"What's your name?" she squeaked.

"Freyja . . . What's yours?"

"Mine is Bella. Where are you goin'?"

Her mother shushed her and asked her to turn around and mind her own business. Bella continued to peer through the crack between the seats to study Freyja.

Home, Freyja thought. *I'm going home.*

Freyja put on her headphones and soon dozed, mesmerized by the trees and the grand Columbia River running into a stream of colorful streaks outside her window. It wasn't long before she and Nash both fell asleep.

* * *

The hour-long trip commenced as Freyja quickly slipped into a sound slumber.

"Hood River Station," called a low voice over the speaker system.

They slowly stirred, noses colliding as they awakened from their nap on each other's shoulders. Nash grinned as Freyja roused. She realized she'd been drooling and wiped her face. The bus creaked and huffed as the engine released itself from the long haul. The stop was near the train station, just a block from Main Street.

"This is it." Freyja scanned the town streets anxiously for signs of the familiar.

Hood River consisted of a five-block town, a few gas stations, and miles of stretching farmland. In the summer, it was abuzz with wind and kite surfers. The rest of the year, gray skies sheltered prized pear and cherry orchards along the fertile valley between the mighty Columbia River and the pristine peaks of Mount Hood.

Freyja and Nash skated out past Main Street, and hiked up to the outskirts where a long country road ran through the orchards and fields for several long crisp miles. The previous days' stressors unfurled with the sun's yawning light.

"Let's take a break here," she said.

They scooted carefully under a barbed wire fence and came into a hayfield. A few cows grazed on the golden wheat and a small glen of trees running towards a river several yards away.

"Do you know where your house is?" Nash said, pulling a snack bar out of his backpack and offering a bite to Freyja.

Freyja walked over to a patch of soft grasses and fell cross-legged into them. "Sort of. It's been a long time . . ."

Autumn had pricked the orchard in palettes of honey and cinnamon reds. Leaves twirled in piles of treasure for the birds and squirrels to hunt for acorns and fallen berries. A blackbird, perched atop a freshly harvested apple tree, called out her coordinates to the canopy of creatures hovering among limbs and boughs. Freyja softened her eyes and listened to the gentle breezes through the treetops and the refreshing tumult of glacial run-off churning through the nearby river.

Freyja remembered this valley and these fields the way one remembers the hug of a beloved relative: warm, pulsing, comforting, steady. So many years, she played in these orchards and dug in this soil. She reached down and touched the dry grasses poking up through pebbles and dirt.

"Mama," she whispered.

A memory struck her suddenly as the sun's rays melted on her head. She recalled her mother's horrified expression as lightning lifted Freyja off the ground.

Mama.

She had been playing near the tree in the yard. Out of nowhere, the fiery hand reached down and yanked her into the sky. In many ways, it was like an eternity as time slowed and every detail froze into molecular space. But it was over in an instant, just long enough for her mom, dad, and aunt Lucy to run outside and reach for her. Her father caught her in mid-air and rushed her into the house for emergency care. Her mother and aunt Lucy shrieked and cried. For some reason, her parents left on a trip soon after that and never returned. Freyja's scars healed, but not her heart. Why did they go? Was it her fault, somehow?

A strange tingling sensation filled her body sitting there in the sun. She wondered if the scars were going to start glowing again as she gazed down at her arm.

Suddenly there was a powerful current flowing straight up her arm and shoulder and into her spine. "What's that . . ." Freyja braced herself for something strange. Her entire being melted into a landscape of colors and sounds.

Suddenly, an egg-sized ball of light exploded behind her eyes, cascading through her mind like falling stars.

"Oh my!" Instantly she remembered Ursa: the crystal she had placed in her head, the conversations, the visions, everything.

"Remember."

The kidnapping, the ancient Eden, the cataclysm, the wars, the Nine.

"Before."

"Wow!"

It all came in an instant; the lab, the guards, the blonde-haired woman, her body shaking and her fingers quivering, a sharp prick at the base of her skull. Freyja raised a hand and touched an odd bump.

"Auuuuuuuummmmm." A low, soothing melody reverberated all around her.

Nash was perched on a large rock overlooking the river, pulling back his arm and tossing in pebbles. The field was still quiet and serene. Gentle clouds floated through the sky above, but the sun was *different*. It was pulsating somehow. Freyja squeezed her eyes and focused as hard as she could at a point away from the sun so that she could absorb it in her periphery. It was contracting and expanding, over and over. As she did this, the hum of the sun grow louder. It was a pulsating rhythm of sound and energy, just as it was a pulsating vision. It was as though the sun was breathing into her. The sun was alive, communing directly with her.

Freyja was overwhelmed by an expansive oneness and connection to everything around her. All the quivering frequencies, fractals of light, beams of matter, and molecules shimmering, every single subjective point of reference was both entwined and pronounced. Life was alive. And she was alive and, even better, fully aware.

"Awake."

She listened again.

"Auuuummmmmmm."

"You *do* realize we're out in the middle of nowhere, and *no one* knows where we are, don't you?" Nash's voice pulled Freyja out of the trance. He skipped another stone into the river.

"I know where we are," she said, pointing across the field.

Just behind the next tree line was a house.

Home.

CHAPTER ELEVEN

WHERE DID THEY GO?

Freyja jumped up from her resting place. Her heart was beating with a rush of excitement. She glimpsed the roofline through the colorful canopy clinging just barely to the orchard bows. She raced through the tall brush, across the lawn, to the perimeter of the brick and stucco farmhouse, caressing the wild neglected hydrangea bushes and ivy-covered walls with her eager hands. The arched doorway framed in oxidized copper presented a heavy molded bear knocker made of brass. She recognized it from so many of her memories. At the height of those memories was Keyo standing, hissing at anyone who approached the house.

"Keeeeyyyyyoooooo . . . Keeeeyyyyyyoooo!" she called out. It was her call to her friend, her wild lynx with her soft spotted fur and wise jet-black eyes. She spoke secret magic of tamed wildness to Freyja's soul: protective, fierce, companion.

Where is she now?

Freyja missed her terribly. She scanned the woods, as if she might suddenly emerge from the forest. Her whole childhood came back in an instant, all the little details that had been buried in mental boxes, keeping the pain of her loss at bay. She thought about coming here so many times. but was afraid of what she might find.

Freyja jiggled the front door latch. She walked around to the side entrance by the garage port, but found that door also locked. Freyja remembered there was a spare key in a terra cotta flowerpot by the doorstep. She bent down and lifted it. There, in the soil, was a thick rusted house key.

"But what if someone lives here now?" Nash protested, as Freyja stood with the key in one hand and used her other hand to brush off clumps of dried soil stuck in between its teeth.

"No one is here," she answered confidently.

"How do you know?"

Freyja turned to Nash. "If anything happened to my aunt, she would have left the house to me..." Her voice trailed off as she wondered if, perhaps, she was mistaken. She decided to proceed with her assumptions anyway.

Nash raised an eyebrow as she attempted to jimmy the lock. "Want me to give it a go?"

"I think... I... got... it," said Freyja, just as the lock gave way and the door creaked open. Freyja glanced at Nash, smiled, and then stepped inside.

They came into a pantry, where Freyja could smell the stale odor of old food and repressed the urge to gag. She flipped the light switch on the wall. The electricity was off. She pulled her phone from her backpack and turned on the flashlight. She held it before her and lit the way into the kitchen. Squalor filled their eyes. Dust coated every surface several inches thick. The sink was still full of the dishes from the day they had left all those years ago. She opened the fridge, but quickly closed it, overwhelmed by the trapped stench of rotting cheese and milk.

"Oh! Gah!" gasped Nash, holding his nose as they turned to leave the kitchen.

Freyja moved into the main hallway to the library and the front hall of the home. "This is where I used to play and study," she said.

By the time she was ten, she had every book and object memorized. That included ivory tusks engraved with ancient hieroglyphs; a multi-colored glass bowl with fossilized eggs, crustaceans, and prehistoric insects; and a magnifying glass on a tripod carved from a bone that she often used to study the micro scripts in some of the ancient texts. Framed to the wall, a map of Central America marked her mother's sites for her work. Freyja studied it for a second, and then returned to the collection of old books on the shelves. She traced her finger over one row of spines, and then raised her dusty finger into Nash's face.

"That's a lot of history," he mused.

On the fourth shelf over, Freyja spied a small black box made of stone. She picked it up and stroked the smooth carvings around its lid and heavy base. Turning it over, she saw a small dial with more markings around it. She used her fingers and clicked the dial around a few times, recalling moments with it in the past. She remembered opening it at some point. As she shook it, something clanked inside. She thought maybe she could give it a go later and unzipped her backpack and dropped it in.

Freyja backed into a large table at the center of the circular library. A pencil box sat spilled open—a silent reminder of the day the police came to take her aunt away and sent her to the Rahuman's. Next to the pencils was a stack of papers. Freyja picked them up and started to read the text.

"This summons shall heretofore declare that Ms. Lucy Stegsen is unfit as the sole custodian of the minor child Juliana Freyja Wolfe and shall relinquish custody to the state of Oregon until such time."

Freyja gasped. This was the letter the police had slipped into their mail slot. Her stomach turned. As she returned the papers to the table, a tiny flickering dot caught her eye. The light was coming from an oculus window at the top of the stairs above the foyer and the library nook.

"Hey, let me show you upstairs." She tugged Nash on the sleeve. He put aside some artifacts he had discovered, and followed her.

Freyja tramped up the stairs, touching the familiar bulk of the railing, worn and soft. Her feet hit each rise with nostalgia. These stairs had carried her up and down for years through breakfast and bedtimes, tantrums and naps, novels and daydreams. At the top were bedrooms to the right and left. Her parents' room was to the left. She remembered peeking in for nighttime cuddles, seeing them both sitting up and reading or working on some project with notes strewn about their bed. She could always find a place between them to curl up safe.

Her old bedroom was the first one on the right. She pressed the old door, which now creaked in surprise at her return. She sighed at the sight of her fluffy patchwork bed. The musty down bedcovers, and all the other tokens of childhood she had been sifting through, weighed on her heart. All the years apart were almost too much to bear. The unavoidable tragedy of events carving through her life were unkind and heartless.

Sensing this, Nash sat down on the bed and pulled her to his side. He put his hand on her back and tried to soothe her in his way. Somehow relieved of her armor, Freyja turned towards him, burying her face into his shoulder. She hadn't allowed herself to be utterly vulnerable with anyone since she had left this place. Somehow, his being here, their connection, gave her permission to let down her guard. She surrendered into him, sobbing.

Nash held her with an unusual strength. "I get it," he said. "No wonder you wanted to come back."

Freyja's heart expanded. He smelled vital and healthy like he was some impenetrable force around her. His blood coursed viscerally through his veins, giving pulse to his heart, a rhythmic breathing. She imagined their hearts beating together, and then, gathering her strength, she lifted her face and gazed into his bright blue eyes. They pulled her into a magnetic orbit of momentary weightlessness. A powerful urge to kiss him washed over her, but she resisted.

"Something is happening to me," she said instead.

"Yeah, I noticed," he replied. His heartbeat rose with the sweet caresses of his warm breath.

Reluctantly, she pushed away from him and said, "No, I mean, my body. I . . . I'm changing."

Nash paused, and then with a smile, he said, "Freyja, that's happening to all of us."

"No, you don't understand," she replied, and pushed herself up and pressed her fingers together. "You have to see this," she whispered, and with that, she furrowed her brow, and a gold streak of light burst from her fingertips.

"Whoa!" Nash yelped, falling backward away from her.

"And there's something else. I have these markings . . ." Slowly, awkwardly, Freyja lifted her shirt and showed him the side of her torso, then her shoulder, and then her arm.

"I thought you got hit by lightning?"

"I did. But something weird is happening now."

Suddenly, as she was explaining this, the tingling sensation began rising again. Then they started glowing. The patterns and swirls, little ornate details, and symbols, flickered and faded over her body, lava flowing and cooling across her flesh.

"Are those . . . tattoos?" He gulped, unable to believe what he was seeing.

"No. It just started . . . happening."

"What do you mean?"

"I don't know. Ben bit me the other day. My hand was bleeding, and there was this *thing*."

"Thing? What thing?"

"This device-looking piece of metal. I pulled it out, and then suddenly, all this started." Freyja gestured down at the markings again.

"Wow. What do you think it is?"

"I don't know. But there's more," Freyja said.

"More?"

"Yeah, I was kidnapped last night."

"What? By whom? Where?"

"I don't know. It's hard to explain. I can't go back to the Rahumans." Freyja held her breath, waiting for his response.

Nash shook his head, his eyes wide. "Dude, this is insane."

Freyja bowed her head. "I know."

"No, I mean . . . It's like, cool, you know? Like a real-life mystery. Hey, maybe you are some super-secret weapon or something." He laughed.

Freyja groaned. "Nash, I'm serious. I'm scared."

"Hey, I'm just kidding. There's got to be some answer. Right?"

"What am I going to do?"

"I don't know. I can't think when I'm hungry. Any food in this house that isn't rotten?"

Freyja smiled and pulled herself off the bed. "Let's go check."

She led him downstairs, relieved for a distraction, and hunted around the pantry. They found some canned cherries and pickles, all the while holding their noses for the stench enveloping the kitchen area. All the food in the freezer was spoilt, so they took the jars they'd found back up to the bedroom, where they could wrap up in big blankets and share their odd bounty. Freyja threw some wood onto a tiny potbelly stove and lit a fire. There, as the flames flickered, they shared their strange but satisfying dinner.

After a few hours passed, Freyja said, "Wait, we should probably get you to the bus station."

"I'll stay. I'll text my dad. I have a project with Grant. He'll cover for me."

Freyja smiled with relief. She didn't want to be alone, and she didn't want to be away from Nash. Freyja, for the first time in a very long time, was not completely alone. "You're the best," she said.

"It's gonna be all right," he said, hitting her with a pillow.

"Yeah." Freyja whacked him back.

Nash hooted and hit her again, initiating a massive pillow fight. Hot, sweaty, and tired, they wrestled, and laughed, and wrestled some until their laughter turned into yawns, and they fell into an exhausted slumber. The moon stood sentry outside the farmhouse, holding them close.

* * *

"Caaawwwww!" a nearby crow called out an alarm.

Both had fallen fast asleep. Freyja woke to Nash's arms around her. She reluctantly moved him and sat up. It was still pitch-black outside.

"Go now!" The voice was urgent.

Still sleepy and not quite sure what was happening, Freyja shook Nash. "Come on; we have to go!"

They grabbed their backpacks and boards and hurried out the back door, locking it as they left. They ran through the dusky field towards the edge of the woods. As they ran, a big black van, headlights off, drove slowly up the long driveway.

CHAPTER TWELVE

LETTERS AND MAPS

The crow's alarm sent adrenaline surging through Freyja's body. She wasn't sure why, but she understood its message. *"Get out now."*

Freyja and Nash sprinted over rocks and shrubs along the property's backside to go deeper into cover, moving quickly towards the forest rim. Freyja turned for a final view at the house. Her heart stopped as shadowy figures were circling it like predators.

"What's going on? Who is that?" gasped Nash, catching his breath as they sat behind the brush, eyeing the ominous figures combing over her family's farm.

"I wish I knew," she said.

"What do we do?" he asked.

Freyja's mind swirled and searched for something to guide her. She had no idea what to do next. It indeed wasn't possible to go back to the Rahumans. A wave of dread cast over her heart. She scanned Nash's face for some ideas. And then something caught her eye—a brisk blur, an oscillating beat, almost like a tiny engine, spinning around them.

"What was that?" she asked out loud.

"Hey!" said Nash pointing and wrenching his torso around to follow the tiny flurry with his eyes.

It was a hummingbird fluttering wildly about, darting close enough to demand attention.

"Whoa!" said Freyja as it darted into her face.

The tiny sapphire bird hovered less than a foot away from her. Its small pin black eyes pierced into Freyja with an otherworldly insistence.

"Hello, there?" said Freyja, half expecting it, especially at this point, to answer.

She was mesmerized by the zipping and zinging sound of her wings, swishing in a constant elliptical churn. Something shivered up through her body. Every nerve ending tingled as if there was a sort of transmission happening between her and this tiny creature. She reflexively inspected her scars to spy any energy movement in her hands.

"Follow me."

"What?" Freyja still wasn't sure if she imagined these things. "Did you hear that?" she asked Nash.

He was transfixed and awed by the bird hovering without fear in front of them, and then he paused and listened. "Uh, what do mean?"

"I heard something. It said, *'Follow me,'* I think."

The bird hovered in front of Nash's face. "I hear buzzing wings ... a consistent breeze .... trees creaking ... and ..." He strained to listen harder. "Yeah, that's about it."

Something was tugging in her skin. And then the tiny hummingbird fled. It flew a few yards down a path through the woods, and then returned as if it were beckoning them to follow. "It's like I can hear the bird's thoughts."

"She's pretty insistent, whatever she's saying," said Nash chuckling.

"I think you are right." Freyja laughed. "Look!" She showed Nash her scars as they began to illuminate beneath her skin.

"What does it mean?"

"I think ... it means ... we are supposed to follow her."

They crept away from the bush and scuttled down the wooded trail just in case the men in black turned to hunt the yard. The tiny hummingbird hovered several feet ahead of them, leading the way through the thick and overgrown forest. A delicate ribbon of gold feathers caught the dappling light around her neck, like a lasso or leash, pulling them onward. The hills and valleys between Hood River and the west were reasonably difficult to traverse with a clear trail. It appeared the tiny bird was attempting to lead them, through her constant weaving motion, to the best route through the thick brush and moss-covered logs.

"Where is she taking us?" asked Nash, huffing alongside her.

"I have no idea," said Freyja, grappling over a log. She landed in a bed of pine needles so soft she sank a foot into the forest floor.

"Ow!" Nash flinched as a thin branch snapped him alongside his head.

They finally reached a reasonably flat clearing of old stumps, truncated emblems of this region's logging industry. Small frail saplings peppered the spaces between, reaching hopefully towards the sun.

Freyja sat on a nearby stump to catch her breath. "We need a plan," she said.

The hummingbird hovered around her, urging them to continue.

"I can't. I have to rest," she said to the tiny fowl, mesmerized by her colorful wings.

Then came a little whisper. *"Sarana."*

"What? Sarana?" Freyja said out loud.

"Who's that?" asked Nash, who had sunk next to another stump, wiping sweat off his brow.

Freyja stood up and asked the bird intently. "Where?"

The hummingbird flew in a circle, and then darted over the hill ahead of them.

"We have to keep going. We are close. I think."

Nash groaned and stood up to follow Freyja and her little messenger friend. "Where? Where do we have to go?"

They hiked up another hundred feet, and reached the top of the hill. Winds were blowing unusually hard through the tree line at the top. Freyja stood, bracing herself against a tall pine. Below them ran the Columbia River and a big highway. There were dozens of cars passing every few minutes. There was a frontage road right below at the base of the hill where they stood. The hummingbird swiveled frantically in front of them and darted towards the road below. They followed her down through the thick forest, buffering themselves from swatting branches and clinging ferns along the way.

Finally, at the roadside, Nash bent over to catch his breath. "Now what?"

Freyja surveyed the road and the forest as the hummingbird fluttering beside them. "What now, little one?"

Her scars were still faintly aglow and tingling softly. It was not unpleasant, and she was beginning to understand that the sensations were always in flux if she paid attention. They moved across her skin like a breeze, pulling or pushing her awareness in one direction or another. As the bird fluttered away, the scars dimmed. As she came closer, they were more pronounced.

"What do we do?" Freyja asked her, confused and impatient for answers.

"*Wait.*" The hummingbird whizzed around her before darting into the woods. Freyja waited for her return, but she didn't come back. They waited and waited. And nothing.

"Where did she go?" asked Nash.

"I wish I knew. I think the bird said to wait," said Freyja, leaning on the sloping hillside on the side of the road. "I'm so tired."

Then a large black SUV with all tinted windows and unusual chrome detailing barreled past. It slowed a hundred yards ahead. As it reversed swiftly back to their precise location, it was clear the driver was a woman. Her dark hair was braided into a thick helmet around her head, drawing attention down to her massively sculpted shoulders and bare muscular arms. There was a tattoo of some kind that Freyja could not make out on her shoulder. Her aviator sunglasses barely masked her furrowed brow.

"Get in," she said.

They stood speechless at this unexpected request.

"Did you need a ride or what?" she asked.

Freyja gulped as her mind raced. Who was this woman? She needed time to think. "We, uh, aren't sure where we are going yet."

"Join the club. Get in."

The hairs on Freyja's neck stood up. Something was intimidating about this woman, and Freyja wasn't sure why she should trust her. Freyja thought back to the men in black circling the farm. Maybe she was one of them.

"We are okay. Thank you." Freyja eyed the hillside for options to escape or hide from this imposing figure who very likely could outrun both.

The woman paused. She took off her glasses and turned to face Freyja with her piercing charcoal eyes. "I suggest you tap into something other than fear, my dear. What does your compass say?"

My compass?

Her scars began tingling again. The fiery prickles swarmed her body and illuminated her arm. She pulled down her sleeve and pressed it against her body to prevent this bold mysterious woman from seeing it.

Nash moved in between them. "We're fine. Thanks anyway."

The woman smiled at Nash and chuckled. "Ah. Okay . . . you're not calibrated yet. Listen, Freyja, if I can find you, they can find you, too. You're going to have to sink or swim here."

How does she know my name? Freyja panicked.

"I picked up the signal to fetch you. But it would be best if you made a choice because I can't hang out here either. What are the coordinates of your destination?"

Freyja drew a blank. Was she perhaps talking about her scars? "Coordinates?" she asked.

"Yeah, where are you going?" she asked.

Freyja realized that this beast of a woman was possibly there to help rather than harm her. "Where *can* I go?" she asked.

"Honey, you're asking the wrong questions."

Something about what she said rang true, though the uneasiness remained. She thought about what the hummingbird may have said to her that Sarana was waiting.

"I think it, the compass, whatever . . . says I need to go to Sarana?"

"Okay. Hop in," the driver said.

Nash and Freyja climbed into the back of the hulking black SUV, sliding into swiveling bucket seats in the all-black interior. Inside the SUV were bolted chests of equipment and gear appropriate for guerrilla warfare. They had barely fastened their seatbelt when the car ran forward with a jolt that pulled them nearly out of their seats, floating as if they had blasted off from Earth. The car raced down the frontage road at near-light speed, sending leaves, debris, and birds fleeing in cyclone trails.

Nash fixed on Freyja with his eyes wide in hopeful anticipation. Outside, the world blurred into a tapestry of mesmerizing color.

CHAPTER THIRTEEN

EVERYONE YOU LOVE IS TRAPPED

Time expanded around Nash and Freyja like a river widening into a vast ocean. The vehicle drifted along the frontage highway, carving and swerving through turbulent uncertainty; its passengers crossed a threshold they couldn't even begin to imagine. The SUV soon found a barely visible gravel road, veering hard to the left, and for several miles up into undeveloped forested terrain. The pits and ruts rattled their resistance and unsteadied any hope of predicting their destination.

Nash turned to Freyja. "Do you trust her?"

Unsure and determined to keep her wits about her, Freyja shrugged and fixed her gaze upon the road ahead.

They reached a large clearing at the top, and the car pulled to a quick stop. The driver turned to Freyja, "This is it. Good luck." She smiled as the SUV doors popped open automatically.

"Uh, thank you." Freyja took a deep breath and peered out.

Nash and Freyja had barely hopped out when the mysterious driver vanished down the long drive, leaving a trail of dust in her wake.

They both gazed around at the thick ramble of trees in the clearing, searching for clues about where they were. No sooner had they begun to think about this when there was a clear scent of campfire.

"You smell that?" said Nash.

"Yes . . ." and it made her homesick for her family campfire days.

Suddenly, Nash pointed over to smoke rising through some trees a few yards away. "Look!"

Just then, a figure walked confidently towards them from the forest edge, beneath where the smoke had been rising. The unusually dressed being came closer. She wore an ornately embroidered hooded evergreen cape like a wizard from a fairytale. She walked with a beautifully carved wooden staff, as though she had traveled great distances to be here at that moment. Her presence was powerful and yet graceful.

"Aho . . . you made it!" the woman smiled warmly, lowering her hood around her shoulders.

Freyja's eyes widened as she realized it was Sarana, the woman from the theater. "I thought you were a hallucination! I didn't know that you were—"

"Real?" Sarana smiled, cutting her off. "What is real, sweetheart?" Sarana took Freyja into her arms and embraced her. Freyja fell into her full warm embrace like a cozy bed. "I knew you would make it!" Sarana whispered into her ear.

Freyja blurted out, "Who was that crazy driver?"

"Oh, that was Eir, a Valkyrie. I sent her. I'm glad she found your signal."

"Valkyrie?" asked Nash. "Like the legend of women warriors from Nordic legend?"

"Yes. These warrior women have many names," said Sarana.

"What signal?" interrupted Freyja, more concerned with what was going on in her body than anything else.

"Oh, it's like a radio signal, I suppose. Your station was not receiving until very recently. That's how we've been able to find you and communicate. Most people are off the grid directly or indirectly. But once you have your cells back online, your signal gets more powerful. And best of all, you can direct it and boost others who, like Nash here, who can't connect on their own."

"I have no idea what you mean," said Freyja bewildered.

"Well, it does sort of make sense since you've been seeing and feeling stuff, right?" said Nash helpfully.

"It's okay, darling. I will explain as we go. Come. Follow me," said Sarana, pointing to a trail behind them.

Freyja and Nash followed Sarana along a twisting wooded path until they came to a serene glade; there was a large campfire a few feet away from an enormous yurt, a round tent made of sturdy leather and fat timbers. The fire pit smoked with a pan of nuts and berries. Surrounding this were several tree stumps like stools artfully smoothed and polished. Beneath all of this, covering the clearing was a thick carpet of beautiful green grass, the cozy oasis nestled in an evergreen hideaway of pines, blackberries, and ferns.

Freyja was entirely enchanted. "Wow! This place is amazing."

Sarana motioned them to sit on the stumps and filled some small cups with hot tea. "Here, you've traveled a great distance with still farther to go. Take this tea; it will help build your strength."

"Thank you." Freyja took her cup, and then asked, "What's happening to me?"

"I am sure you are confused. There is more afoot than I can explain in one night, but I will get you started," she said, smiling reassuringly. "Do you have the key?"

"Um . . . yes, I do," Freyja said, reaching into her backpack to prove it.

"Keep it there. Keep it safe." Sarana then turned towards Nash. "Well, young man, you aren't quite sure what you got yourself into, are you?"

Nash laughed uncomfortably. "Uh . . . yeah, not really."

"Well, buckle your seatbelt." She laughed and squeezed him on the shoulder. "There is a lot I must convey to Freyja, but this is all applicable to you as well. In time, you may become sensitive. For now, just pay attention and don't get lost."

Nash was confused. "Sensitive?"

Sarana nodded. "Sometimes, Adepts can trigger spontaneous repair in those around them. We don't fully understand how or why. Just pay attention. Often, our gifts lie in the things we do without too much effort. You have an ear for music, no? Perhaps you will begin to develop clairaudience. It's unpredictable at this stage." She turned to Freyja and solemnly asked her, "Are you ready for this?"

Uncomfortable with the pointed question and still not sure what was going on, Freyja shrugged. "I think so."

"You do know, dear. You do. Listen deeply," Sarana said and touched Freyja on the arm as she sat down on a carved stool next to her and peered closely into her eyes.

Freyja was startled with this directness. Sarana's eyes were warm and dark, full of richness and reason. The more Freyja investigated them, the more they had a familiar sparkle. It was as though they had known each other longer than any lifetime.

"I am just kind of in shock. I don't know what's happening . . ." Freyja hesitated.

Sarana leaned in. "Freyja, this is the path your soul chose. Your path is a brave one, but not easy."

Her words hung around Freyja's shoulders like a heavy cloak. She wasn't sure what those words meant. How could *she* have chosen all the crazy things that had happened so far? What sort of path had she chosen precisely?

Sarana stoked the flames of the fire pit and reached under her cape. She pulled from a pocket an old envelope. It was creased and yellow. "This is for you."

Freyja's eyes widened. The words on the envelope, the handwriting—she recognized it. "You knew my mother?" Freyja's eyes searched Sarana's face for more, but Sarana remained calm and tranquil, so Freyja anxiously grabbed the envelope and ripped it open.

She could still remember her mother's buttery-soft skin and how she smelled like fresh roses. The memory ignited a dull ache deep inside Freyja's chest. As a child, she had memorized the few photos she had of her parents. One was of her mother and father at an archeological site, smiling up at the camera as they stood beside a large stone relic from some ancient culture. Her mother was so beautiful in her plain tank top and wild windblown hair. Her father's dark eyes pierced her memories for the long hikes through ravines or laughing at her knock-knock jokes. They were in love and doing the thing that they loved together. They couldn't have been happier. Yet Freyja's favorite photo of all was one of her entwined in her mother's arms, taken only months before they disappeared. Freyja had tried, but she never remembered being as happy as she was in that picture, ever.

Inside the envelope was a letter and what appeared to be an ancient map. Freyja pulled open the letter so furiously that little tears ripped at the sides. Then she fixed her eyes on the words as if they were glittering jewels:

My sweet Freyja,

If you are reading this, then you already know that something happened to your father and me. You are no doubt afraid and confused right now. I know you are braver than you feel, little star.

I have spent my entire life searching for an ancient global matrix described in countless myths and sacred texts. This grid may be the only hope to restore balance on our planet before it's too late.

Included here is a copy of a map that reveals some of the ancient sites or portals once used to power this matrix. Earth energy is measured by the Schumann Resonance, which is affected by solar flares from our sun. Energy levels are spiking now. We believe someone built these sites to harness and transmit this energy like a shield around the planet.

Some men want to keep this knowledge hidden and use it for their own purposes and benefit. You may already be in danger. Learn to trust your instincts. Everything is shifting. That's all I can say for sure.

Contact Professor Darnell, the head of Neolithic archeology at the University of Lima. You can trust him. He gave me the map and a stone box for safekeeping. Aunt Lucy, if she is still with you, can help with the box.

Be strong, little star.

I love you,

Mom

Freyja reread the letter a few times. Her eyes were wet and heavy with longing. A volcano of emotions erupted inside her. Letting the letter fall to the ground, Freyja bowed her head and allowed the sobs to come. Nash shifted awkwardly on a stump. Sarana remained seated, her face tranquil.

Freyja raised her head and wiped away tears. "How did you get this letter?"

"Your mother left it for you. I kept it safe."

"Safe?" Freyja demanded.

"You were being watched very closely. I couldn't let this get into the wrong hands," Sarana said sternly.

"Watched? By whom?" Freyja asked. Instantly, she remembered the implant, the Rahumans, the lab, the doctor.

"Exactly, my dear." Sarana had read her thoughts. "The implant you removed from your hand functioned like a cellular jammer and tracker. The lightning strike when you were a child triggered your latent genes to turn on. These genes are your connection, like wi-fi, into a great matrix cloud of multidimensional information. Some humans have accessed small parts with a tremendous effort, but they don't realize what they are experiencing. This powerful knowledge is something the people tracking you want to control. Like every power grab in history, you are a resource they want to own for their gain. Your parents tried to hide you, and unfortunately, they gave up their freedom to do so."

"So, the Rahumans were not foster parents, were they?"

"No."

"Are my parents still alive?" Freyja asked.

"They are still on Earth, but . . . I would caution you against seeking them out until you have progressed much farther in training."

"Wait—what? I don't understand. Are they alive? Where are they? Why did they leave me?" Her mind raced with questions that had longed plagued her.

"Freyja, Listen to me. There is so much you don't know, and it will take time to understand. Your parents love you. They had no choice." Sarana eyed Freyja's body, focusing on something dangling on her shoulders. "You've seen the dark web?"

"Yes . . . at my school. There was something creepy there," said Freyja, turning around to see where Sarana had been staring.

"This web will continue to grow, infect, and enslave humanity if we do nothing to stop it. Billions of people will needlessly suffer and die. The Nine are not immune. The only humans with any hope to reverse the black web are the Adepts waking up now. No one is sure why so many are being born with the ancient codes. But you are here, and we have work to do."

Freyja wanted to understand what she meant, both the work to do and why. Why was she being called to this? There was an alarmingly familiar reflection in Sarana's eyes. Freyja gasped. Could it be so?

"Yes, you are correct," answered Sarana. "My real name was always Sarana even though you called me Keyo."

Freyja sat stunned on her stump. Nash was confused about where the conversation had gone.

"How is that possible?" asked Freyja staring with her mouth open in shock. "How can you be Keyo?"

"Who is Keyo?" asked Nash.

"My lynx . . . my pet lynx," stammered Freyja.

Nash scratched his head, bewildered.

"Some of us can shapeshift. I am too weak to shift again. I left my lynx form shortly after the Nine came for you. I promised your parents I would protect you when they left. I honor my obligations." Sarana leaned closer to Freyja and put her hand on top of hers. Keyo morphed into Sarana's face, a shocking and yet comforting sight.

"Whoa!" Freyja sat dumbfounded. She took a deep breath as questions raced through her mind. "What about my aunt Lucy? Where is she?"

Sarana rose off her stump and crouched in front of Freyja. "Lucy is heavily medicated and under tight surveillance ever since they took her away. They didn't want her to contact you or any of the others. She's only alive because she has the knowledge they want. But she would rather die than tell them anything. I have contemplated when and how we might contact her. We need to be very careful, so we don't put her life in danger."

"Others? Danger?" Freyja said, eyes wide.

"There is much you don't yet know. One step at a time."

Sarana returned to her seat and moved a small teapot on a grill over the crackling fire. Freyja turned her focus to the map and unfolded it carefully in her lap. The paper was very thin, fragile and hundreds of years old. She studied the lines and symbols curiously.

This topography could be anywhere, she thought.

Then she remembered the box she had brought with her from the house and pulled it out of her backpack. She studied it again: it was about the size of a small brick, though the stone surface was warm to the touch and indeed not as heavy as one would expect. The soft, worn edges were mesmerizing. Twisting it in her hands, she played with the small dial again, running her fingers over the curious cuneiform inscriptions or runic symbols. She guessed that the script was something like that anyway.

"What is this?" Freyja asked.

"It is an ancient device," Sarana said, smiling gently. ""It may help you find the answers you seek."

Sarana stood up and moved the teapot off the fire and poured the water into the open pot to let it simmer. She strode into a yurt, and came out with a basket full of dried herbs and feathers. "Now, it is time to begin your training," she said.

"Training? What training?" Sarana had said that earlier, but Freyja was overwhelmed with all the revelations that she hadn't processed what that meant.

"Yes, you don't want to keep blasting holes in ceilings, do you?"

Freyja was wide-eyed. "How . . ." she began, searching for the words, "how did you know about that?"

"Look at your hands." Sarana smiled.

Freyja obliged, inspecting her hands. They were reasonably pale, thin, ordinary. She was curious why she should be evaluating her hands.

"'Look,' as in 'sense through' the skin layer, into the energetic layer, that tingles there below your normal senses. Look to see what is there. What holds them but doesn't touch them? Listen to the energy buzzing between your cells."

Freyja focused her eyes on her hands. Tiny hairline threads of something iridescent flowed throughout her hands and arms, parallel to veins and other muscle tissue. Several of these threads appeared blackened and bruised.

"Yes. That is your energy body. It weaves through the facia layers and stretches far outside you, like the mycelium network that connects every plant on Earth. These fractures happen when you overdo it. When you send uncontrolled energy through your body, you can damage it. So, we are going to learn a thing or two about this system now."

Sarana stood over the pan and dropped some of the herbs into it. Then she cupped some of the rising steam and motioned to Freyja and Nash to come to join her.

Freyja shot Nash a wide-eyed shrug.

"What is that?" Nash wrinkled his nose and turning away from the usual smells.

"Medicine," purred Sarana.

As she approached, Sarana moved her hands in a circle over the pan, stirring from it a small tornado of steam. Sarana continued to push the growing column with her hands in a figure-eight motion. She slowly shifted her hands, and the smoke took the shape of a large fierce cat, like a jaguar. Without warning, Sarana pulled her arm back and shot the misty jaguar straight at Freyja. Instinctively, Freyja sprang up and dove out of the way, coming to a hard crash on the ground.

"Hey!" Freyja shouted, pushing herself up from the thick grass.

Nash instinctively moved into a defensive posture he had learned from karate in grade school.

But Sarana was busy pulling another little smoke being out of the steam, smiling wryly, as she formed it into something new. Before Freyja could comprehend what that was, or what had just happened, Sarana sent another mist creature hurling towards her.

"Freyja, watch out!" shouted Nash.

But it was too late. The bullet of steam, shaped like a bear, barreled over Freyja, knocking her to the ground once more. Freyja gritted her teeth in a fury. These assaults didn't hurt, but they alarmed and humiliated her. She lifted her head as Sarana pitched another, and another.

"Stop it!" she shouted.

Freyja closed her eyes and threw up her hands, fingers splayed, expecting them to be knocked over by the volley. But they didn't. After a few moments, she opened her eyes and peered in the direction of the onslaught. "What . . .?" she whispered.

To her amazement, there was a luminous force field, like a shield, glowing around her hands. Sarana's steam bullets pressed hard against her hands, but she held them at bay. Freyja's eyes grew wider as the atoms exploded over them, like fireworks. "It's amazing!" she said excitedly, laughing in surprise and wonder and her apparent achievement.

But the more Freyja marveled, the weaker her energetic shield became. And in seconds, the boar-shaped mist creature ripped through and bowled her over, sending her tumbling across the grasses.

Sarana walked over to Freyja and offered her a hand up. "Concentration is important, dear. You had it until you left your body and went into your mind."

"What are you trying to do to me?" Freyja scowled, half afraid, half in awe.

"Your body is a lightning rod. You must ground yourself and allow this energy to flow through you. You need to know who you are," Sarana stated firmly.

"What do you mean? I know who I am," she insisted.

"No, you don't." Sarana lifted her middle finger and touched Freyja in the center of her forehead.

A jolt of knowing gave her sight but not understanding. A woman with a cape of feathers, a fierce helmet, and spear, with two giant cats at her flanks, appeared to her mind's eye.

"Who is that?" asked Freyja.

"She is the ancient goddess Freyja. Your namesake. That was intentional by your mother. She knew of your ancestral origin."

"What does that mean?" Freyja asked.

"It means that you have the potential to manifest the same power and purpose. Goddess Freyja lives within your genes."

"A goddess lives in my genes?" said Freyja incredulously.

"Yes, but don't get too cocky. Your genes are not yet fully active, and the stories of gods and goddesses are more myth than reality." Sarana smiled at Freyja. "Now . . . take off your shoes. It's easy at first. You too, Nash. I will give you a lesson in Energy Control 101."

Freyja and Nash dusted themselves down and kicked off their shoes to the side. Then Sarana began to show them how to ground their bodies with bare feet in the earth.

"Visualize your energy," she said, adjusting her posture. "Allow it to build and move up your spine."

Freyja's chest buzzed. "Oh, wow . . ."

"Yes, but reach that down into the earth, to grow and build the energy, then draw it back up! Use your mind's eye to see it and then feel it in your body. Imagine a golden cord from your own heart reaching down into the earth and tapping into the healthy golden veins of mother earth. Then see her pulsing life force up through all the layers of earth, oceans, rivers, and mountains, filling your body with peace and power. Imagine this cord now growing up into the heavens, opening your crown to the celestial healing light that illuminates across all time and space. Notice the flowing up and down between these powerful forces, filling up every space in your being and radiating outwards like the little sun that you are."

Freyja followed Sarana's words as best as she could. Her body continued buzzing and expanding. A powerful warmth washed over her skin and lifted her mind and heart as though she were floating. A beam of light rained down on her head, like a spotlight, though as she cracked her eyes open to peer, the daylight was unchanged.

Sarana began moving her arms in big sweeping arcs from the ground up over her head. "Your body can receive, ground, and project all the energy available in this realm. And there is a lot of it as you have discovered. Learning to channel it with intention and control is the key."

Freyja stood in the center of the circle as her feet begin to buzz. It tickled at first and even made her giggle. She was amazed she had never had this feeling before.

"Pay attention!" Sarana scolded her. "Look up at the rays of the cosmos radiating down, searching for a receiver. You, my dear, are that receiver."

Freyja closed her eyes and focused on a small magnetic tug at the center of her head. It circled from the front of her forehead and up through the top of her skull. There was a warmth there, a warmth that filled her body with powerful vibrations that cascaded down through her spine and coiled like a roaring fire in her belly. Her body simmered in feverish waves, crashing ever outward, touching the boundaries of her skin. Then the waves moved beyond her outer layers and into a field of space around her body, like Earth's atmosphere. A sense of physical connection beyond her body was impossible to miss. Steadying herself into the ground, she held out her hands as the energy began to form into small hot orbs against her palms.

"Whoa!"

"Yes, that's it." Sarana smiled.

Nash looked around dumbly, first at his feet and then his empty hands. He closed his eyes. "I don't think I'm getting it," he said sadly.

"You will," said Sarana. "Be one with the earth. Allow it to crawl up your legs and body. Let it simmer a while. Stop trying to force it; instead try to attract it. Call it to you. Allow and open yourself."

Sarana walked into the circle with Freyja and held up a flat square polished piece of crystal. "Look here. Do you see yourself?" asked Sarana.

There was a reflection, but it wasn't a typical reflection that one finds of themselves in a mirror. In this reflection, she appeared like a bright tree of light. The trees circling their camp waved their arms around her, mimicking the fanning veins of their leaves.

"What is that?" Freyja asked, astonished.

"That's you. That's how we are."

Their roots were luminous. They flowed with an energy that filled their trunks and boughs and branches the same way as Freyja's body was now radiating with intensity. The pulsating plasma tendrils reaching around Freyja's head to precisely form a crown like a forest canopy.

"Now, pull *all* this energy into your heart center *and* hold it there," Sarana said in between deep lasting breaths. "Let that energy build and overflow your heart."

Freyja was walking on a tightrope, barely balancing above a vast canyon. She sucked in, and squeezed her upper body to draw in every ounce of the energy above her into her chest. "Uh . . . um . . ." Something happened, but the spectacle quickly vanished in a poof. "Darn it!" Freyja's shoulders slumped. "This is so hard!"

"It's okay. Don't try to force anything. Allow it to flow," Sarana urged.

Again and again, Freyja practiced as the day wore on. She opened herself to the energy in the hope of drawing it all into her heart. Again and again, she lost her grip, becoming frustrated with each defeat. She wanted to take a break.

"I'm terrible at this." She sighed, taking a seat on one of the stumps.

Sarana approached and sat on the stump next to her. "Let me tell you a story, Freyja. When I was a young girl, I thought the boys in our village were much better than me, so why should I bother? When we were practicing harnessing energy, my teacher put me in the ring with the best boy in our group. I was terrified and danced around, trying not to get hit. Rather than defending myself, I allowed him to practice his aim in which he always eventually struck me. After everyone recoiled in laughter and I was red as a beet, my teacher took me aside and scolded me. 'Sarana, you are a lion, not a turtle. Stand proud, ground yourself, and face your challenger.'

"So, when this boy had crafted the largest energy ball you have ever seen, I connected my energy into the earth like a tree's roots and faced him squarely, ready to catch and return whatever he sent my way. That boy's fiercest energy missiles bounced off me and ricocheted back and hit him. The lesson—power does not come from force. It comes from will and intention. Intend to be a lion, Freyja, and it will be so."

Freyja furrowed her brow and nodded. "Okay . . . Let's do it again."

She circled back and re-grounded herself, her face etched with fierce determination. "I can do this," she whispered. "I can."

Focusing her mind on the energy all around her, Freyja relaxed and, rather than trying to demand it, simply invited it into her body at the crown of her head, and then whooshing into her heart. Energy ran through her spine, crackling like an atomic combustion engine about to blast off without the rest of the rocket. Freyja struggled to contain the energy pulsing in like a vibrating fire hose. Currents of light suddenly burst out through her hands like missiles. They split the atoms of the air and exploded against some of the rocks around them.

"Holy mackerel!" Nash yelled as stray sparks of current flew off Freyja's body in every direction. He ran for cover behind one of the tree stumps.

Sarana stood peacefully outside the circle behind her protective wall of energy. Next, Sarana set up a small target several feet in front of Freyja. On a stool, she placed a simple birdcage.

"I want you to imagine that everyone you love is in that cage, trapped, and you are the only one who can open the lock to free them. Focus your intentions on that lock," Sarana explained.

"What? I can't do that." She hesitated.

"Yes, you can."

"But it's complicated with me. It's—"

"Hard? I know. That is why it is powerful."

Freyja took a few breaths, gulped hard, and steadied herself. Closing her eyes, her parents appeared, the black loving eyes of Keyo, now Sarana, the smile of her aunt, and then, even the face of Nash. Sarana smiled and urged her to go for it. Freyja tried once more, this time focusing all her effort on those faces and imagining the energy swooshing into her heart. She aimed her finger at the lock as she did this, like a pistol at a target. A bolt flowed down her arm and out the tip of her index finger straight at the cage. When Freyja opened her eyes, the door of the cage was sizzling on the ground.

"Ha!" she laughed in amazement.

"Brava! But next time, don't kill your family in the process!" said Sarana with a wink. "Now, that will be all for today. It is time to rest."

"But that was incredible. I want to do it again!"

Sarana chuckled. "Patience, my dear. Tomorrow we will continue with training."

Sarana put several logs on the fire and stirred a big pot on the grill. The smell of rich smoky stew filled the clearing as the sun began to dip below the treetops.

CHAPTER FOURTEEN

THE BOX

The fire crackled into a lulling, darkening rhythm as crickets sang the sun to bed. Freyja and Nash soaked up the last drops of stew from their bowls. Afterward, Sarana offered them a refill of her delicious sweet tea.

"I recommend sleeping out here under the stars," she said, "but I do have beds inside if you prefer." Sarana motioned to the wool blankets and sleeping pads next to the campsite, indicating their bedding for the night. "I am going to retire now. Do let me know if you need anything else."

Freyja was so weary from her training but also somehow energized.

"Wow." Nash laughed. "I had no idea you were Wonder Woman."

"Come on," Freyja said indignantly, "I am not . . ."

"You are. You are Wonder Woman. I don't see anyone else who can shoot lightning bolts out of their fingers. Do you?"

Freyja shrugged. "Well, *no* . . ." she conceded.

"Do you think your parents were like you?" Nash asked as he laid down some wool blankets and prepared his bed beneath the stars.

"Not that I know of," she said. She scanned her memories of them and couldn't think of any time in her childhood where she had seen them do anything out of the ordinary. "They were just regular parents, I think."

Her head was beginning to hurt, and her ears started ringing. She remembered the box in her backpack and pulled it out. She studied every inch of it in the warm firelight, brow furrowed in concentration. She pulled her phone out of her bag and focused the flashlight beam on the figures.

"What is that thing anyway?" he asked.

"Well, it's a box," Freyja replied. She pinched her fingers and spun the small dial on the bottom again.

Nash rolled his eyes. "Yeah, I can see that. But what's special about it? What are all those markings? Do they mean something?"

"I have no idea."

The symbols *were* familiar somehow, but she had no idea what they meant. To her, they were as vague and indecipherable as a line of French, or Mandarin characters, or any other language, like math, they tried to teach her at Roosevelt. The top of the black stone had a smoothly carved lid with a pattern of foreign yet familiar shapes that were interlocking and very precise. There was a thin border of raised stone, like a frame around the lid. Inside this frame was a large circle, like a wheel, with divided pie-slice sections. Inside these sections were delicately carved shapes. The way they wove together, layered in repeating patterns, was almost Celtic. She couldn't quite figure out which ancient symbolic language they most resembled. One section appeared to have shapes like the letters "S." They were artfully carved into layers and arranged symmetrically. The figures were more right-angled in another area, like the letter "E" with little indentions and bumps inside the forms. The other six sections had similarly carved shapes, but they were less familiar. The larger space on either side of the wheel had a column, sort of hieroglyphic like stylized forms of animals: a bird, a cat, a scarab or beetle, a snake, a flower blossom, a bee, and other creatures she couldn't quite decipher.

"I'm just trying to remember something my aunt taught me," Freyja murmured out loud. "We used to solve puzzles and study symbols all the time. She remembered that the key to deciphering any code was to know something about the maker, the symbols, and its purpose."

"Huh?" said Nash, only half listening. He lay in the grasses with his arms behind his head, staring up at the night sky.

Freyja flipped the box over to study the small dial again. Something caught her eye. The dial contained a perfect spiral surrounded by a series of symbols that mirrored those on the front. Freyja turned the small dial with her thumb. *Click, click.*

Is this it? Is this a combination lock?

At the edge of the spiral arm was another mark like an arrow, or at least a tiny indented line. Freyja pressed the line so that it aligned with the other symbols. *Clack!* The dial caught on one of the symbols, particularly one that resembled a squiggly "X."

Freyja gasped. Had she done it? Thinking back to her padlock she used for school, she turned it the other way. That usually unlocked it. But there was no click, no sound at all. And the box's contents remained trapped.

"These symbols make no sense!" Freyja complained, and then she huffed and stuffed the box back in her backpack, too tired to mess with it any longer.

By now, the sky had filled with crimson clouds, the air around the camp cooling with each disappearing ray of sun. The sound of the nearby lake, just through the trees beyond the camp, called to Freyja. The waves lapped a mesmerizing beat.

"Want to go check out the lake?"

Nash shrugged. "Yeah, sure."

They found a tiny little path through the trees and meandered just a few yards to the lake's edge, their bare feet brushing through young saplings and moss-covered stones. Standing together by the shore, the first hint of peace in a long time spread through her body. Exhausted, but basking there, in that moment of simple dusky bliss, made her forget the traumas she had suffered and the uncertainty of what was to come.

They both sat down on the soft grassy edge of the lake, digging their feet into the narrow sandy shore. With water lapping their feet, Freyja closed her eyes and let her mind stretch into the quieting edges.

Suddenly, a low rumbling sensation—so low she wasn't sure if it was a sound or a tremor—disturbed her meditation. It sounded like a distant stampede or an oncoming train.

"Do you hear that?" asked Nash ominously.

Freyja nodded. "You heard it, too?"

"Yeah," he said, lips parted, eyes wide, an expression of fear of what was to come. But just as Freyja was about to try to soothe him, to say sorry for getting him caught up in the middle of all this, he said, "There is a sick bullfrog moaning for some lovin' out there." Then his lips broke into a wide grin.

Freyja punched him on the arm and said, "You idiot! I thought you were serious."

They both laughed and turned their gaze back to the lake. Freyja gazed at Nash; her goofy friend was suddenly something else. His quiet, handsome features were more appealing and endearing to her, the way his eyes pinched with delight and happiness and now softened towards her, giving her strength without words. Had she just never noticed this before? She was suddenly amazed he was there. Here he was at this camp in the middle of nowhere, taking all this energy, shape-shifting, matrix hunting stuff as just another day.

"Aren't you a little freaked out by all this?" she asked, afraid of his answer. What if he thought she was completely crazy? How did all of this strike him? Nothing in their lives had prepared them for this parallel world that was so real but so impossible too.

Nash chuckled and shoved his hands into his pockets. He kicked a small pebble into the lake. "Yeah, maybe a little . . . and no," he finally said. "I don't know what's going on, but I also think it's pretty cool. You know, I don't know. I always knew there was something different, special, about you . . ."

"Really?" She wanted to cry, but her throat was too dry. "It means a lot to me that you're here. I . . . I don't know what I would do without you." Her voice tightened as the last word slipped out like a whisper. Her cheeks burned. What was this? She crossed her arms and held herself tightly, overwhelmed by these experiences.

"So . . . you think Sarana can teach me that stuff?" he mused, bending down to pick up another stone that he then threw sideways, trying to skip it across the surface of the lake.

"Oh, er, maybe," Freyja replied, stepping back, and shaking off the tension that had accumulated in her chest and stomach. She wanted him with her, but was wary and unsure of what lay ahead. "Perhaps we should head back to the campfire."

Nash tossed one last stone into the lake before they turned to go. The fading firelight slipped over their sleeping bags, calling them to slumber.

CHAPTER FIFTEEN

YOUR THOUGHTS ARE NOT YOURS

"What?" Freyja woke disoriented by the crow of a rooster. She groped around the strange blanket and the fading campfire aroma, orienting herself to Sarana's yurt. Early sunlight oozed like honey through the light canvas walls. Freyja peeked over her blanket. Nash slept with one leg draped off the bed and his mouth agape, snoring loudly.

"Wake up, noisy freak!" Freyja croaked. "I need water." She rolled off the bed and flopped on the floor.

"Coffee?" Nash moaned. "Anyone? Anyone? Is that too much to ask?"

Freyja laughed and slapped his foot sticking out of his bedding as she crawled to stand. She planned to act normal and pretend that the little moment, or whatever it was, by the lake hadn't happened.

A womanly hand pulled the flap aside, and Sarana peeked in. "Come join me for breakfast." She smiled and winked mischievously to her sleepy guests.

Freyja lumbered out into the crisp morning air, pulling a wool blanket around her shoulders. Sarana sat facing the rising sun, cross-legged on a mat. In front of her mat was a spread of playing cards, a small tray with two glasses, and a bowl of fruit and nuts.

Nash followed Freyja, squinting. "Brrrrr. Who turned off the heat?"

Freyja took a sip of one of the teas. "Wow. That is amazing."

"It's juniper bark and thistle." Sarana smiled. "It'll warm you right up."

Nash grimaced and swallowed hard. "Never had tree bark tea before."

Freyja sipped from the cup and studied Sarana, wondering what was next.

"Sit here, my dear." Sarana waved Freyja to join her on a folded blanket beside her. A semicircular spread of cards lay splayed in front of Sarana. "Pick one."

Freyja reached across the spread and picked one of the cards. She held it for a moment, and then Sarana motioned for her to look at it. It was an ace of spades.

"What does it mean?" Freyja asked.

Sarana studied Freyja's face and smiled. "It's your card."

"Okay. But what does that *mean?*"

"It's your life purpose, my dear. The card you draw is what you do now. It is your sign that your soul is ready. Your path is to align spirit and matter. Your challenge is to balance them within yourself. When you can do so, you will be able to move heaven and earth, mountains, and more."

Sarana sprang up from her seated position like a ballerina. She moved with such poise and elegance it was hard to imagine her any older than twenty-five. Perhaps that was the lynx in her. She picked up a worn and bulky leather glove and slipped it onto her hand, and then made a loud whistle with the fingers of her other hand. After this, she gazed around at the forest with searching eyes. In a moment, a large bird with dark brown and red feathers came swooping into their camp and landed on the glove.

"Whoa!" said Nash.

"Tommy, say hello to Freyja," said Sarana, who spoke to the bird in all seriousness.

"What is he?" Freyja asked.

"He is a red tail hawk. More specifically, he is a messenger and a Guardian."

What is a Guardian, she thought?

Sarana motioned to Nash, who was utterly enamored with Tommy. "Would you like to feed him?"

"Sure!"

Sarana handed Nash a big hunk of flesh. "Just watch your fingers, please." She laughed.

"Ew ... What is this? Chicken fillet?" Nash tried to find a way to hold the meat out without extending too much of himself. Tommy snatched the pale flesh, tossed it back, and slowly gulped it down.

"Excellent, thank you, Nash." Sarana kissed the hawk's beak. She whispered something to him and lifted her arm back high into the air. With a heavy beat of his wings, the hawk pushed off and soared into the sky.

"Where is he going?" Nash asked.

"He's taking care of some business for us." Sarana took a deep breath, and then turned to Freyja as if to answer her earlier mental question. "The Guardians are a very ancient order. They come from all animal groups to protect the earth and every creature on it. It is a sacred duty that is a high honor. Sadly, the human species has not been part of this order for some time." Sarana paused, peering more intently at Freyja. "When did you go to the void?"

"What?" asked Freyja, surprised, but realized what she meant.

"The void. There is an echo in your field. Was it the box? Are you okay?"

Freyja realized she must have been talking about that strange dream she had had the night before by the campfire. She scanned her body for markings. Her arm was tingling and shimmering. "How do you know about my dream?" she asked curiously.

Sarana shook her head, and her features became very grave. "That was no dream, my dear."

"What do you mean? Not a dream? Then what—" She was about to ask what it was, but Sarana interrupted.

"Tell me, what happened?"

"The box, yes, I had it. I just touched it. And then, I went to this dark place. There was this voice—haunting, cold. But I couldn't tell what it was. I thought I had dreamt it all up."

"No, dear, no. You did not dream this. Not the way you think of dreams. You are awake now. You have much to do before you return there. Be careful. Many who go do not return at all."

"I certainly didn't mean to go anywhere, let alone there." Faint and weary, Freyja decided to be much more careful with the box in the future.

"Alright then, shall we begin?" Sarana walked over and tapped Freyja on the arms. "Lift. You, too, Nash. This exercise is powerful for everyone."

Freyja lifted her arms. Sarana pulled them up, straight above, and put her hands together.

"That's it . . . *Press* the fingers to . . . get . . . there. Like a prayer, but higher. Come on, Nash. You can do this, too." Sarana deeply inhaled and exhaled to demonstrate, waving her arms in a flourish of animation. "In . . . and . . . out . . ."

Nash sat down next to Freyja and measured himself in a posture to hers, trying to follow along. Freyja mimicked her breathing as best as she could. Suddenly, a wave of love flowing in rivers down from the sky ran straight into her heart.

"That's it. Do you feel that?" asked Sarana.

"Yeah, I think so," Freyja answered.

"How about you, Nash?"

"Uh . . . I think my arms are falling asleep," he answered with his eyes squeezed so he could concentrate better.

"Good. That is a speedy way to pull down energy from the cosmos into your temple, your body. It's more than energy, but we will go over that later. You should begin your days and end your days this way, if possible. You are in control. This is your life. No one can deprive you of this. Breathe in, through your nostrils, from the belly, from your core. Then breathe out through your mouth, quickly. Hard! Say, 'Hawwwww.' Breathe in again from your heart and then out: two breaths in, one breath out. Do this for at least ten minutes. It will clean your mind of all the rubbish."

"Rubbish?" Nash asked.

"Yes, all those so-called thoughts, you call them. They are like viruses, making everyone sick. They are usually quite dense, untrue, and negative, too, yes? Most of your thoughts do not even belong to you . . ." Sarana paused as the two kids had their arms over their heads.

"Like an earworm?" Nash laughed.

"I'm not sure I know what you mean," said Sarana.

"It's like a bad song or joke that you can't get out of your head," explained Nash.

"I suppose it is like that. How do you remove an earworm?" Sarana prodded him.

"I play something else. Get on the piano. I guess I give myself a better earworm to replace it."

"Yes, so, here we are replacing earworms with a vibrant breath of life that fills your entire body with higher energy. And with this new frequency, the thoughts or knowledge will be completely different. Perhaps you could say, better quality?" explained Sarana.

Freyja continued the breathing pattern and started to relax as her body and mind let go. In a few minutes, her body was buzzing, like electricity running currents up and down her limbs. Somehow her boundaries had expanded in concentric circles, going further, and stretching out into infinite fields beyond her. Like a wave cresting and falling back into the ocean, she could touch the borders of everything around her. Huge, enormous, and expansive waves were dissolving into the air around her.

"Do you feel it?" Sarana whispered excitedly.

Freyja nodded slowly.

Sarana moved her arms down in front of her, and then adjusted Nash as well. "Now, notice the flow between two polarities. Left and right. Reach out and hold on."

Freyja experienced a deep pulsing of energy building between her palms. It was like two magnets pulling towards each other.

"Yes," Sarana cheered. "Yes!"

A great knot of tension started in Freyja's chest, but then shifted into other areas of her body. She mentally pictured it as a large living organism. It was angry and dark and raged against whatever Freyja was doing. It was tight, and it throbbed and ached the more she stayed with it. She wanted to let go.

"No, stay with it! You must!" came Sarana's voice. "Put your focus there and witness it."

Freyja gritted her teeth and did so, absorbing all the pain it caused. Like a wound, an emotional clot that needed air and light to heal, she wanted it to leave her. No, she *needed* it to leave her. Freyja began to sob. Tears were flowing down her cheeks.

"Your body is clearing out stuck emotions," Sarana roared with delight. "All this energy you are pulling in and moving around is cleansing you. Like a flowing river, your body flows with life. Stay with it."

Sarana walked forward and touched Freyja gently on the collar bone, tapping right over where her heart would be, to encourage her to continue breathing deeply. "Let your breath move this thing. Honor it and release it."

She could not concentrate on Sarana's words. Tears streamed down Freyja's face; the emotions swelling in her body were too great. Giant boulders of sorrow dislodged from all around and crashed through her heart. Freyja was haunted by the faces and voices flashing through her mind. Most of it made no sense, but it was real. Sobbing uncontrollably, she was desperate for relief. She tried to stop breathing, but it left her marooned in the grief, so she kept breathing, until she realized the weight of it had shifted. In the space where grief had lodged, there was now expansive freedom and peace. Like freshwater cleansing a wound, love swirled into the black hole in her chest, filling her with light.

"What was that?" she gasped, almost afraid to know.

"Just ask. A word or name will come."

"Mom . . . Dad . . . ?"

"Of course, dear. Of course."

"So, my grief over them just vanished?"

"Not vanished. Your memory and concern remain, but the bound energy of that sorrow has moved. You freed up space in your temple for more love and energy, like cleaning out the pipes so freshwater can flow."

"Okay . . . I don't know what that means . . ."

"I know this is very new to you. Be patient. Think of unconscious pain as chains or shackles on your body. It weighs you down so that you cannot move through life with power and purpose. And power is what you need most right now."

Freyja nodded. It was hard to get what was happening, but she couldn't argue with the results; her body was lighter and stronger, her mood more serene.

"So . . . very simply, everything is energy: all matter, all thoughts, all feelings, every creature, every sound. Absolutely everything is energy, with unique signatures in a complex yet simple symphony of frequency. We are the music in motion. Our blueprints encode at birth, and we accept them without question. You are what we call an Adept. Adepts are only different from the rest of us in that they have the original cosmic human gene intact. Your frequency may vibrate at a clear tone, while others can't quite tune in due to the genetic tampering. While they are on AM, you are on a digital satellite. Get it?"

Freyja shrugged. "I guess?"

"I like that. Music in motion," mused Nash.

"Because your blueprint is attuned and fully *on*," Sarana continued, "you can work with the energies of the universe more easily and with greater access. Most can only think about these concepts. You can *experience* them. It's like you can perceive a rainbow of colors, one that the average human today cannot. They are, in essence, color blind. For you, the wind is a being; you can listen to *her*, receive *her* messages, call on *her* to go where you ask. Lightning is an extension of your energy field, an element that you may communicate with like words or a rock you might throw. You can, with time and practice, move mountains. It is not impossible for an Adept. This was the way many thousands of years before. You are in tune with Earth energies. Everyone else is tone-deaf, at least for now . . ." Sarana dropped her eyes. "You just need to learn how to use your instrument. Does that make sense?"

"Hey, I want to play with the cosmos," laughed Nash. "What's my instrument?"

"Nash, dear, you are going to have to improvise for now. But do pay attention as you already demonstrate a natural affinity for sound and frequency. This is likely a clue to your gifts." Sarana smiled at him.

Nash beamed with hopeful pride. "But why are my genes on and everyone else's off?"

"Everyone had their genes tampered with long ago," Sarana said. "What today's scientists call junk DNA . . . But that's a misnomer. It is not junk at all, far from it. That term is nothing more than a deceptive category to dissuade amateur geneticists from discovering more about the genome. Every single gene has a function; they don't understand. Like putting up a detour sign on the highway, no one questions it. And when they do, the Nine discover it and shut it down."

"The Nine? They were men or something?" said Freyja remembering the dream vaguely or whatever happened to her in the lab.

"Well, the original elders who ultimately began what you call the Nine, yes. But those in charge today consider most of humanity as livestock. However, in the last couple of decades, for whatever reason, more and more Adepts are being born with the ancient genes on. Some fear an army may rise to upset the balance of their power. They are desperate to control or even stop humanity's awakening because of the inevitable end to their reign. They want it on their terms. The implant did protect you for the time being."

"Protect me?"

Sarana smiled and continued, "There are many different companies in the human advancement division that the Nine control globally. They are all seeking to understand how and why you were born with these genes turned on. The whole purpose of the global gene project is to locate and control kids like you. You are not the only one. For eons, the Nine and others have worked to suppress and hide this knowledge to avoid misuse. Ironically, they are now the ones misusing the gifts."

"Is that why they kidnapped me?"

"Yes. You are property to the Nine, in the way they now think about resources on our planet."

"Property? Why?"

"Because you are powerful, Freyja. Uncontrolled, you are dangerous to them and their goals. These companies are all in competition to learn how to turn the ancient genes on or off. They are playing god. They want to control who has them, like breeding elite animals or genetically modified humans. To them, you are a secret weapon."

"Because I can blow things up?"

Sarana laughed. "Just the tip of the iceberg, dear. For now, I've blocked the new implant they put in your head so they can't track you." Sarana became very quiet and serious.

"In my head?" Freyja gasped, touching her skull while recalling the soreness. Her fingers passed over the small bump on the lower edge. "No! Get it out!"

Sarana hugged Freyja tight. "Listen, I fear that this implant may have a timer, and my abilities are not such that I can safely remove it. It's much more complex than the original version. I can only buy you some time, but I don't know how much. I have put a shield around it so that it is invisible to them. It should hold a few days." Sarana then continued talking about collective timelines and how everything was in flux.

"I don't understand. Timeline?" Freyja asked, bewildered.

"Yes, we are all tethered to a shared timeline, but powerful forces are shifting it at unprecedented levels. I can usually foresee the primary forces unfolding, like seasons or cycles. I cannot see anything right now." Sarana sighed, staring off into the distance wistfully.

"Sarana, are you an Adept, too?" Freyja whispered, realizing that she hadn't asked her before. She must be.

Sarana smiled and hugged her tighter. "You are full of questions, aren't you?"

Why was Sarana so coy? "What do you mean? Are you like that driver of the car—what's her name, Eir? A Valkyrie?"

"Ah, yes, the Valkyries. They are a tribe of warriors who have taken the sacred oath of the Guardians. There are Adepts among them, yes. The ones who support the network are Adepts. That's how Eir found you. I sent her your coordinates as

I knew you would not yet be able to do that. We'll work on that on our way," smiled Sarana. "As your mother said, you need to find a professor and your aunt."

Freyja lit up. "My aunt?"

"Yes. You must be excited, but I must warn you, we could be putting your aunt's life in danger. My sources tell me she's at the state hospital. The only way you can safely communicate with Lucy is in the yard, just before lunch. That is our window of opportunity. They dope everyone up right after that. There's constant surveillance, but Nash and I can create the necessary diversions."

Nash perked up, hearing his name in the plot. "Yeah! Diversions!"

"You won't have much time, though. Are you ready?" asked Sarana studying Freyja's face.

Freyja nodded and grabbed her backpack. Her heart soared at the thought of reuniting, finally, with Aunt Lucy. She feared for what she might find, but she had no choice. She was the only family she had left.

"Okay, then. Off we go."

CHAPTER SIXTEEN

WE ARE ALL PATIENTS HERE

They hiked through the forest rim and into a clearing. Freyja studied the landscape and realized they were in the field by the Rahumans' house! Had the house in the trees been Sarana's yurt the whole time? They marched through the grasses, and half a mile down the edge of the street. The old real estate sign on the empty lot swung lazily in the morning breezes. A few cars passed by as they stood waiting for Sarana's next command.

"We're so close to my house!" marveled Freyja.

"Yes, well, things are always different than we imagine, aren't they? I set up camp to keep an eye on you after your abduction."

"Really?" Sarana's face was warm and kind. Freyja wanted to hug her old friend Keyo now standing before her in luscious grandmotherly form, and never let go. "Thank you."

"Of course, dear." Sarana put her hand on Freyja's shoulder, squeezing her in affirmation while scanning the roadside.

Nash piped up from behind. "Hey, do we have time to pick up some fresh clothes, and um, maybe some food, from my house?"

"Unfortunately, we do not. However, if you would like to return home, now is a perfect time," said Sarana.

Freyja was curious and anxious for Nash's response. He quickly shrugged his shoulders. "Nah, that's okay. I'm down for this. Are you kidding me? I'd wear a plastic bag to see what happens next." He turned and grinned at Freyja, a sincere twinkle in his eyes.

"Won't your parents worry about you?" asked Freyja.

"I can help you with that." Sarana dug into her large pockets in her tunic and pulled out a small finch. She whispered something to it and sent it on its way. "They will not worry a moment until you return. By then, we'll have an alibi."

Nash did a fist bump in the air as though he had just won the lottery. Freyja was grateful for his companionship.

"Now, Freyja, if we are going to get to the hospital, we need a ride. I do not recommend public transportation as there are cameras now in most buses and cabs. And you are unlikely to find a willing stranger to drive all of us to the state hospital. So, you are getting a crash course in modulating now."

"Modulating? What do you mean?" Freyja asked.

"Modulating is when you dial into the Adept network. You can broadcast or get information. It's an ever-expanding network of frequencies that orients you within the matrix of all things. Have you noticed that your scars illuminate yet?"

"Ha," Freyja laughed, "yeah. I've noticed."

"Yeah, she showed me. What is that about?" asked Nash.

"Show me your arm, dear." Sarana touched Freyja's arm and urged her to remove her sweatshirt. She inspected the scars traveling up and around her arm to her shoulders. She smiled and gave her arm a solid pat. "Good. Good."

"Why are my scars lighting up?" asked Freyja.

"We aren't sure, dear. Many believe that lightning was used to jump-start the genetic repairs, like a power surge that turned on a new neural pathway. Every Adept has a unique pattern, and not all were struck by lightning, though many were. In time you will see that they are not just scars, but are ancient codes that will help you navigate and, of course, modulate. Your scars connect you to the nervous system of the planet and all those who can tap into it."

"Like spidey senses." Nash wiggled his fingers like little spiders running up a wall.

Freyja ribbed him. She had to think maybe there were others out there she could find.

"Yes, so what you need to do is to imagine in your mind this place you need to go. It doesn't matter that you don't know exactly where it is. Your body has this compass that is now building connections. These connections flow through every atom on the earth ultimately. Every time you use it, it will get stronger and reach farther. It's easier to dial into locations that are close to you, or you have already been. Like muscle memory. So, new locations will be more difficult, but I will help you this time. So, try this now. Think about your aunt. Tap into your memory of her, like her last known coordinates; allow your energy body to search for her. If that makes sense?"

Freyja wondered how close her aunt had been all this time. She remembered her beautiful, soulful eyes, the last time they were together. Her heart ached. She began to picture her aunt's face in her mind. Then she remembered her smell and how she walked with a graceful nonchalance. She began building a picture of her in her mind, a bit older, perhaps ill, considering how she was now a strung-out prisoner. Her scars began to tingle. As the tingling grew, she noticed that some spots sparkled more than others.

"That's it. See! There it is. Excellent." Sarana clapped her hands together with excitement. "Stay with it. Now, listen very carefully. Let the momentum guide you and say very clearly in your mind or maybe out loud to start, 'Adept Wolfe, destination assistance.'"

"Like, out loud?" asked Freyja.

"Yes. Exactly. Except, it's not to yourself. You are broadcasting. In time you might pick up on others broadcasting. Think of it like the old ham radio. There is a network of Adepts who listen on the line and try to help the others out. The problem is that the Nine and others are listening, too. They have found a way to track some of the Adepts. Or we fear some Adepts are working with them. So, the lines are not always secure. It's not a guarantee of help, but it's something you can use when you need to."

"That is so cool!" said Nash.

"Um. Okay. So, here goes." Freyja cleared her throat and concentrated again on Aunt Lucy.

As her body began to hum and tingle, an area around her shoulder radiated the most. It reminded her of Aunt Lucy, strangely. Her heart swelled with knowing so powerful, she figured it must be pretty darn close.

"Adept Wolfe, destination assistance!" she said with uncompromising clarity as though she were commanding a robot to move.

She searched her body sensations and listened for anything, maybe the cackling of radio waves or some sort of ring or click or confirmation. There was nothing but the fading radiation in her shoulder. The scars were like a web of squiggly lines. What did they mean? Freyja searched Sarana's face for guidance. Sarana nodded towards the roadway.

Then, roaring around the bend, came an odd and unexpected vehicle. It appeared to be an old VW bus, painted yellow with hippy flowers and a smiley face on the front window. A bearded man stuck his head out the window and hollered, "Destination assistance?"

Sarana smiled and waved. "Frank!" She turned to Freyja. "Now, this is very important. You cannot accept destination assistance without first confirming who you are. You must do this for everyone's safety. So be sure to confirm your identity."

"Okay, but how do I know he, Frank, is um, the network or whatever?" asked Freyja, overwhelmed by the rules and oddity of summoning a ride with her scars.

"Frank, how do you verify your ride?" Sarana asked, motioning for Freyja and Nash to climb aboard.

"Hehe, welp. And I am pretty good at homing in on the signal, but if I'm not sure, I have this little scanner deal-y." Frank pointed to a big rock on his dashboard.

The bearded man wore a tie-dyed Grateful Dead t-shirt with khaki cargo shorts and bare feet. Frank filled his bus to the brim with army duffle bags, boxes of flea market treasures, random pieces of musical equipment, and linens draped over the windows. It appeared he lived inside this bus.

"Um. That's a rock," said Nash.

Sarana smiled. "Oh, it's a rock, alright. It's also a mineral core that only hums when an Adept activates it. Go ahead, Freyja, touch it."

Freyja moved her hand over the big flat rock and pulled back, startled. There was a pleasant but an unexpected curling hum. The rock held a faint glow that disappeared as soon as she removed her hand. "Wow. That is amazing."

"Would you like to try, Nash?" asked Sarana.

Nash moved his hand over the rock and frowned. The rock did not illuminate in any way. "It's just a rock to me, I guess." Nash was disappointed.

"Be patient, Nash. Activation, even for Adepts, takes practice. And it's a way for the network to operate safely. If you are with Freyja, you are part of the team." Sarana waved them on board to find a place to sit among the cluttered seats.

"Where are we going?" asked Frank.

"Oregon state hospital!" Sarana purred.

"Okie dokie." Frank adjusted his oversized sunglasses and shifted into drive, whistling a familiar melody as they sped off through the neighborhood.

"Hey, that's Rolling Stones, 'Ruby Tuesday.'" Nash laughed.

"Yup. You know the Stones?"

"Yeah, I play in a band with my dad."

"Yeah? I got some instruments in the back if you wanna play. Keeping time is what I do, too," said Frank.

"Sweet. Okay!" Nash turned and eyeballed the piles of junk, unsure where to start. He picked up a guitar headstock that was sticking up under some coats. He pulled it out and started tuning and strumming.

In a matter of time, the bus was humming along the highway towards Salem. Freyja's mind was filling with so many questions.

"Why did they take Aunt Lucy?" she finally asked Sarana.

"As soon as the lightning struck you, your parents knew it was only a matter of time before the Nine would want you. They left you with Aunt Lucy so they could try and keep them away longer. Once they figured out you were still in

Oregon, the only way they could get a hold of you was to remove her. The Nine try to operate within the rules and laws to avoid any spectacle or news they must suppress. Since the age of the Internet, information spreads quickly, and they've had to spend far too much time producing counter conspiracies to drown out the real information. Given your aunt was known as a shut-in recluse, it wasn't difficult to have her committed and place you with a fake foster family."

Out of nowhere, a surge of kinetic irritation, like hearing someone scratch their fingers on a chalkboard ran through Freyja's body. "Whoa! What was that?" She realized that she was reacting to Nash playing something off-key on the guitar.

Nash was curious, too. "Yeah, these strings are bad."

"No, that was worse than bad. It made my everything in me cringe," said Freyja. "Please stop!"

Nash smiled. "You mean, stop this?" He strummed the same dissonant chord, and Freyja immediately writhed in discomfort.

"I mean it. That's awful!" said Freyja.

Amused by his new power, Nash played a few more chords moving swiftly into an ethereal jam. The melody was both enchanting and disturbing, leaving Freyja unable to sit still. Every cell vibrated.

"Stop! What is that?"

Sarana was staring at Nash curiously. "Nash, honey, where did you learn that?"

"What? How to play guitar?"

"No, that melody?" she asked.

"I just made it up," he said.

"Huh," said Sarana. She smiled and winked. "Nash, you have a lot more potential than I thought.

"Potential to drive me nuts!" said Freyja starting to settle down again.

Nash didn't care much about what Freyja said and continued jamming into some well-known chords for classic rock. Frank hollered his approval from the steering wheel.

Freyja felt perturbed. "Why is that bothering me so much?"

"Well, there are all kinds of chords in the cosmos. Everything exists in vibration: chords, sounds, frequencies. He just played a chord that was dissonant for you. However, notes can be combined in limitless ways. Some combinations soothe; some disrupt. All of them create an effect. All of material reality is essentially a vibration at different levels of density. I'm wondering if proximity to you is enhancing his natural gifts."

"Oh, great. So, Nash has the gift to annoy me. Just what I need," said Freyja trying to shake off the sensations.

"Here we are!" said Frank.

The yellow wagon bus pulled up at the corner of American essentials, a 7-Eleven built into a gas station and a Denny's restaurant next to a run-down Motor Inn. Sarana led the way as they hiked along an industrial roadway, past empty grass lots and warehouse buildings. The historic mental hospital lay just beyond a forested hidden but well-manicured drive. Built in 1862, the Oregon Mental Hospital was a well-known backdrop in pop culture, but was very run down. Patients ranged from severe bipolar, schizophrenic, to hardened criminals, including serial killers, who were deemed insane. It was the perfect place to hide a perfectly sane person from the rest of the world. Sanity was strange to anyone there.

As they approached the security booth at the entrance, Freyja's feet became lead weights. Was her aunt here?

"Now, we go inside," Sarana said, waving as she approached the gate.

Sarana stopped Nash and Freyja a few yards away and walked up to the guard. He tipped his hat and studied his clipboard as he listened to Sarana. He began to smile and laugh, making a note and waving as he ducked inside. The gates began to open slowly. Sarana turned and motioned for them to proceed ahead. She bowed graciously at the guard and joined them on the other side.

"What did you say?" asked Freyja.

"It's not what I said, Freyja dear; it's what he heard," Sarana said, and her lips spread into a faint smile.

"Seriously? That's all you're going to tell me?"

Leaning in, Nash whispered, "Did you put him under a spell or something?" his eyes blazing with awe.

Sarana smiled. "That's an interesting question, Nash. But the concept of *spelling* is a curious one. What even is spelling?"

His eyes flickered in curiosity at her prompt. "Spelling is when you spell words," he confirmed.

Sarana shook her head. "When we speak our intentions, we are using words, are we not? Words that we spell. So, yes, in a way, I am creating a spell. I used words to help him with his beliefs. He believes we are counselors, and we have patients to see. He believes he saw our credentials. Therefore, his beliefs and rules are intact. There is no conflict within him. That is why he let us pass."

"Isn't that just a fancy way of lying?" said Nash with a crooked smile.

"Truth has many levels. The material level is the most concrete and where most people demand *the facts* and consider anything outside of that to be untrue. Then, the brave souls allow the emotional and spiritual level to inform them of what is truth. Unfortunately, most find tremendous conflict here because these realms are unique to everyone. Most truth on this level is by popular belief, not because there is an inherent factual basis. If there can be a thousand versions of the truth, how do you determine which one is more credible than the next? You can't."

"So, we pretend to be counselors?" asked Freyja.

"What is a counselor? A person who brings counsel, solace, advice, support? We are giving support to your aunt if we can get past the others. Truthfulness is honoring another's coherence and intending for mutually beneficial outcomes. The mind gets hung up on facts and data. But remember that reality is energy, and energy is in a constant state of flux. Our measuring devices are inherently limited. Only the heart can navigate us to mutual coherence, a common experience of reality that honors each soul equally."

Nash gave a long sigh. "But we *aren't* counselors, not the way they think anyway," he said, folding his arms and shaking his head.

"The way they *think*—exactly. We are not breaking his rules. He is not disturbed. So, let's go!"

The trio continued up the drive and walked towards the back of the grounds, where another fence encircled the yard. There were patients out walking the grounds, gazing off into the distance, or sitting on the grass uninterested in exercise. All the while, caregivers in white uniforms supervised them intently.

Just as Freyja puzzled over how they would climb over the fence, Sarana slipping into a nearby storage shed. The crudely constructed shed was a jumble of wood paneling and broken windows fixed together with rusty nails. A loud click from a lock inside prompted the side door to creak open. Sarana emerged on top of a large lawnmower.

"So, who wants to be the landscaper?"

Nash, nodding his head and smiling, raised his hand.

"Okay." She smiled, and then turned to Freyja and tossed her a glinting bunch of keys. Freyja caught them in surprise. Then, Sarana said, "Now, it is our job to find the entrance."

With Nash puttering on the mower, Sarana and Freyja followed a narrow path until they came to a large iron gate that led into the yard. Freyja fiddled with the keys, trying each one until the last turned with a satisfying click in the large metal lock. She and Sarana shared eager glances, and then pulled on the heavy doors, holding them open for Nash to enter. As he went by, Sarana hollered something to Nash over the loud motor. He nodded and went on.

After he had gone through, Sarana pulled Freyja close, and together, they walked briskly through the grounds, staying close to the trees, evading the gaze of the guards.

"Your aunt is very likely sitting alone," Sarana said as their feet crunched over loose twigs. "Do you think you might recognize her?"

"I am sure I would," Freyja said, her heart beating wildly.

She scanned the yard for her aunt, but did not find her. An older gentleman sat on a bench in his robe and black slippers; he was staring blankly into space. He had a paper bag that he reached into to feed the birds, but there were no crumbs in the bag, and only one or two birds lingered nearby. Another shriveled very old woman sat so far hunched over in her wheelchair Freyja wasn't sure if she might have collapsed. She was being pushed down a lush rose garden path by a tall sharply dressed woman singing a very extemporaneous interpretation of *Phantom of the Opera*.

Another giant pole of a man wandered barefoot in the middle of a patch of grass, just walking in a circle. He was speaking to himself in detail about something or other. Close to some large doors at the aging hospital building entrance, there were a couple of women dressed in medical uniforms. One was smoking, and the other ranting, waving her arms about, and speaking excitedly about something. It was difficult to tell which were the patients and which were staff members.

And then, at that moment, the web appeared: blankets of thick blackness draped like a fog bank across the building and gardens. Freyja's eyes filled with the dreadful image of those long oily leaders attached to every individual who roamed the grounds. It infected all of them, trailing their ankles, hands, hair-like slithering snakes, sniffing out each body for a place to nestle in for a while. She followed one to a bench by the pond. She hadn't seen the web since that day at school. She wanted to ask Sarana about it until someone caught her eye. It was a woman with grey hair twisted up into a bun, sitting slouched and tilted slightly. Her sloped shoulders, narrow neckline, and the way she crossed her feet were so familiar. Freyja's heart thumped harder.

Just then, eyes fixed on the woman, Sarana's voice whispered in her ear. "You don't have much time. Her brain is very foggy. Get the facts you need. I will signal you with a bird call when we must leave."

Freyja took a deep breath, and moved quickly towards the woman by the pond. As she approached, Aunt Lucy's profile came into view. The arch of her nose, the soft gentle slope of her brow . . . it was like an avalanche of emotions, casting open in her heart memories of stoic Scandinavian hugs, mythical starry filled eyes, and the melodious alto singing voice of her only remaining family. Freyja slid up to her side and hovered, wanting to fall into her arms or pull her up and race away. But she couldn't. She knew what she had to do.

"Aunt Lucy . . ." she uttered in barely a whisper.

"I knew you would find me." The woman smiled, without moving. "Come, sit here next to me before they see you."

Freyja obediently crouched down next to her and immediately recognized the scent of her almond skin, though now soaked in chemicals and a foreign smell of decline.

"Aunt Lucy, is it you?" Freyja's voice quivered with emotion.

"Yes. Mostly . . ." Lucy said, patting Freyja on her knee, in a familiar and comforting way. "It's so good to see you, dear."

Freyja's eyes filled with tears. The reality of the past few years rolled over her.

"I'm okay. No need to worry." She coughed. "You look well. Are you well, dear?"

"I guess so. I'm scared. There's so much I want to tell you. And ask you . . ."

"I know. I'm sure you have many questions. Do you have the map?"

"Yes . . . but I want to get you out of here." The streaks of black web draped around Aunt Lucy's shoulders. Freyja swatted them off her. Slowly the color started to return to her face.

"I've missed you, too. I love you so, sweet Freyja dear," Aunt Lucy wheezed and coughed again.

"What have they done to you?"

Her aunt laughed and said, "Freyja, this is all they can do. They have nothing else. Do not be fooled by their tactics."

"But they are killing you," Freyja cried.

Aunt Lucy soothed her and reasoned, "If they wanted to kill me, I would be dead already. They need me alive. And so do you. All they can do is drug me and try to keep you ignorant. But here you are, my brilliant girl." Lucy turned her tear-dashed eyes to Freya, full of warmth and love.

Freyja leaned into Aunt Lucy's side and squeezed her, and at the same time peering over her shoulder to see if anyone was watching them. When they parted, she pulled her backpack from her shoulders and placed it into her lap. She drew from it the envelope with the letter and the map.

"Do you know Sarana?" Freyja asked her.

"Sarana?" Lucy said, brow furrowed, repeating the name several times. "No, I don't know . . . I don't remember," she said meekly, somehow pained—an anguished pain that turned her skin stiff. Then she coughed and said, "Let's see that map."

Freyja unfolded the yellowed edges and laid the map before them. Several large masses were likely islands, while other lines arched around like mountains, and some smaller circles might have been water forms. There were symbols in each of the four corners and down each side, like coordinates on a graph. In the lower island were pyramids, with a large one in the middle and a cluster of writing around it.

"Ah," Aunt Lucy said. "This is the Quechua map. So, that's what she decided." Aunt Lucy mumbled a bit to herself, and then turned to her niece. "Listen carefully. These are portals," she said, pointing to a marking of a spiral target. "Portals are like nodes or hubs. We only have theories, but legend says these portals were places and were part of an ancient power grid, very powerful vortices all connected. Your mom called it the ancient power matrix, like the PG&E of Atlantis. You see?" She pointed to several spots on the map. "All these spots, or portals, are found near powerful energy spots, often where ley lines cross, but not always. That's no accident. Many ancient sites are near these locations and are even well known, but most are buried, built upon, or deactivated."

Freyja pointed to a large geometric flower symbol. "What is that one?" she asked.

"The Flower of Life. That is a sacred place. Very ancient. Heart place. Possibly a temple location or something else."

Freyja pulled her backpack open and showed Aunt Lucy the box inside, and the key was lying next to it.

"Ahhhhh. Have you opened the box?"

"Not yet . . . but . . ." Freyja hesitated to share the story of her experience with the box. She wanted to get as much information as she could from Aunt Lucy.

"That key will fit one of these places. The stones that activate the key will align with one of them." She paused, and then added, "Well, theoretically anyway … This was your mother's research before she disappeared. Your mother believed she found one of the missing crystals. It's probably in that box." Lucy pointed to the empty holes on the key.

"What do you mean, disappeared?" asked Freyja. "I thought they both died in a climbing accident?"

Lucy laced her fingers nervously. "No … no …" She finally sighed. "Your parents, they were far too careful about that. I never believed the university's story about the whole thing. Their bodies never returned, only a box of ashes. It wasn't theirs. I know it."

Her head was splitting. Her parents possibly not dead? "Why did you tell me they were dead?" she said with sudden sternness.

"I couldn't leave you with them missing. Imagine if you had known all this time? You would go mad trying to find them, wouldn't you? I know you." She shifted and peered intently at Freyja. Lifting a hand to her face to squelch a cough, she pulled her sweater tighter around her shoulders.

"So, this map …?" Freyja said.

"Yes, here." Aunt Lucy pointed at it. "This area indicates a desert and fertile valley filled with a complex of pyramids, dozens. Probably most of them are buried today. It says it lies across the ocean from the Kingdom of Ra, which is likely Egypt. Now, just before your parents disappeared, your mother was very excited about a discovery in a place called Caral in Peru. Her colleague, Ruth Shady, managed to get the approvals to excavate a series of buried pyramids part of a much larger complex, at least five thousand years old. I believe this map is from there."

"Okay, but," Freyja shook her head, unsure what to do with this information, "how do I get to Peru? And how do I open this thing?" Freyja reached into her bag to pull out the box.

"Freyja, don't you remember?" smiled Aunt Lucy.

"No?" Freyja said. "Remember what?"

"Cawww. Caaaawwww." Suddenly, a loud birdcall disturbed their conversation. Sarana was standing next to a distant tree waving at her wildly. It was time to go.

"Dear, you must go," Aunt Lucy said, stroking Freyja's arm.

Freyja reached around and hugged her aunt tightly, crying into her shoulder. "I can't leave you here," she cried, starting to panic. "Come with us."

"I'm in no shape to run from these goons. I believe in you. Your mother does, too."

"No. You must come." Freyja's heart was splitting, and her eyes streamed with warm tears that her aunt wiped from her cheeks.

"Caaawww! Caaawww!"

One of the guards in the yard shouted at them, "Hey!"

"Go!" Aunt Lucy shoved Freyja away from her.

Freyja sprang off to the fence line, tripping over herself, running half-blinded by tears. She watched her aunt over her shoulder while searching for Sarana and Nash. Nash was fleeing from guards on the lawnmower, while both Freyja and Sarana were sprinting for the gate. Nash came riding up behind them, just as they made it through the gate, closed the door, and locked the bolt. The security guards ran feverishly towards them, grabbing for their keys to the gate.

"Hurry!" said Sarana.

They sprinted around the building towards the entrance. The guard who had been under Sarana's spell was now standing with his weapon drawn, pointed straight at them. Sarana waved her hand, and the gun flew into the bushes. The shocked guard ran to his gatehouse, dialing on his phone. As they approached the closed perimeter gates, Sarana stood with her hands in a cocked position around the lock. She turned it just so, and the lock fell away. The gate opened slowly.

She hissed at Freyja and Nash. "Squeeze through and run!"

They ran as fast as they could down the drive, and out into the road, turning to see that Sarana was not behind them. The guards had surrounded her.

"We've gotta help her!" Freyja gasped.

"If she can't help herself, how are we gonna help her?" Nash yelled.

"I know, but . . ." Panic rose inside Freyja. It commingled with the guilt at leaving her aunt, and the two emotions were breaking her apart. She started walking towards the gate, determined to help.

"No! You are in danger. Go now!" Sarana stared sternly at her through the gate.

Freyja instantly realized what was happening. Sarana was communicating with her mind.

"She said we have to leave her," Freyja sobbed, her body convulsing as if in a fight with itself.

Suddenly, sirens filled the air, like the sound of an emergency drill from school. Freyja grabbed Nash, and they sprinted further down the road into an empty overgrown lot across the street. She realized that they could be spotted, and rolled to the ground in the tall grasses and pulled Nash down with her. They lay on the ground panting with adrenaline.

"Shhhhhh!" she said as if he could stop breathing. Sirens grew louder and passed by them before turning into the hospital driveway.

"Now what?" asked Nash.

"I think we wait here until they give up," she said. "Or until it's dark."

They turned on their backs, holding hands and staring at each other. Freyja began the breathing exercise Sarana had taught her in the forest. Nash joined in. There they tried to fall into a peaceful meditation until enough time passed, and Freyja realized the sirens were long gone and that her skin was burning. The scars on her arm glowed brightly.

"I wish I knew what it meant," she mumbled.

Nash paused and then broke the silence, "Is it saying time to eat?"

Freyja laughed. "My stomach's magical blinking billboard."

Then together, in dusky shadows, they crept towards the 7-Eleven.

CHAPTER SEVENTEEN

THINKING IS DANGEROUS

The phone rang several times before he picked it up.

"Yes..."

He listened to the voice on the other end without responding, and hung up. He was tired of this. He would much rather be out in his waders throwing a line across the river current, luring a fish. He had long ago surrendered to this path. Though he didn't pick it, it chose him. The science was indisputable, irresistible. The risks were great, but he could not resist the challenge. The potential to impact the world, to create a legacy for all time, was too great a reward. No matter the price.

The buzzer clicked, and the door opened.

"I suppose you know about the escape?"

"Yes."

A tall, imposing figure in an ill-fitting jacket walked directly to a leather bucket seat to the right of Drake's desk. He sat and crossed his extraordinarily long legs, puffing on a pipe and wiping his chin with an old-fashioned handkerchief.

"Why do you bring that filthy thing in here?" Drake complained.

The man ignored him, gazing out of the tall windows to the left. "That view never gets old, does it?"

"What do you want?" Drake said, crossing his arms.

"I want to hear that NuTech can handle this. I want to hear that NuTech is in line with the Nine's policies. I want to hear that your head is still in the game, Drake."

"Of course, it is," Drake scoffed, and then he stood up and paced next to the windows, realizing it was time for his bourbon on the rocks. He walked to the small bar sink in the back corner of his office. "Would you care for one?" he asked reluctantly.

"I would. I would also like to hear more reassurance. I know you. This has hit you hard. What are you thinking about?"

Drake sighed. He was not interested in discussing this with him. He wasn't up for it. Nothing was the same. Clarity was gone. The genome projects had gone wild. Too many competitors, and somehow, they all knew. They knew something was coming to the surface. It was a tinder box about to explode.

"Thinking is dangerous. I trust the numbers. We stick with the plan. Nothing else to say." He dropped an extra ice cube in the highball and handed it to the man.

"They will want more than that. You know it. The girl. Where is she?"

Drake had just finished hearing about her escape. He was surprised it hadn't happened earlier. But Arktik wasn't working yet. He did not want to shut her down, not yet. "We are tracking her."

"How can you track an Adept with no implant?"

"She has Arktik."

"I know. And it's not working."

Drake inhaled sharply, aware that his teacher, his mentor, was studying every movement, the man who taught him everything about reading non-verbal communication. It was one of his favorite subjects in training, to profile the unconscious habitual behaviors and mannerisms of humans. *Everyone has a tell—* that was the bottom line. You will know everything about a man by what he values, and when the stakes are on display, he will always tell you what that is. *Everyone has a tell.* He shuffled a deck of cards on his desk, flipping one and then another over until he had five cards arranged on the surface. "We think she's got help."

The man chuckled. "Drake, this could be your downfall. I would hate to see that happen." He took the last sip of his bourbon and set it down forcefully. "You're one of the good ones."

Drake clicked his tongue and shook his head.

The man got up and headed towards the door. "Let me know as soon as you find her."

As he left and shut the door, Drake flicked a card angrily at the door.

CHAPTER EIGHTEEN

THE FREEST MAN BEHIND BARS

The 7-Eleven parking lot was empty except for one old white Honda motorcycle. The ceiling lights flickered inside the convenience store, illuminating the colorfully packaged processed candies, sodas, and chips.

As Freyja grabbed the shop door, someone spoke. She paused but didn't see anyone, so she went to grab the handle again.

"Don't go in there."

She spied a figure hunched over near the pay phones. The person had a wool blanket wrapped around his shoulders and a brown leather cowboy hat with a white feather tucked in the band.

Freyja paused, and then asked, "What did you say?"

The hat barely moved. "You are hungry now, but if you enter this place, they will find you." His voice was somber and eerie, spoken in such a way as to raise the hairs on the back of Freyja's neck.

"Excuse me?" she said in a breathy whisper.

"I said I wouldn't go in there if I were you."

Freyja took a step forward. "What do you mean they will find me?"

The mysterious man sighed heavily. He shifted where he was, and then cocked his hat and revealed a piercing set of eyes that gazed out from an angular weathered profile. His skin was buttery and creased, the way a well-loved glove or favorite leather chair might be, and he had a grey braid tucked around his neck.

"Those who hunt the Adepts, that's who you'll find in there. Adepts like you, Freyja."

Shocked, she asked, "How do you know me?"

There was something about the man, something familiar in his eyes, and the authority he held, which was strong and powerful, yet not threatening. "My sister . . . Sarana," he said.

Freyja gasped and stepped closer, and then said, "You are Sarana's brother?" Her heart leaped at the possibility.

"Yes, and I have shelter and food. You should follow me."

The man rose like a limber sapling, using a worn and knobby stick to steady himself. He stood no more than five-and-a-half feet tall. His lumberjack shirt and work jeans hung clean and oversized, but fumed of pitch and pine smoke. He was an odd mix of hearty woodsman and street hobo. "I can explain more on the way," he said, waving them along.

Freyja and Nash reluctantly left the 7-Eleven shop and followed behind the mysterious elder. They trekked behind the building through a dirt path into some trees. Not far behind the tree line was a train track. They walked along the rail lines for half a mile until they came upon a long line-up of parked train cars. The man tossed a bag he carried into the last container car and pulled himself in with surprising swiftness. Once in, he turned and reached out his hand to Freyja. Then, just as Nash's legs were clambering up the ledge of the dusty car, it began to scoot forward slowly.

"Is this legal?" asked Freyja.

The man laughed. "Man-made laws are suggestions at best and immoral at worst. This train's existence violates natural laws." He dealt her a wink and lowered himself gently into a corner.

The train car was full of shadows and flickering light as the city went passing by. Freyja studied the man, staring quietly out the open door. He appeared to be an older Native American man, though he could have been of many origins. His eyes sparkled like diamonds, shining and full of absolute wisdom. Freyja watched him for a while in silence.

Nash was staring out at the accelerating landscape. "Um, do we know where we are going?"

"I think he knows," said Freyja gazing at the man. "What's your name anyway?"

"Tommy," the man said. "You can call me Tommy." He lifted his pack, pulled out a few wrapped sandwiches, and handed them to Freyja and Nash. "I am grateful you listened to my warning. Those stores are wall to wall with cameras. They would have swarmed on you in an instant. Now we are invisible for a while."

Freyja shuddered, thinking of the mysterious people pursuing them. It was overwhelming to consider that, until she pulled the implant out of her hand, she had been utterly ignorant of anything unusual in her life or the world, that there was some mysterious group tracking her and others like her, that she had so narrowly escaped from who knows what. Freyja rubbed the base of her skull where the new implant was. She remembered Sarana's words about the timer. How much time did she even have? "Who are they? What do they want with me?"

"Well, as Sarana told you, I think they are misguided men. They think they can control the forces of life. You will understand your place in all this soon enough."

"So, Sarana is your sister?" asked Freyja.

"Of course. We are all relations in this realm. All of us are moving within a shared web. Long ago, humanity danced with the light of the web, calling in the magic of all the elements and beings woven together. You've seen it now, haven't you?"

"You mean the web? I only see it sometimes."

The man nodded and then pointed over to a corner of the train car. Freyja followed his extended finger's direction to a spider's web suspended halfway up, pale and silky. "They are not like this. Those you speak of, the black ones, are infected, diseased. Dis-eased. You will understand more as you learn."

Moonlight glistened on the fine silken threads, women in hexagonal shapes. Each spiral was delicately attached in somewhat random but balanced segments, holding the entire fabric splayed out to capture the nutrients this spider needed to survive. Small beads of water sparkled and slipped along the maze. Beautiful shapes emerged from the pattern, shifting and flexing in the breeze.

Freyja gasped. "It's beautiful."

"Yes, and like every being in our cosmos, we all have a little corner of the web where we weave our experiences and cast our nets." Tommy gently touched one of the support strands with his finger. It bounced and swayed in the gusts that rushed in from outside. "Life is ever-expanding and growing," he said, sitting back down against the wall. "Grandmother Spider teaches us to be open to the creative potential of the universe. She symbolizes the infinite patterns and fundamental nature of polarity in our world. There are dark webs and light webs, and cradling all of them is an infinite web of life."

"Why can't we all see it?" asked Freyja.

"Our web is out of balance. It has been so for long that our only memory of balance is in our myths and fairytales. We have forgotten who we are. Humanity has a disease that makes us keep forgetting. Collective amnesia." Tommy beheld the moon shimmering over the mountain ridge. "Do you know about the liver flukes?" he asked.

"The liver flukes. No . . ." Freyja replied.

"This is a common parasite. The only way it can survive is to turn ants, the forest floor workers, into zombies. Normally, ants would never position themselves on a flower near a mammal that could eat them. When infested with liver fluke, ants stop whatever they are doing, climb to the top of the nearest flowers and grasses, and wait to be eaten. The liver fluke can only reproduce in the liver of large mammals. Humanity has a parasite, an inner demon. It came many moons ago from meteors that rained down on the earth. There are many zombie people now, very easy to control. The infection does not know it's an infection. A zombie does not know it's a zombie."

"And Adepts?" Freyja said, impatient to hear him out.

"The Adepts, like you, are immune to this. All healing requires is exposure to pure Earth energies, unpolluted. But our Earth is now in chains. Her veins have been ripped open and mined, just like the hearts and minds of people. The body of a man, like the body of Earth, is in distress because we have forgotten our connection. We seek reunion with each other and all of creation through awareness, with the grace of the Great Spirit. The purpose of our lives is to awaken, to remember who we are. Great Mother has been working slowly within this world. She has summoned you."

"Summoned?" asked Freyja, alarmed at seeing Tommy's speech grow bolder.

"Yes. You must repair the grid."

"What is the grid?" asked Nash.

Tommy wiped his chin and gazed out at the passing fields. "The grid," he began calmly, "is the nervous system that will awaken humanity and begin healing of those who have forgotten. It's a connection of powerful energy centers around the earth. These stations receive cosmic source energy and amplify it along to other stations. The frequencies are healing and purifying, like freshwater from the mountains. It's a lot like when you are in a good mood and infect others with the same mood. These stations magnify these energies millions of times greater."

"So, like when you feel better, you do better?" asked Freyja.

Tommy nodded, pleased with her understanding.

Freyja sat quietly, considering the web. She was struck by how cruel it was that some negative entity or energy could somehow infect an entire planet.

"So, we just need to hook up some speakers and play some sick tunes to heal the world?" said Nash.

"Perhaps 'well tunes' would be best." Tommy smiled softly and starred out into the dusky skies. He had so much more to say, but was holding it back.

The train left the city and traveled east along the Columbia River, passed the thickly forested Willamette Valley, and then towards the Gorge's national scenic areas. Turkey vultures soared overhead, hunting for small rodents to feast upon. The rapids of the river roared over itself the farther they journeyed into the east wind, sending frothy waves across the channel.

"You need to find the mother crystal for the key, no?" Tommy said.

"Mother? It was called Pachamama or something."

"Yes... Mother Earth, Gaia, Pachamama, all names for the Great Mother of Earth and matter. Matter, matter, mother. Pachamama is from the people of the Andes, but it means the same thing," said Tommy.

"There might be one in this box, but I have no idea how to open it and no clue where to get others," she said, shaking her head.

"I have some ideas," Tommy answered mysteriously.

Soon the train slowed, and Tommy pointed to the grasses outside. "Jump!" he yelled.

Freyja and Nash crouched and then sprang out of the train car, cold air whooshing past their ears. They landed hard, rolling onto their sides on the slope of dewy grass, as the train gradually slowed into a proper station further down the track. Tommy stood, wiping his muddy knees with his hands, and motioned for them to follow him across the tracks and down the river.

"Hurry; they don't like people on the tracks," he whispered.

Once they reached the riverbank, they saw a motorboat anchored near the rocks, gently swaying in the tide through thick brush. They hopped in the boat, and Tommy shoved out into the river current. The water was flowing west, but they needed to go east, so he drifted for twenty feet or so into the middle of the broad and deep Columbia River, and then pulled the cord and started the engine. It rumbled to start and purred like a kitten. The boat come to life beneath her. Freyja sat down at one end of it and held her knees as they passed several large ports and smaller docks. Industrial warehouses of every kind lined both sides of the river. There were old repurposed canneries now docking logging carriers and tugboats. The teens shivered in the night air, cooled more so over the water.

"Here." Tommy tossed them his blanket as they ferried farther upriver.

Soon cliffs were rising on either side with old campers on the southside, single-wide trailers, motor homes, beat-up trucks, and clotheslines situated along a narrow strip.

"What's that?" asked Freyja.

"Those are reservation fishing grounds," Tommy said, his words cutting through the sound of the powerful rapids. The corner of the massive Dalles Dam complex had a giant painted American flag on the dam's wall glowing in the moonlight. Tommy steered the boat into a cove below the cliffside. "We will have to hike to the sacred grounds. We can't get through the dam lock."

They crawled along a rocky shoreline. Above the shore were little promontories wedged out from the rocks where fishers once stood to catch the salmon. In the days of the tribes, the river flowed wild, and the salmon leaped victoriously over the stones, with their single goal to reach their sacred mating grounds. The local tribes honored this migration and only fished the second run of every season. With ropes tied around their waists, the fishermen crept out onto rickety platforms, dipping their nets into the frothing rapids to catch the mighty salmon. When the federal government built the dam, it flooded the river and submerged an entire way of life.

"This water is under official federal control," Tommy said, staring at it bitterly. "It generates 10 percent of the whole country's electrical supply."

"Ten percent. That's impressive," said Nash, nodding.

Freyja scowled at him.

"What?" he added innocently, shrugging his shoulders.

Tommy continued, "The ancient fishing grounds now lie lost, submerged below its depths. Every home and business in this whole state draws power from this dam."

The block of curving stone holding back the flow of the river was either an industrial marvel or a monstrosity, depending on your point of view. Freyja could vividly imagine those times: of the leaping salmon and of the place that people had once called home. The rocks were slick and cold from the misty air drifting between the river channels. She gripped the uneven ledges carefully, watching her footing, holding her breath. Nash slipped as loose rocks tumbled into the water.

"Be careful!" she scolded.

Tommy had gone on ahead of them and was turning around a stony corner. Freyja had no idea how much farther they had to go. Cold, tired, and weak, she trudged on, and soon enough, they arrived at a rocky beach.

"Take my hand!" yelled Tommy, reaching with outstretched fingers around the rocky face.

Freyja took the hand, and Tommy pulled her to a large flat ledge. Nash followed right behind, not requiring Tommy's hand. He sprang onto it as cleanly as a mountain goat.

They jogged quickly along the beach, and then ducked into some trees where a warm fire was burning at the center of a little clearing.

"Here we rest." Tommy put his pack down and motioned for them to sit by the fire. Freyja sat down, crossing her legs, and leaned forward. She warmed her hands over the crackling fire as Nash lay down on one elbow, pulling his shoes and socks off with one hand, and then pointing his toes at the flames. After a few minutes, Tommy handed them each a tin cup full of some sweet tea.

"Thank you," said Freyja.

The moon illuminated the clearing with mystic wonder. The stars gathered around their shoulders like old friends stopping by. The heavens and Earth touched down around this humble camp that, at that moment, was the center of the entire universe. And no one could have convinced them otherwise.

"This is amazing," said Nash, his eyes wheeling around at the silvered leaves and shiny grass.

"This is an ancient place," Tommy said. "It is the oldest continuously inhabited area in North America, and it was once a great place, a center of massive cosmic energy. Many tribes met here. They traded and fished and sang and danced. Many were people of the river, the Wyam'pum," he added, pointing through the trees at the inky waters of the Columbia.

"My grandfather taught me the history of the earth. He told me about the time when massive rocks fell from the sky and destroyed everything. He showed me the giant rock called Willamette Meteorite. Some thought it was the wreckage of a spaceship or Stargate, a door to other planets or dimensions. Many believed these meteorites held deep power and could alter time and space. Now it lives in a museum in New York City."

"Whoa . . . So, like Jefferson Starship?" chuckled Nash. Tommy cocked his head quizzically. "You know, like, rock band . . . rock and roll? It was a joke." Nash shrugged, turning his gaze back out to the stars.

Tommy continued, "The cosmic storm that attacked the earth changed everything. Many tribes all over the world used these rocks to open doorways that should not have been open. The seers say we can heal these breaches and restore our integrity," Tommy paused then and began staring intensely into the flames before adding, "if we repair the grid."

Tommy continued, "Grandfather also showed me some special crystals. He called them star crystals. He said they fed is Great Mother the strength of the universe. I believe this what you seek, Freyja. Pachamama is Great Mother in the language of the Andes people."

Freyja bolted up with excitement. "Do you know where to find them?"

Tommy began to pace. "Because our livelihood was fishing, we were always showing our deep gratitude to the salmon. Grandfather kept the stones in a special altar in the rocks to show thanks for our protection and nourish us. But, when the United States built the Dalles Dam and flooded the most ancient sacred place in North America, that was the end of our way of life. Those crystals and our history lie deep under the waters there now."

Tommy had spoken so somberly. "It's like we keep burying our history, like we don't want to know who we are."

"Freyja, our elders and chiefs foresaw this, the great forgetting. The tragedy now is that our people should still remember the old ways, but are suffering and dying. Most of all, they have forgotten who they are. We've all gone down the same way."

Freyja stood up and gave Tommy a deep hug. She was more determined than ever to help. "What can I do? I'm just one person."

"Inside the one is the whole. When one is moving towards change, the one gathers momentum on the path. Momentum builds. One is magnified by purpose. One plus one becomes two. One plus two is three. Three plus two is five. Three plus five is eight. Do you see?"

"I'm not sure I get what you are saying," Freyja said.

"I get it," said Nash. "Like that story in science class about the butterfly. She flaps her wings in Shanghai, and eventually that action creates a hurricane in Kansas. Right? The energy expands, like massively, to create a much larger force."

"Yes," smiled Tommy. "Very good."

Freyja tried to take it all in, to process the experience as totally normal even though it was unlike anything she had ever imagined.

"Are you ready to find your stones?" asked Tommy.

"Yes, but how?"

"Let me take you on a journey."

"Aren't I already on a journey?"

"A different kind of journey . . . this is to your freedom. The freest man, or woman, behind bars is the one who knows the bars are an illusion . . ."

Tommy shook out a large wool blanket, rolled it in his hands, and laid it down as a pillow. "Lay down here," he said before grabbing a thin drum out of his backpack and then waited for her to get comfortable. "Now, close your eyes."

CHAPTER NINETEEN

TO FIND PEARLS, DIVE DEEP

Tommy stoked the fire next to them and ran his hand through the flame. He put a few more pieces of wood on the fire, and then started to shake a rattle. Tommy walked around the fire slowly, chanting an ancient song, and then turned to face the flickering flames. He began to pray.

"Mother Earth, hear your children. Let us come to you to learn and receive your lessons. Let us hear your voices in the winds. From the east, we seek clarity and vision, the lessons of childhood, to see with innocence, the lessons of Spirit, given in love by Creator. From the south, we learn the way of questioning our past and programming, the fire, and the independence of adolescence. Help us to grow on this path. From the west, Grandfather teaches us to accept our responsibility, to learn from the years of marriage and family. From the north, our elders show us their wisdom and knowledge and teach us to walk in balance with our Mother, the earth.

Mother Earth, Great Spirit, ancestors, four-legged, two legends, the furred, the clawed, the winged, and even the creepy crawlers—I honor all who have gone before and all who come after. We are one in this great dream. We invite you to this sacred fire to show us the way for sister Freyja."

Tommy took a deep breath and stood for a moment holding the space around the fire. Then he reached his hand through the fire and smiled. He picked up the thin drum and firmly struck the rattle against its taut surface. With each beat, their blood pulsed in unison.

"We call on all our ancestors and the star nations to help you on your journey." He did a slow stomping dance around the fire pit, calling out a haunting song with unfamiliar words. The soothing mantra lulled her into a hypnotic state. Tommy paused and ran his hand through the fire.

Freyja was surprised. "Doesn't that hurt?"

"When the fire is friendly, it will not burn you. We have asked for the support of the spirit and Earth worlds, and they have granted it. This is one way to show respect and awareness for all the forces around us."

"Wow. So, the fire is like a celestial messaging service?" Freja asked.

"Yes, in a way . . ." Tommy said mysteriously. "Ready to walk between worlds?"

"Walk between worlds? Like leaving my body?"

"Yes, I will guide you there." Tommy winked. "Some call it astral travel. I like to call it spirit cloud. Your spirit self will find a way there, and you will see what you are ready to see. Just trust yourself. This space is protected and very safe."

"You are going to leave your body? Like, for real?" Nash asked, incredulous.

Freyja giggled at Nash's question. She was also surprised, but then she wondered, "Can I take Nash with me?" Was that even possible?

Tommy peered sternly at them both. "He can journey, too, but you each will have your path and destination . . ." The man rubbed his chin thoughtfully, turned towards Nash, and asked, "You have a gift for the tonal, no?"

Nash shrugged. "Well, I play music."

"Hmm. Perhaps another time weaver," he murmured to himself. Tommy touched him on the shoulder. "I want you to relax and set your intent to listen. Okay? Listen with your whole being, not just your ears. You may discover something that you both need."

Nash set his chin and nodded.

A few moments later, as Tommy continued to drum and chant, both Freyja and Nash lay side by side on the blanket, their ears filled with nothing else than the hypnotic beats emanating from the small clearing in the woods.

"Relax your body and your mind," Tommy repeated. "Let your arms and legs go heavy. Let them melt into the ground . . . You are going deeper and deeper. Your bodies are sinking heavier and heavier into the grass, the soil, the roots of our Mother. Soon, you will be absorbed by Earth, into a river that carries you deeper . . ."

Every word he said was as if he were conjuring them into life with only his voice. Freyja drifted into a dark but comfortable sleep, a dream state. Soon she realized she was sitting at the edge of the river, watching the water lap against the small rocks, gently pulling her into its grasp. She stepped into the calm waters where the hard pebbles massaged the bottoms of her feet. Just ahead of her, something caught her eye. She peered into the dark surface of the water where there was a small flash. She could not quite make it out. There was a cliff along the ridge next to the river, facing the enormous dam below. Was there a cave at the bottom?

"What's that?" she said to herself.

"Keep drifting down deeper. Allow yourself to follow the path that unfolds before you . . ." Tommy comforted her, his voice rich and deep, and beginning to fade.

Freyja spied the glimmering ripples fanning across the water, reflecting the ghostly rays of the moon that hung like celestial ropes in the night. One dangled into her reach, and she twisted it around her. As the cool velvet water deepened, she dove into the black depths. Then, effortlessly, she began to sink into an illuminated haunting underworld. She swam up to the ancient submerged fishing platforms, rocking in the tomb-like currents, the native fisherman once balanced on dangerous tethers to catch salmon leaping through the rapids. Now it was only stony crags jutting like gnashing jaws at lonely Chinook and catfish.

Freyja swam farther and farther into the busy river belly. A curious five-foot sturgeon and juvenile salmon darted in and around her. The river grasses swayed in thick groves. Freyja spied something sparkling among the rocks and platform ruins, so she grabbed on to a plank and pushed off, propelling herself forward. Just between two platforms, wedged between the rocks, was something flickering like a flame. She kicked hard to get in closer, reaching out to pull herself towards it. As she did so, a platform above rocked in the current and slammed down on her head. She was knocked out cold, going into another level of trance.

"You are going deeper and deeper . . ." Tommy's voice was faint in the far distance of her mind.

She sank deep into the black abyss. A swirl of blood danced from her scalp from where she had hit the platform. The river currents swirled around her, like a twirling dancer. Below was a growing darkness, blacker and thicker than oil, and deeper than any deep she could imagine. She struggled and clawed at the liquid sheets enveloping her body as a great drum echoed in her head. She gasped, desperate for air. A rush of icy water flowed into her lungs. In revulsion and panic, she tried to stop the pulsing knives from tearing into her chest.

"Relax into the depths of the river," chanted Tommy in a low calm whisper.

His voice called forth the light. Freyja squinted at little specks in the water all around her. The tiny fragments of matter suddenly imploded and vanished, sucking all light out of the blackest space, consuming her. She was both in the space and of it. Freyja herself was like a vibration on a wire, but not the boundaries of what her body was. She wiggled her fingers and toes. Then she tried to speak, but all she could hear was the hollow echo of her voice in a watery echo.

Where am I?

A low humming grew into a horrible growl. Freyja floated helplessly. Then suddenly, a silhouette appeared from the black cloak of the deep. It roared a tidal wave of current towards her and sent her tumbling and spinning wildly. The very presence of the shadow was beastly. It dashed and whipped around her. Freyja was beyond terrified. There was nothing she could do. But as the vile thing continued to thrash around her, Freyja turned her mind inward to her heart and remembered Sarana's training. Slowly, she did as she remembered: she breathed the universal energy into her heart. It was there, against a presence that threatened to engulf her, the inward truth that everything is connected.

Slowly, the waters calmed to a ripple, and Freyja found her equilibrium. There was only silence and peace. The presence was still there. But like an exhausted lion, it waited just on the periphery, in the corners of the darkness.

"Who are you?" Freyja said.

"We are the river."

"The river?"

"Yes, we are the spirit of the river. We are trapped here by your dams. We are forsaken and forgotten."

"You are trapped here? Is that why you are so angry?"

"We are sad. We are alone. Why have you forsaken us?"

"I . . . I mean, *we* haven't forsaken you. I didn't even know you existed!" Freyja wondered for a moment if maybe this river spirit could help her get the crystals. "Do you know of the Pachamama crystals?" she said.

There was a long silence. *"Pachamama is every crystal, every mineral, every creature. She is us. We are she."*

"Okay. But I have this key to an ancient site in Peru. And I need a special crystal. Do you know it?"

There was a long pause. And Freyja wondered if they'd gone.

"Yes, we can show you the way if you free us."

Freyja asked with excitement, "Of course! How can I free you?"

"Destroy the dam."

"What? How?"

"We must be freed."

Freyja's head swam. Destroy a dam? How on earth would she bring down a massive cement and steel structure? It wasn't possible.

As she drifted, the river breathed and buoyed her up into a vast and watery cradle. There was a rumble of thunder far off over the hills. A bluster of wind kicked up the surface of the water with tiny waves. Star light traced the scars and symbols on her shoulder like small paintbrushes on a milky canvas. The moon's rays washed over her like ribbons of joy. A sparkling line of moonlight highlighted a crescent-shaped scar on her arm. Was that scar somehow linked to the moon? Her heart was burning inside her chest and a flower-shaped scar on her arm pulsed in amber. The water around her body slightly simmered with a comforting warmth.

There was energy drawing into her body from everywhere, even the constellations above. The pressure was building as though she might explode.

A giant current of lightning cracked from the scattered clouds in the sky.

Freyja gasped.

The lighting organized itself quickly and coursed straight at her. She ducked underwater as it struck the water surface with a jolt.

Another bolt cracked nearby, glancing off into the rocks. Freyja floated, stunned, and fearful for the enormous storm cackling just over her head. A third bolt fired down and hit her hands, and she quickly covered her head. It did not hurt her. She absorbed the energy.

Freyja steadied herself and wondered if perhaps she *could* channel this, contain it, direct it. She waited for another bolt, and waited. She became impatient and held her hand in the air. A ball of energy pulsed from the palm of her hand. Instinctively, she directed her aim at the dam.

The energetic bolt exploded from her palm like an awkward yoyo leaving its spool. Freyja gasped, her body recoiling in the water, and watched with wide eyes as a hole the size of a tanker truck blasted through the wall of turbines, more than half a mile away. The river started to flood through the gaping hole, escaping towards the Pacific. Immediately sirens went off, and Freyja realized she could now touch the river bottom with her feet.

"Thank you, sister."

The river spirits giggled with delight and danced along the surface of the now rapidly flowing river. Their joy and mirth restored.

"Hey, what about those crystals?" she asked.

"There."

She turned around to behold a magnificent alcove within the rocks. She walked carefully across the shallow riverbed and studied the opening. It was half her height, so she bent over to peer inside. Crawling on her belly, she discovered a small carved bowl. She pulled the bowl with a bright, sparkling purple stone and a perfect star beaming from its center into her lap. Freyja turned to show Nash and Tommy as if they were right there beside her, but she was alone in the rocks. In a moment, the river rose around her and carried her into a large swirling eddy.

The drumbeat steadied in her blood.

Bom. Bom. Bom.

Freyja sank back into her body by the fire. The crackling grew louder and louder as she wiggled her fingers and toes. She opened her eyes to Tommy still pacing with his drum. Nash was sitting beside her, with a grin on his face.

"Welcome back," said Nash.

Freyja blinked hard and tried to get her bearings. "Wow. That was crazy," she said.

Tommy made a quick closing prayer around the fire and began to cover it with sand. "You must go . . . Now, you must go!" Tommy said hastily.

Sirens were going off, with emergency vehicles speeding down the highways on either side of the river. Spotlights were scanning the river in the vicinity of where they had been.

"What's going on?" Freyja asked him.

"You were successful," Tommy said, nudging her hand.

Freyja opened her palm to study the star garnet resting in her hand. But her clothes were dry. "Wait! That wasn't a dream?"

"What is not a dream?" Tommy laughed.

Utterly perplexed, Nash pulled her up to her feet. They gathered their bags as riverboats with powerful spotlights roared up the river in their direction.

"I don't have time to explain," Tommy said. "We can't let them catch you."

Moments later, they were hurrying quickly down the beach, through a small grove of trees, and up into the hillside going east. Tommy pointed out a cave at the base of the hillside. There was a stack of haphazard old railroad ties covering the mouth of the long-abandoned tunnel.

"Okay, now to find the blood-sucking vampires, I guess . . ." said Nash.

"We are going in there?" asked Freyja.

"I will make a diversion. Here is an abandoned mining tunnel. There is an outlet about two miles on the other side. Be careful and stay out of sight." Tommy handed them two small torches. "May Great Spirit protect you both."

As soon as Nash and Freyja got inside, Tommy heaved the railroad ties back over the tunnel opening. Freyja watched Tommy turn and hop down the trail back towards the water. But for the little pockets of light that glowed from the torches, darkness surrounded them.

CHAPTER TWENTY

THE SOUL ALWAYS KNOWS

Under cover of the tunnel entrance, Freyja stopped and faced Nash.

She trembled. "Okay. What happened back there?"

"Are you okay?" he asked, grabbing her firmly with his free hand. His eyes were piercing and calm even though his shaking body was jostling the torch and creating an eerie silhouette on the tunnel walls.

"I think so." She exhaled deeply and searched her memory of what she had just experienced. "I don't understand what just happened." Her throat was impossibly dry and tight. She tried to take in a deep breath and calm herself.

Nash squeezed her arm. "I was there, too. I saw you."

Freyja blushed. "You were?" She stared wide-eyed and curious. "Tell me. What did you see?" She wanted his confirmation, either that what she experienced happened or that it didn't. This dreaming awake stuff was very strange and new.

"Yeah, in my journey or whatever it's called, we were together at the beginning. Except, I kept losing you. And when I found you, you had changed into something else, like a flame or something. I tried to reach out to you, but I got kicked out, I guess." He started walking into the long dark tunnel, holding her hand and the torch, moving anxiously away from the sounds of sirens and danger outside.

"A flame? Maybe you witnessed me get struck by lightning?" The recent events were pulsing loudly in her mind, full of energy and emotion.

"Is that why you blew up the dam?"

Freyja sputtered at the absurdity. "Oh, my God! Yeah. I met these water spirits. They asked me to free them. They were somehow imprisoned by the dam. How crazy is that? And then they showed me the crystal."

"Wow . . ." Nash was entirely used to hearing about these things now.

They ambled, trying to focus on the path just ahead of them. The old railroad tracks were rusted, but continued along in a straight line. The air was stale, full of burnt kerosene and damp earth. Suddenly, a high shriek of anguish ruptured the air, cracking particles apart like nutshells.

"Arrrgggghhhh."

Nash gasped. "Did you hear that?"

They froze.

"Yeah," Freyja whispered. "Whatever it is, I don't want to meet it."

Freyja and Nash waved their torches, searching for a way out and away from whatever it was that had howled so menacingly.

"Here! Look! It might be a way out!" said Nash, his voice a mixture of hope and despair.

Freyja turned her eyes to the light of Nash's torch on the outline of a door that led into a little wooden structure. They gasped.

"Go on," said Freyja.

Nash nodded, and his trembling hand reached out for the rusty handle. "Yeah, maybe a storage shed or something?" he whispered, and then as he tried to turn it, the handle came loose and fell to the ground in a loud clink.

"Aaaaarrrrggghhhh."

"What the hell?" Nash fell back on his butt, trying to move away from the sound.

"Is someone there?" Freyja called out.

"Leave!" came a bellow.

Freyja jumped, and the torch dropped to the ground. Nash hoisted himself up in alarm, his limbs stiff.

"Who are you?" demanded Freyja.

"You trespass!" came the voice. It was harsh and rattling the very ground where Freyja and Nash stood.

"We're just . . . we're passing through!" Nash blurted anxiously.

"Get . . . out!" the voice seethed.

Suddenly, the door beside them burst open like an explosion, startling Freyja, and sending Nash tumbling back onto the ground in a heap. Through the dust, Freyja glimpsed a small light on a table inside the room. A black shadow leaped across the room.

"Sorry! We are leaving!" Freyja screamed, pulling Nash to his feet.

"Go back the way you came! Leave!" roared the voice once more.

"There is no other exit. We would if we could. We can't go back that way!" Freyja pled; she didn't know what to do.

A long silence followed. Then Freyja had a thought: what if she tried to befriend it? "I am Freyja, and this is—" Freyja started to explain.

"Aye . . ." the voice trailed off into the distance.

Suddenly, there was some thrashing about, odd sounds for a cavern in the middle of a cliff. They were domestic sounds. Bottles or chairs were falling over. Cupboards were slammed shut. Cutlery rattled on the hard floor.

"Show yourself," the voice demanded.

Freyja shivered. Nash gulped hard, but he couldn't muster a single word. Everything in them wanted to run away from whatever it was. But they couldn't go back out; they couldn't leave. Police would be roaming everywhere.

"Um. Maybe you could come out and meet us first?" Freyja offered.

Nash froze wide-eyed hoping she had not just consigned them to their deaths.

"No!" the angry voice said. There was a long silence as Freyja and Nash stood there, unsure of what they should do. "That would be difficult for me," his voice softened. "I know who you are, Freyja Wolfe. I've been waiting for you."

His words sent chills. "What do you mean?" Freyja asked, alarmed.

"I knew your mother."

Freyja gasped and stared at Nash in total shock. "You, what?"

Determined to learn more about who this person was, Freyja stepped carefully through the doorway, holding her torch in front of her to illuminate the room as best as she could. The flame cast large shadows upon the stone-blasted walls and a hallway that led further into the rocky dwelling. A squat wood table made from warped planks and a couple of rickety stools sat in the center of the room. On the opposite wall stood a stack of broken frames, bottomless chairs, and lobster cages, random artifacts of a fisherman. Freyja and Nash stood on either side of the door with wide eyes for the gruff voice to emerge physically.

In a few moments, two lights appeared to twinkle from the dark hallway. There was an abrasive sound, like sandpaper running across a plank.

"You are as beautiful as your mother," he said. By now, the voice began to sound more human. It was undoubtedly male.

"How do you know my mother?"

A shadowy silhouette hovered in the doorway. The lights appeared to be eyes that were attached to a slightly larger than average head.

"Who are you?" asked Freyja.

"I am Seamus. Perhaps what you mean to ask is *what* am I?" he said.

Seamus moved slightly out of the shadows. As he did so, he revealed a grotesquely shaped body that was sickly grayish pink and half covered in a tattered winter coat and wool hat, which, as he pulled off out of respect, revealed a substantial hairless head covered in scales. And though he had legs, they were misshapen and tiny, attached to a much larger tail propping up the rest of his body. "I don't get out much these days," he said.

"What the hell?" gasped Nash, turning white at the sight of him.

"It is a kind of hell. But you need not be afraid," he said, more softly now, before launching into his story. "You see, my kind used to rule the seas, a very long time ago. We were the legendary merpeople, an ancient race of beings who lived in the ocean but could live on land for short periods. We were the ones who taught men of land how to sail and fish and use the energy of water to power other systems. Water is one of the primary elements of our world, and we were its masters.

We were once a respected race among the races who lived on this planet. And then, the great apocalypse that destroyed all our homes.

"Now we are part of the science pool. Not exactly a step up, if you know what I mean." Seamus hobbled into the torchlight and lay in a water-filled tub sculpted from the rock wall.

"I knew your mother a long time ago," he said, as he splashed himself with water. "We met in the caves where she was studying some old petroglyphs. I escaped the labs near the Colorado River and eventually found a place to hide. I went from one cage to another." The creature laughed bitterly.

"You knew my mom?" Freyja said. "What experiments?" She had so many questions she didn't know which to ask first.

"The stories of man beasts are true, Freyja. They have extensive underground labs all over the world. These people love to play with genetics, the blueprints of creation." He laughed awkwardly. "They are trying to create beings with powers no others have. So far, they are succeeding only in torturing and bastardizing life. They are too dumb to understand anything but brute force."

"You mean, you were a genetic experiment—" Freyja began to say, but Nash interrupted.

"Yeah, like Frankenstein?" he asked.

Freyja frowned at his rude interruption.

"Yes and no. I am primarily a merman," said the creature. "Your scientists found our remains from the old wars and genetically engineered me back to life. But because of their idiocy, they didn't quite get it right. And indeed, they had no idea the power we possessed. So, like any foolish scientist, they assumed they had control.

"Some part of me knew that there was more to this world than sitting in a cage and listening to the anguished cries of deformed life. So, I started exploring and found that there were many others like me. These labs are like a living hell. Most of their creations die before they are even born. Those who survive are so malformed and have so many maladies that they remove them—you know, kill 'em. I decided to free all of those who could move on their own. I sparked a mass breakout. About fifty of us were able to escape. The scientists called on their militias to hunt us down. I don't know how many of the others got away."

"That's incredible," mumbled Nash, his eyes wide.

"Your mother hiked into the caves where I was ready to die. She was scared at first, like you. But she felt pity for me. She wrapped me in wet blankets and drove me here so I could live the rest of my life in peace. She used to visit and bring me mangos and books. And one day, the visits stopped." The merman paused and began to cough fitfully.

"How do you survive here?" Freyja asked quietly.

"I only go out at night to avoid men. This river, while increasingly polluted by your greedy culture, has plenty to offer me for sustenance. And, thankfully, I never tire of the classics," he said, pointing at the now visible shelves of books just behind them.

"But surely you're lonely?" Freyja asked.

"I am far better company than the vile beings that created me." Seamus shrugged.

Freyja's heart swelled with compassion. She walked closer, drawn to his eyes, and sensing something was not right with him. He had a square face and a lumpy head, with a sparse curly beard and icy blue eyes. He was scary to behold, but there was gentle kindness there. His chest heaved erratically. "You're ill?" Something appeared to her eye in his chest, like reading a fuzzy X-ray. There was something in his heart, blocking the flow. A dark spot twisted around his artery. "May I?" Freyja asked him as she raised her hand to his chest.

He pulled back, but was too weak to resist. Freyja's hand became warm as the symbols or scars lit up. It wasn't all the symbols, just some: a ">" sign, and the "⚡" lightning sign.

"Freyja, your arm." Nash pointed.

Freyja followed her intuition and held her hand over his chest. A glowing light grew around his heart. His body softened as a wave of gentle warmth washed over him. A minute later, he slumped down onto the floor, with his eyes closed. His body shook slightly.

"My heart . . ." Tears were falling down Seamus's face.

Freyja turned towards Nash, unsure, fearful that she injured him further.

Seamus reached up for Freyja's hand. She knelt by his side.

Then, sounding somewhat automated, he said, "You are born to this world, not of it. You are Valkyrie. You are Goddess. Whatever else they call you, you are the daughter of Gaia, as was your mother. You are a warrior. Rise, child. It is written in your blood."

His words fell hard on her, like a message from beyond. Then he grew suddenly limp. He just collapsed without any apparent reason. Freyja squeezed his hand and then shoved his body, trying to wrestle him alert.

"Seamus? Seamus? What's happening?" Seamus' body became icy cold and still. She pulled his coat up around him. Alarmed, Freyja yelled at Nash, "Get a blanket!"

She panicked, watching him slip away. Seamus lay eerily silent. His breath was barely perceptible. His skin slowly changed from a clammy pink to translucent silver. His scaly flesh appeared to repel the life from itself, as though his spirit was climbing out and abandoning ship.

"Please, Seamus. Stay with us. We need you," Freyja pleaded.

She instinctively started to scoop water from his shallow bath and pour it onto his body. Instinctively, she touched his head and heart simultaneously. His body was nearly frozen and utterly lifeless. She lowered her head with a foreign desire to pray. Her throat tensed as her voice coiled and broke through.

"Dear God, or Goddess, or Great Spirit Being, whatever name you go by, please help Seamus. He doesn't deserve this. He deserves, like, a real home, with clean water and fresh air, somewhere he doesn't have to hide. Please, take his pain; give it to me. I'll take it. Please, help him." Freyja sobbed, "What do I do?"

Nash moved closer to them both and put his hands on her shoulders for warmth and support. He was as mystified as she was. The horror of this being dying right before their eyes was almost too much to bear. Nash whispered, "Come on, dude. Stay with us."

Freyja didn't know what more she could take. Her entire life was upside down. Nothing was as she expected it to be. In the past few days, she had found out that she had an implant that might blow up her head, that she could channel energy, that she had some old genes that helped her sense stuff, that her parents weren't dead. And somehow, she had to get to Peru and find an ancient place that would somehow give answers.

She slumped down next to Seamus, who was clammy and cold, barely breathing. She felt warmth in her heart for him beyond his odd form. He was just part of this insane story. He was trying to survive like her. She couldn't think of anything more she could do. Defeated, Freyja slumped down on the floor, pulling her jacket tight, willing the chill and the confusion away.

Nash curled up next to her, wrapping his arms around her. Eventually, they drifted into a fitful sleep.

Freyja slowly stirred. Was someone watching them?

She gasped, "You're alive!"

"I am ... very ... Thank you." Seamus pulled himself out of the bath and slithered to a cabinet nearby. He grabbed a small chest off the shelf. "Your mother saved my life. And now you. I want you to have this." He handed her a necklace with a small polished stone. "This will allow you to breathe underwater, in this world."

Freyja stood and took the necklace, bowing so that Seamus could put it over her head.

"Your mother said that my life had value. Now I understand." Seamus coughed and touched his heart. "Thank you for showing me."

Relieved, Freyja said, "I don't want to leave you like this."

"Freyja, I had given up. Now, I understand that there is hope. Hope is stronger than fear. You and others like you are changing the field. I may not live to see it, but I must remain to help anchor this potential here."

Freyja hugged Seamus with joy. "I will never forget you."

"Down this hallway, there is a narrow tunnel that will lead you to the river. Use this necklace to stay out of sight underwater until you reach the train tracks. You can share it by holding hands with Nash."

Nash feigned shock about holding hands.

Freyja laughed and punched Nash. She turned one last time to Seamus. "Goodbye, friend."

Seamus smiled. His entire face had changed. He appeared serene and angelic, with a bright pink glow and a glimmer in his eyes. He gave her a deep hug. "God speed, Freyja."

They moved quickly down the hall. It wasn't very high or wide, just enough for their bodies to waddle down. There were a few smaller alcoves with cans or boxes of things, and then it was just a straight shot into the darkness. They ran as far as they could before the hallway became too narrow and short, and they had to crawl. There was a dim light ahead where water crashed into the rocks.

"We're almost there!" she said.

CHAPTER TWENTY-ONE

ANYTHING IS POSSIBLE IF YOU CAN IMAGINE IT

The tiny tunnel opened just above a grassy ledge that dipped straight into a human-made reservoir between the angular basalt hillside and the train tracks. Dawn crept slowly over the western desert, chasing the shadows and inviting the ducks and birds to herald a new day.

"Now what?" asked Nash.

"Man, I don't know." Freyja sighed. She sat opposite Nash, shivering next to the water.

"Where do we go?"

"Peru, I guess." Freyja laughed at the absurdity of it all. She didn't even have a passport. She hadn't been out of the country since she was a small child. And now she was reaching into her backpack and pulling out a map to plot a route to South America. "You don't have to come with me, you know," she said, lowering her eyes, and then gazing up at Nash, hoping with all her heart for one answer.

"Yeah, well, I want to come," Nash said. "The world's fate is in *your* hands," he added, poking her in the side. "And I've got nothing better to do. Plus, don't you need a wingman? Do you know, like Bonnie and Clyde? Luke and Leia? Joker and Harley Quinn?" Nash laughed at his joke, but was equally inspired: his eyes grew wide with the wonder of possibility. "Yeah, maybe I can learn a few things. You know, charge up my junk DNA…"

They gazed silently at each other until it was a little awkward. Freyja's body buzzed with warmth. She realized then and there just how much his companionship meant to her, having him close, knowing she wasn't alone like poor Seamus had been for so long.

"Thanks," she finally said. "Now, let's get going."

Freyja scanned the area. There were trucks on the highway running along the northern road, not more than a hundred yards from where they sat. Anyone could see them from the roadway in the water. Then, the unmistakable thunder of helicopters rose overhead.

"Watch out!" She grabbed Nash's arm and backpedaled, pulling him into the tunnel. They crouched in the corner of the cave and peered out. Chopping rotor sounds grew louder and louder until, finally, they spotted five dark spots on the horizon. They were military choppers, shiny black, and moving fast. In formation, they pointed their noses down and dipped low, and then continued over the river.

"The cops are still out there." Nash sighed.

"Well, we got this," said Freyja, holding the necklace Seamus gave her. "Hold on to me. I hope this works."

She grabbed Nash's hand, and they slipped into the water quickly, hanging on to the side as the depth was unknown. As they dipped in, they remained dry, as though there was a force field around them. They took a big gulp of air just in case, but there was no mistaking that, whatever it was, it functioned like a cocoon. The chill of the water hugged them briskly, like a soggy coat. But as they both struggled to swim across the small reservoir one-handed, they never grew damp. Freyja's eyes, meanwhile, were darting around with wonder. There were all kinds of trout swimming in slow circles. Beneath them, algae and river grasses groped at their ankles as they pushed forward. Freyja pointed towards a rocky bank about thirty feet ahead of them.

She turned towards Nash. "This is so cool."

He exhaled and realized he could talk, too. "Yeah, man, I got to get one of these necklaces!"

They reached the rocky embankment and crept slowly up to the surface of the water. Freyja poked her head up to see what she could see. The choppers had faded to the west. Freyja and Nash clambered over the rocks and up towards the train tracks. They made out a line of trees where they could hike unseen just a dozen feet ahead. Crouching like panthers, they scrambled up and along the tracks. There was a weigh station not too far ahead, but first, they had to cross a freeway stretch without being seen.

"There's one getting ready to leave!" Nash yelled.

"Run!" Freyja sprinted towards the line of train cars that were slowly inching west towards Portland. "That one! There!" she shouted between heavy breaths, pointing towards an open container car near the end. They ran as hard as they could. Nash was faster and reached the car's handle first, swinging himself up and inside it. He turned and reached out to grab Freyja's arm as she pumped her legs faster and faster.

"Grab my hand!" Nash urged her.

Freyja stretched and kicked her feet to lunge towards him as the train's speed increased. He caught her fingers. "Gotcha!" Freyja swung around in the wind for a moment, until with a sharp tug Nash pulled as hard as he could and jerked Freyja towards him. She flew up and into Nash's chest, pinning him down against the timber surface.

"Holy hell." She gasped, breathing heavily on top of him.

Nash peered into her eyes. The two of them were silent, just gazing at each other, until Freyja coughed awkwardly and hoisted herself up.

Over the next few minutes, the silence remained. They sat crouched against the wall of the train car, hugging their knees as it bumped through town, making its way towards the Pacific. The hypnotic thumping of the mile-long train cars over rail ties held them in a moment of peace, just enough to forget everything for a moment—all the confusion—but only for a moment.

Whitecaps to the right grew into percussive hands, clapping and crashing in a rhythmic beat, reaching up into the wind and slapping down on the roiling blue river. Their crescendo met the clackity clack of the metal wheels and rails as the train careened down the gorge with persistent tact.

The train cut through whistling winds along the cliffs like a torpedo on track. The sky yawned bird song, and the sun nudged bear and elk to stir and stretch. A beautiful eagle soared alongside the river, surfing on the currents of the wind, along the shores of the Columbia, with not a human or building in sight. Freyja was like a time traveler, flying into a realm where nature speaks and humans are not separate or asleep. The river rejoiced in a colorful melody of hope and strength.

"So, what's the plan?" asked Nash, breaking the spell.

"We need a plane, I guess. Can't exactly hitchhike to Peru," she said, staring out at the passing landscapes and hoping for an idea. She remembered the implant in her neck, gently touching the area timidly. She reached for her cell phone. It was nearly out of battery. "Let me see what flights might be leaving. What about your parents?" she asked Nash.

"Oh, I'll text them and tell them I'm at Jake's. He'll cover for me until I can explain more. We can be outlaws on the run, cut off our hair, dye it and whatever, you know…" said Nash, jabbing her in the side. "Hey, we should probably power off, too. We don't want to make it easier to track us."

Freyja's mind was awhirl with possibilities as they rattled along the tracks, with the ebb and flow of the Columbia River and then the industrial parks of the outlying suburbs. It wasn't long before they pulled in towards the city boundaries and signs for the airport.

"We need to get off here," said Freyja. The traffic control tower of the airport was visible in the distance. There were plenty of back roads to get there.

The train was going way too fast to jump out of it. Freyja leaned out the car with wind whipping through her face and hair. When would this train stop?

"We're going too fast."

Freyja sat and thought and thought. Her mind bounced between a vision of the train stopping and figuring out how to backtrack once it did stop. Suddenly, the train's horn blared. A second blare and the train began to brake suddenly. Freyja and Nash flew to the other end of the container, tumbling over and landing on their backs.

"What the …?" Nash shrieked.

"Get out! Quick!" Freyja yelled and hurried up to the door. "We have to jump!"

And then they did, whistling through the air and coming to land hard on the ground before rolling a few feet farther. When they came to a stop, they gingerly pulled themselves up and dusted off their damp jeans and slightly bruised knees. As they did so, a large doe on the other side of the train tracks appeared.

"Look. Over there."

Freyja's eyes followed the direction of Nash's index finger, which pointed into the distance.

"Well, hello there," Freyja smiled. The doe raised her head watching them quietly while chewing on some shoots or leaves. She did this for a minute or so before running off into the nearby glade of trees.

"So now you're an animal whisperer, too!" said Nash, laughing.

"Right," she said, pushing him ahead of her.

The two hiked towards a frontage road along the main highway, watching the early morning commuters speed by with blinding headlights. A jet screamed overhead, preparing for landing. They spotted an airport bus shelter and sat with their heads down to avoid getting detected by the cameras parked all over the grounds.

Freyja could barely remember the last time she had been on a plane.

She remembered how the engines rumbled, the seats jostled. Scratchy fabric. Cool stale air. Her ears popping, and she staring out the chilly windows at white fluffy clouds and the bluest sky. Her mother's hand on her leg. *"Sit down, Freyja. We'll be there soon."*

Her memory was interrupted by a green bus.

"Hop in. We'll get you there." The driver, with twigs in his beard and a twinkle in his eyes, waved them onboard.

Freyja howled at the absurd and utterly appropriate sight of him, "Of course," she laughed.

"No way!" said Nash.

"Welcome to Portland International Airport," said the driver. "Hope your travels have been pleasant today. Next stop, Falcon Air."

The driver winked at Freyja through the rear mirror as he hummed a tune and steered the bus to a side road behind the airport. "So, Falcon Air is a special network. You will have to play along," he said.

"What do you mean?"

The bus pulled up in front of the main doors of the departure wing of the airport. "Find Max and Smoochie. They will get you there. But be careful of the cameras. Don't be seen."

Freyja paused. She wanted more information, but he waved them off the bus with a big grin. "God speed, my dear."

Nash winked and pulled his hoodie over his head. Freyja had only her jean jacket. A man checking in his luggage at curbside dropped his 49ers hat. The wind scooped it up and flew it into her hands. He hadn't seen it. She pulled it over her forehead.

"Thank you? Well, it is for a good cause . . ." she whispered as they crept stealthily through the revolving doors.

Inside, there were the usual major airline booths and overhead monitors showing flight arrival and departure times. Freyja scanned the front hall: United, Horizon, Alaska, Delta. A huge line at the Delta counter had a dozen people with dogs. Freyja read the departure boards and found that Delta had a flight going to Lima on *Falcon Air*! The flight was boarding in an hour. Then, a commotion started to form before them.

"My Smoochie, Smoochie! You mustn't be afraid, baby. Mommy is going to see you on the other side. Okie dokies?" A huge woman dressed in polka dots with a large white sun hat made a horrendous kissy face at her equally giant Great Dane.

"Nash! Smoochie!" Freyja elbowed him, and they inched closer to the area with the dogs. "Act natural."

"Madam, you will need to put your dog away now. We have other customers waiting." An airline attendant gazed at the large polka-dot-dressed woman and pointed to an enormous dog crate next to the check-in counter. It was on a wheeled platform and tagged for Peru via Falcon Air.

"What? Am I supposed to get in there?" asked Nash.

"Shhhh . . . Maybe!" said Freyja, studying the scene.

The woman walked her dog over to the side of the counter and opened the crate door.

"Mommy! It's going to be so fun! I can't wait!" squealed the woman's daughter. She waved at her mother, putting Smoochie in her crate. The girl's backpack had a large flier sticking out of the top that said, "Grand Nationals, Lima, Peru."

Freyja studied a lineup of people, a couple who had Great Danes on a leash, awaiting their crates. She laughed, realizing this was their way to Peru.

Freyja grabbed Nash. "This is Smoochie. As the driver said, these dogs are all going to Lima. We can slip into their crates. It's the only way to get on the plane."

"They'll see us," said Nash as Freyja pulled him closer to the conveyor belt.

"Smoochie and Max. They are helpers. We can do this! Why not? What other choice do we have?" Freyja said as she nudged him forward.

As the large woman said her overly dramatic farewells to Smoochie, Freyja and Nash snuck along the wall and waited for their chance. They crept behind her as she walked away and crouched to get something from her overstuffed carry-on bag. The attendant was just far enough away to not notice them. Freyja grabbed the dog door and motioned to Nash. He hesitated.

"Freyja, I can't. This plan is nuts."

Adrenaline surged through her body as she realized her window of opportunity was quickly closing. "What? But I thought . . ." She panicked.

Nash acted like he might sprint out the door. His face was flushed. Fear had him paralyzed. Freyja realized that maybe he was right.

"Okay. It's fine," Freyja said hastily. "Thank you . . . you know, for coming this far." She started to duck in when Nash grabbed her elbow.

"No. I'm okay. Just panicked," Nash said, and took a deep breath and smiled. "I'm in."

Before Freyja could say anything, he had already ducked down into Smoochie's crate. There was a large blanket in the back, which he threw over himself, and Smoochie did not mind at all. He just leaned up against Nash and the blanket as if it was a bolster for him. She quickly closed Smoochie's door and latched it tight, holding back tears as she banished the fear that Nash would end up stranded in Peru without her or that they would get caught. She couldn't bear anything happening to him because of her. As frightening as all of this was, she couldn't turn back. There was nowhere to go except forward.

Nash and Smoochie were loaded by a couple of attendants onto the conveyor belt and slowly rolled away. Tension and hope bound in a knot in her chest.

"Now to find Max," Freyja muttered mostly to herself.

The next crate rolled on to the loader near the conveyor belt.

A disheveled middle-aged stick figure with wild curls, wrapped in a long purple coat made of velvet, was arguing with the attendant about the proper loading of dogs for air travel. "It is a miracle you are in business at all. I mean, really. We give you a lot of business. I would expect much better service." She scolded the attendant, and then turned to her gawky teenage son to lead to a humongous white Great Dane. "Franklin, get Izzie in her crate. Carefully!"

Franklin ambled over to the crate and kissed Izzie on the snout. He shoved her inside and closed the latch. There were no other dogs in the line; they'd all loaded. Freyja didn't want to risk not getting on the plane. As soon as the boy left, she snuck to the crate and reached for the door. Izzie growled. Startled, Freyja backed off.

Uh-oh.

Freyja stepped quickly away and walked in a circle near the departure sign. She tried not to panic as Nash was well on his way through the conveyor system to their plane.

Then, a man wearing a jogging suit and glasses sprinted up with an elegant black Great Dane. He was nearly out of breath. "We made it, Max!"

The airline attendant held out her hand. "Passport."

Once they had their tickets, the man turned towards the last crate and opened it up for Max to get in.

"Okay, Maxwell, this is the easy part." He pried open the dog's jowls with one hand and popped a small white pill into the dog's mouth. He patted him on the head afterward and shut the crate door. "Be a good boy. I'll see you on the other side."

As the man turned to head back to the ticket agent, Freyja grabbed the door and, without hesitating, dove into the back, turning just briefly enough to shut it.

"Oh, I forgot the lock," said Max's owner. Max whimpered. His owner put the tiny padlock on the front. "You're okay, bud."

Freyja had barely slipped underneath a thin airline blanket that was in the back of the crate when he did this. Max sat up with his snout pressing on the door grate as they were loaded up on the conveyor belt. Freyja ducked quickly into the shadows as a child standing by her mother at check-in spied Freyja inside the crate. "Mama, dere is a girl," she said.

"Uh-huh. I know, sweetie," said her mother.

Maxwell licked Freyja's face and settled down into a small circle with just enough room for her to lie down next to him.

"Thanks, Max," she said, genuinely grateful for his protection.

The kennel wobbled along the conveyor belt, sliding down some long tunnels until finally reaching a loading dock.

"Another crate!" yelled a gruff manly voice. "Oh no, these Great Danes are seriously heavy! Dude, get over here!"

Two large men lifted the kennel and dumped it rather harshly onto another large rolling cart. Freyja ducked as far down under the blankets as she could. Other than the pervasive dog smell, the kennel was remarkably secure inside.

In moments, Freyja was riding up another conveyor into the plane itself. Someone pulled the crate into the hull and slid it forcefully against a lineup of the other containers. Freyja listened to the sounds of more heavy boxes and bags tossed into heaps all around them. By now, Maxwell was snoring happily. A few minutes more, and the outer doors were shut and sealed. Freyja and Nash found themselves in darkness once more. After a long while, the engines roared to life around them.

Freyja peaked through the grate and, focusing hard, could make out the faint outline of some bags and a host of dog crates all along the wall. Freyja's stomach grumbled. How long are flights to Peru? She didn't know.

"Nash?" Freyja called out tentatively.

"Hey, you made it!" said Nash.

"Yeah. You okay?"

"I'm great. Smoochie is a little fresh, though," he said, wrinkling his nose.

"I was afraid I wasn't going to find Max. I guess this is it until Lima, huh?"

"Yeah. Hey, it's going to be alright," Nash said.

"I know." Freyja agreed as the airplane rumbled backing up from the gate. "Get some rest. Who knows what's next?"

"Adventure," Nash replied.

Freyja and Nash bounced softly as the Falcon Air flight taxied towards the runway. After a few minutes, the engines roared, and soon enough, the plane sped away and lifted into the air. Their stomachs lurched and their ears popped. As they reached altitude, the cabin became very cool. Freyja huddled closer to Maxwell and tucked herself in the blanket.

Ding.

Something sounded like a door, and then footsteps. Heart thumping, she threw the blanket over her head.

"How are my puppies doing?" came a sweet, melodious voice. The lady rattled the doors on each cage to check on the dogs. Freyja held her breath. One dog started barking furiously.

"Okay, now. You're fine there," the attendant said sternly. Then she walked back towards the door where she had entered, glanced back over her shoulder, and shrilled, "Sweet dreams, everyone. Have a great flight."

CHAPTER TWENTY-TWO

BIGGER THAN YOU

The screens flickered in the control room. A dozen analysts searched through camera footage and listened to headsets.

"Sir, we got her."

One of the analysts hit a button on a larger console and sent an image of a young woman in a 49ers hat to a large central screen. A flutter of images raced across smaller screens, flowing through a facial recognition program.

"She's at Portland International . . . ten minutes ago."

Drake took a sip of his lukewarm coffee and put it down in disgust. "Which plane?"

"We are searching now. That was the Delta camera," said the lieutenant as she stretched her neck side to side. She was used to Drake hovering, but now he was practically taking over her desk.

The screen suddenly filled with a flutter of pigeon wings. On the next screen, she was gone.

"Find another angle. Don't lose her," grumbled Drake.

The lieutenant turned to face him. "We detected electromagnetic anomalies prior to the Dalles Dam blast."

Drake listened. "I'm not surprised. Track the data. We need to know how quickly she's growing."

He tapped the image of the 49ers hat on the screen to get a closeup of a hooded young man. "Who is that?"

"We believe it is her friend, Nathaniel Shaw. We were tracking his phone, but it appears to be offline now."

Drake adjusted his cornflower Lloyd's of London shirt, exposing a deep scar on his neck. He turned back to the lieutenant's desk and pounded it angrily. "Did she get on a plane?"

"We haven't determined that yet, sir."

Drake paced back and forth like a caged lion. He knew that the longer they delayed, the harder it would be to intercept her. "Get me Colonel Wayne," he said.

"Yes, sir." The lieutenant began rapidly tapping into her keyboard.

Drake pulled a playing card out of his pocket and flipped it around his fingers. "Ping me when you have something." He marched out of the control room, and into his office through the glass doors.

The glass doors opened through a long stretch of glass that divided the intel arena from his soundproof office space. The analysts were like an extension of his own body, on 24/7 surveillance of all the Adepts and assets they tracked around the world. He wanted to know the minute anything shifted. For him, the movements and activities of the Adepts were the blood in his veins.

Drake glanced at the illuminated wall behind his desk, which cued him for a bourbon on the rocks. He turned sharply to the corner bar he kept handily stocked with his favorite beverages when he caught sight of the man's legs crossed in the corner chair. It was his chair, the Nine's consulate to NuTech. He appeared whenever he liked.

"Seems your technology failed, Drake," came the raspy voice of the man in the shadows.

Drake refused to respond. He had a strong suspicion about where Freyja might be going. "She won't get far."

"You are quite the risk taker, aren't you?" The man stood up and moved towards the flat screen panel hanging on the wall adjacent to Drake's desk. The board was streaming every screen in the arena in smaller windows. He pointed to a control button along the bottom of the screen. It said, "Terminate."

Drake coughed nervously. "We're not there yet."

"Don't let your heart cloud your judgment. This mission is bigger than you. You know that."

"I am very clear about what we are doing," Drake replied, barely concealing his irritation.

The man sighed. "She is not like the others. I don't think you understand what she is capable of."

"I do know. Let us do our jobs."

The man turned and left the room, the airtight door suctioning shut behind him.

"Colonel Wayne is on the line, Director Drake," said the lieutenant.

Drake picked up the headset lying on his desk and barked, "Wayne! Where are you?"

"Sir, I'm where you want me," said Colonel Wayne.

"Check your box. I just sent you coordinates and a file on a critical Adept. Get her back to base," ordered Drake.

"Yes, sir," Wayne answered.

"Oh, and colonel . . . she's not alone. We need them all."

"Of course, sir," replied the colonel.

CHAPTER TWENTY-THREE

WHISPERS OF THE SOUL

The cargo hold kept a chilly temperature, but the dogs were warm, and soon Freyja was very drowsy. She tried to process all the events in the past few days: discovering the energy in her body, the way she could harness it, and how she had connected to some, the truth about her parents, that her aunt was still alive, that nothing was as it seemed. Then there was the key, the box, the stones, Sarana, Tommy, and Seamus. The world was a strange new puzzle. She couldn't imagine what her role might be. She knew that she had to do her part, especially if she could find and help her parents.

Soon, Freyja was asleep, but dreaming very lucidly. She was aware she was dreaming.

Soaring on the wings of a falcon, Freyja grabbed on around the bird's neck, noticing the feathers and how rigid and soft they were. The falcon was quite enormous, or Freyja was relatively small. The falcon soared effortlessly through the clouds, dipping and climbing the jet stream, spinning and diving. Freyja opened her senses to experience the ride as fully as she could. The air was cool, but filled with the tiniest particles of light, grazing her skin like wispy feathers. She could smell the moisture from the seas below, fusing with the air into droplets that clung to her body and evaporated just as quickly. The atmosphere pulsed in waves that moved in sync with the falcon's shifting pattern. There was a swath of air current dissipating behind them like ocean waves crashing over a giant reef. There was a magnetic field, like a map of waves, between sky and earth. A fire burned brightly in the falcon's eye.

It turned towards her and said, "See . . ." Then, the falcon's face morphed into Ben, the boy from Room 101. He said, "You see now . . ."

Freyja shuddered.

She had an intense déjà vu soaring over the hills and valleys, and a shoreline dotted with small villages and stepped pyramidal stone buildings. The falcon flew over a fertile valley cradled by mountains on either side. Along the river were small encampments, all leading back to a collection of larger buildings. In the center of one grand structure was a beam of light, split into rays going across the earth and straight into the heavens. Water flowed from around the top down into a pool near the bottom. The light was warm and inviting. The falcon flew through the beam, and Freyja's body tingled and expanded. It was peace and bliss.

Suddenly, dark clouds rolled in, and a hailstorm of rocks and dust swirled through the valley. In the darkness were clear screams from the people below. The falcon swerved and dove to avoid getting hit by the falling stones. At the top of a tower or pyramid stood a man, covering his head as the stones and sand hailed down around him. The temple was somehow significant, and someone was trying to destroy it, bury them there. He held a small black box and appeared to be trying to bury it in the stones at the tower's top. She sensed that the box contained a dark secret. The falcon flew her in close enough to see that inside the box that the man held was a woman, crouched in the fetal position, a prisoner. Freyja screamed. She looked just like her mother. The falcon turned sharply and began flying towards the earth.

Bump. Bump.

The airplane landed abruptly, snapping Freyja awake. Did she scream out loud?

"Damas y Caballeros, Bienvenidos a Lima. Ladies and gentlemen, welcome to Lima."

Freyja listened to the faint Spanish announcement from the cabin overhead as the plane taxied to the arrival gate. Twenty minutes later, the luggage hatch opened, and cool ocean air wafted inside the hull. It was pitch black outside.

Sounds of large men huffing and puffing moving the bags and crates onto the conveyor belts filled the large hull. Maxwell stirred. He licked Freyja's face, his tail wagging enthusiastically.

"Shhhh," Freyja said.

"*Oh Dios Mio. Estas cajas pesan Como la mierda* (These bags are bloody heavy)," said a male voice, heaving the crate up in his arms.

Soon, Freyja was sliding down a conveyor belt and thumping on the ground. Maxwell started growling. Freyja was worried the loaders would come to investigate why he was upset. She hid under the blanket, petting Maxwell. "Shhhh . . . it's okay."

After sitting on the tarmac in silence for a few minutes, Freyja decided to make a run for it. "Nash!" she whispered loudly.

"I'm over here!" he replied, creeping close to her crate. His face appeared, and he said, "Hey, we made it!"

The black web laced around the cargo, creeping towards hers. "I have a lock on my crate," she said, wiggling her door. "Hurry!"

Nash grabbed it and studied it for a moment. Though it was dark, there were enough scattered buildings and tarmac lamps around to cast some light. In a reflection from the metal surface, numbers engraved on the back of the lock were visible.

"Here! Try this: 3,5,7,9."

Nash fiddled with the lock, and it finally gave way. He swung the door open.

Maxwell started to exit, but Freyja grabbed his collar to hold him back. "Whoa there, Max. Thank you for letting me stow away. Good luck with your competition. I hope you win."

Max licked her face. He was proud to be of service.

Freyja and Nash dashed towards the airport building, dodging staff and ducking behind luggage trucks and building columns. Freyja's heart pounded furiously as heavy steps approached from behind them. Seeing a flight of stairs that led towards a cracked door, they sprinted, skipping steps and hurrying inside. Ahead of them was a long empty walkway into the main terminal. Freyja collected herself and proceeded, putting on her "I'm supposed to be here" face.

CHAPTER TWENTY-FOUR

STRANGER IN A STRANGE LAND

Lima International was like many airports, except it was filled with the smell of sea and spice, pungent tide pools, fishing boats, and their nets home from the day's catch: a stew of mollusks and seaweed wafting over them like a foggy stew. Travelers were coming and going through the security gates, with familiar airline placards. A giant mural of Machu Picchu filled one wall. Opposite that, the scent of roasting coffee drifted from a Starbucks, while heavy feet shuffled in and out of gift shops and food courts, massage stations, and shower stalls. Though it was nearly midnight, the airport brimmed with arrivals and departures.

Freyja was shocked by the time on the departure sign. "Nash, it's almost midnight!"

"Seriously?"

"Yeah, and I'm starving. I can't think. I need food."

"That way," said Nash, pointing to signs overhead that led to the food court.

They weaved through travelers and came to a McDonald's. Freyja fished in her backpack, hoping to find some cash. Nash held out a wad of crumpled bills. They approached the counter.

"Um . . . do you know Spanish?" Freyja asked him as they waited behind a couple ordering fries.

"No, I'm doing Mandarin."

"Okay, well . . . I'm doing French. But I did do a year of Spanish in junior high, so here we go."

As the couple in front walked away, clutching their bag of fries, Freyja watched the girl behind the McDonald's counter. She was thin, with dark eyes and short hair, and wore a red uniform.

"Uh, uno . . . oh no, I mean . . . *dos hamburgosa?*"

"*Dos hamburguesa. Que mas?*" The girl spoke on autopilot, gazing into the sea of travelers just behind Freyja.

"*Dos cola et dos French fries?*" said Freyja sheepishly.

"*Si. Que mas?*"

"Um . . . C'est tout. That's it," Freyja said, muddling up languages.

"*Si, viente soles, por favor.*"

Freyja cupped her hands and pushed the mixture of crumpled dollar bills and coins towards the girl, who then muttered something indecipherable while pushing the pile back to Freyja.

"She said she could not take dollars," came a rich, buttery voice from behind her. Turning, Freyja took in a young man with sparkling eyes and black hair. He was tall, with broad shoulders and dimples set either side of a serious but handsome face. He appeared to be about their age and was dressed in a tailored jacket over jeans, and he was oddly interested in them.

"My name is Eduardo. Listen to me carefully," he said in a lowered tone. "You are being followed. I can get you out of here, but you need to move quickly and act normally." He paused, staring into Freyja's eyes.

"What?" her heart started to race.

"Who is following us?" asked Nash.

"There is no time to explain. There is an exchange machine over there. Once you have your food, follow my lead. And act naturally." He pointed over his shoulder at the far wall.

Freyja gulped hesitantly and elbowed Nash. "Let's go."

"Uh, yeah . . ." Nash scooped up the change, which the girl had spurned, from off the counter and walked with Freyja to the cash machine. "Do you trust him?" Nash asked her as he began smoothing out the notes with shaky hands and feeding them into the machine.

"I don't know. I mean, how would I know?" Freyja paced, trying to act as naturally as possible but unable to thoroughly dampen her anxious energy.

"Can't you, like, read his mind or something?" Nash said as he scooped up the Nuevo sol currency that the machine delivered out the exchange slot.

"What? I don't know . . ." she said impatiently, annoyed that she should somehow know everything. Freyja searched her mind and gut for some read on him. "I think he's okay," she said, somewhat unconvinced.

They headed back to the McDonald's counter to pay the cashier. Nash grabbed the food, and Freyja scanned the room for anything strange. Eduardo was moving swiftly towards a hallway across the large open space. He stopped to check if they were following him. Then his expression changed to panic. "Hurry!" He waved frantically at them.

A couple of dark uniformed men with sidearms moved menacingly into the food court. She grabbed Nash, as they rushed through all the tables and chairs, making a beeline for the hallway.

Once they reached the hallway, they sprinted after Eduardo, dropping their food bag, and flew towards the door. As they swung around, Eduardo shut the door and locked the big bolt behind them.

"Follow me!" he said. They shuttled down two flights of stairs, and out another door to an outside tarmac. They were right next to the airport's main building, and the parking lot to exit lay a few hundred yards ahead. "You guys need to stay close and run when I tell you," he said.

The three of them walked at a rapid clip towards the parking lot. Cars and buses were moving steadily past the arrival and departure lanes in front of the seaside airport. The fishy ocean smells were at odds with jet engines' sound taking off from the distant runway. They sprinted past the crowded baggage claim and out towards a black sedan waiting near the taxi lineup. Eduardo grabbed the back door of the sedan and motioned for Freyja and Nash to hop in.

""Okay, my American friends, let's go." Eduardo slid in beside them. He said something in a foreign language to the driver, who nodded. "This is my driver, Carole," Eduardo said, to break the tension as they sped rapidly out of the airport industrial area towards the city center.

"You have a driver?" Nash asked, half annoyed and half impressed.

"Yes, of course. Everyone has a driver here," he smiled. "Um, everyone with some money, anyway. So, again, my name is Eduardo. What are your names?" he said turning towards Freyja first.

"Freyja."

"Ah, what a beautiful name. The Norse goddess. And you?" Eduardo turned to Nash. "Perhaps a Norse god?"

Nash smirked. "Nathaniel."

"I don't think that's a Norse god." Eduardo chuckled.

"No, it isn't. Would you mind explaining who you are and why you are helping us?" asked Nash.

Freyja was dying to ask that, but was still trying to catch her breath. She looked anxiously out the back window of the sedan.

Eduardo laughed. "Of course. Officially, I'm a diplomat's kid. I am into DJ and avoiding my studies. Unofficially, I am a hacker. I happened to intercept an encoded message tonight from a black ops group that is always up to no good here, running drugs and trafficking people. It said to apprehend a young girl and boy from America. Did you stow away on Falcon Air? That's impressive. I figured you might have a good story to tell. And if you are running from them, you probably need some help."

Nash sat there stunned by what this kid just said. "Hacker?"

"Okay, but how did you know it was us?"

"I didn't see any other American kids, did you? And you smell like big hairy dogs right now, which is odd. Why do you smell like that?" Eduardo laughed.

Freyja was suddenly self-conscious. "Uh, that's a long story."

"So, what's your story?" asked Eduardo.

"Story? Um. We are here to visit a professor that my mother knows and find some—" Freyja stopped herself. She wasn't sure if she should tell him anything about why they were there. "We came to see some ancient sites, you know . . . like Machu Picchu . . . and you know, um, retrace my mother's work, maybe . . ." Freyja realized she was not very good at improvisational lying.

"Wow. Okay, that's interesting. You'll have to tell me more later," said Eduardo. "Have you been to Lima before? Would you like a tour?" He smiled and waved his arms towards the city of Lima that they were approaching.

"Nope," said Nash eyeing Eduardo suspiciously.

Freyja asked, "So, what language was that you just spoke?"

"Ah, not familiar with that one, huh?" he said, smiling. "That is Portuguese. It is a language related to the old Latin spoken by the Romans. I am from Portugal. My driver is Portuguese, too."

"Ah. Well, it sounds beautiful," Freyja said in a soft voice.

Eduardo asked the driver to take them along a central route. As they rolled through the city, he turned from side to side, pointing out pretty parks, prominent museums, the capitol building, most of them in an area he called "Miraflores," or the "flower view" neighborhood. Outside, the salty sea air gave way to a cool misty fog. Eduardo signaled to the driver to stop near a park. They got out to walk around.

"This is my favorite place," he said. "This is the Parque Kennedy, named after your unfortunate president. There are over three hundred cats that live here. Some neighbors come to feed them, but otherwise, they live on their own."

The streetlights glowed as Freyja scanned the area for life, seeing an unusual number of cats wandering about. Shops and restaurants surrounded the sizeable triangular park, most of them still full of patrons eating and drinking though it was well past midnight. Suddenly quite tired, and not as refreshed as she would have liked after sleeping in a dog crate, Freyja tried to stretch her arms above her head with a long yawn.

"Perhaps we get some rest?" asked Eduardo.

Freyja studied this young man who was being so kind. How could she trust someone she had only just met, especially given everything that was happening? Anyone could suddenly become a threat at any time and in any place.

"What is it?" he asked softly.

She thought about her options, and then said, "We don't have a plan . . ."

"Well, why don't you stay with me? We have plenty of room. You can use my facilities and find your professor in the morning."

"But won't your parents mind?" Freyja asked.

Eduardo chuckled. "No, they're not even in the country right now. It's fine. Diplomats, remember?"

Nash was clearly uneasy about the invitation, as he eyed the stranger. "Thanks, but we can stay at a hotel," he said sternly. ""You can just drop us off at the nearest one. We don't want to bother you anymore."

"No, I insist. Plus, you aren't safe if those goons are trying to find you. They have no jurisdiction in our building. Diplomatic immunity, you know. Easy to throw them off, too, with Carole driving," Eduardo replied, clapping his hands together and smiling brightly. ""You are welcome at my home. It is my honor. *Vamos!*" Eduardo opened the door and jumped back in the car. Freyja smiled at Nash innocently, who sighed as they climbed back into the sedan.

As they sped along the shoreline highway towards Eduardo's home, Carole the driver fiddled with the knobs on the radio until the notes of some Peruvian guitar music started to lilt through the speakers. Freyja gave a heavy sigh of relief and satisfaction, staring out the window at the dark seas rolling in across the beaches below. She tried to count the barely visible whitecaps washing ashore. She almost forgot where she was for a brief sleepy moment.

Suddenly the car swerved hard away from an oncoming vehicle.

"Cuidado!" Eduardo yelled at the driver.

The driver spoke rapidly and swerved the car again and sped up along the highway. Suddenly, another car came up quickly from behind, and Freyja jolted forward and gave a little scream as it thumped into the back of them. Lights were flashing all around them, and everything in the windows was a blur. Freyja, grabbing hold of the door handle, wondered about barrel rolling out of there. Was Nash thinking the same thing?

Eduardo yelled something else at Carole, who nodded and stepped on the gas. "Don't worry," he said. "These guys are amateurs. Hang on!"

The car smashed into the back of them again just as Carole, apparently an ex-race car driver, sped into oncoming traffic and merged in front of several vehicles. They raced at breakneck speeds up the highway, putting some distance between them and the pursuing car. Carole turned sharply under an overpass near the seaport, driving between piers, and then veering another sharp left through a group of warehouse buildings. At the end of a long row, a door opened, and he charged inside quickly, letting the door fall behind them.

"What the hell? Have you done this before?" asked Nash.

"There are some bad guys in this town. Carole is a pro," said Eduardo.

Freyja feared that the implant in her head was tracking her movements. She remembered Sarana said she had roughly two days of invisibility. Had it been two days yet? How would they even know she was in Peru, let alone in that car? Vulnerability wrapped around her with an icy grip.

Driving for some time in an underground tunnel, Carole pulled up onto another side street and into another underground garage, part of a modest skyscraper. At the bottom of the garage was a large elevator.

Carole swiftly got out and opened the door for the kids. He bowed and waved his arms in a welcoming gesture. "*Bem-vinda*. It was my pleasure. Senhor e Senhornita. Boa note."

Carole murmured something to Eduardo, who nodded and said something back. Carole had a sidearm tucked under his jacket, the handle just poking out. He spied her gaze and buttoned up his coat.

Eduardo pointed Nash and Freyja to a bank of elevators. "We go that way..."

"Now what?" asked Nash, leaning into Freyja's ear.

"I wish I knew..." she answered.

"Are we going to be safe here?" asked Nash.

"What choice do we have?" said Freyja.

Eduardo ushered them to the elevator doors and punched the call button. "Hah, well... never a dull moment in Lima, no?"

Once the doors opened, he waved them inside and hit the button for floor thirty. The force of the express elevator made Freyja's stomach lurch. She grabbed hold of the rail as the cityscape flashed behind the glass window facing the building's exterior.

The door opened to a hallway leading straight to the front door. Freyja gasped as they entered the apartment. Gold medallion wallpaper lined the walls where two massive abstract oil paintings of human nudes hung. A sparkling crystal chandelier hung overhead on either side of the entrance. There were antique gilded tables beneath the paintings with ornately carved stone bowls filled with succulents and orchids. Freyja had never seen such a luxurious apartment or home in her life.

"Wow," she whispered.

Eduardo walked briskly through the entry, and into a large foyer with rooms to the left and right. A large staircase led up to other rooms. Directly ahead was an incredible view of the ocean and the city on either side.

Eduardo motioned her to the left, past the dining and living areas. He led them down the hallway where there was a bedroom, and inside it was a sizeable lush bed possessing a view of the sea.

"Hope this will be comfortable for you," Eduardo said, sweeping his elegant palm through the air.

"Yeah. This is nice." Freyja smiled in wonder.

"If you need a change of clothes, I can have Carole fetch you something. We have a brilliant tailor. Just call or text your size and what you need to this number." He left a card on the desk.

Just then, Freyja realized they had their phones. Was it wise to use them? "Can they track our phones?"

Nash was wide-eyed as it dawned on him, too. "I turned my phone off, but they might still be able to track them." Freyja and Nash simultaneously fished for their phones, to disable them.

Eduardo studied them partially amused, and then said, "You're probably wise to ditch those. Let me see if I can get you untraceable ones to use while you're here."

They quickly and sheepishly put their phones in his open hand, comprehending how foolish they had been not to think of that earlier. The intense race to leave home, the training camp, visiting Aunt Lucy, meeting Seamus, and then trying to stow away on an airplane—thinking of phones wasn't exactly on top of their minds.

Eduardo motioned to Nash. "You will be very comfortable in the den. Come."

Nash followed Eduardo down the hall to another room. Freyja listened as their voices trailed off and surveyed the room before her. She sat on the bed, torn between the beautiful view and the plush pillows calling her name. She fell back into the ornate Peruvian quilt. Her body slowly and reluctantly relaxed; all the tension of the past couple of days unfurled in fitful thuds as her limbs released and collapsed one by one.

* * *

Cool waves crashed on the shores of the beach. Although Freyja had no memory of how she got there, she was at ease. It was as though this was a place she had always been. Her toes sank into the wet sand as the winds filled her lungs and tousled her hair. Only her mind suggested she should be cold. She inhaled the buttery smooth air. A beautiful melody crested along the shoreline, filling her head and heart with a lovely peace. It was all so familiar, like something her mother might have sung to her perhaps.

"Psssst! Wake up."

There were miles of sea, beach, and a distant field with hazy trees behind her, but no other person.

"Freyja!"

In a split second, Freyja's awareness returned to her body. Nash crouched down next to her dangling arm and face and tickled her arm. Freyja was on her stomach, hanging half off her heavenly bed. She shot up, grounding herself to the bed and the room to get her bearings.

There it was again—the melody. It drifted in from somewhere else.

"Do you hear that?" she asked.

"Hear what?" Nash asked. "I don't like this guy. Let's get out of here before he wakes up."

"Yeah, okay."

Freyja grabbed her backpack, ran her fingers through her dirty, tangled hair, and sniffed her sleeves: *sweat and dog*. She was more than overdue for a shower. They crept out the door and tip-toed down the hallway towards the elevator they had come in the night before.

As they moved quickly towards the elevator and punched the button mercilessly, the scent of pancakes filled the air.

"You aren't leaving, are you?" came a voice from out of one of the rooms. It belonged to Eduardo.

Startled, Freyja was tongue-tied, head on a swivel, eyes searching for any sign of Eduardo. Just then, and the high *ping* of the elevator almost made her heart explode. It was Carole, Eduardo's driver, who stepped out from the sleek brass doors. He stopped and studied Freyja and Nash with curiosity.

"Carole can drive you to your professor whenever you like," came Eduardo's voice once more. Closer now, his head poked out from a room down the hall. "You can't leave now . . . I've made you my mother's famous strawberry crepes for breakfast. Come and join me." He smiled and winked at her. He appeared to be wearing an apron over some black sweatpants, or perhaps they were his pajamas. The sun was coming up and beaming warmly through a window down the hall.

There was nothing else they could do. So, she grabbed Nash by the hand, and they walked into the kitchen. Pots and bowls full of batter and flour littered the marble countertops. "Please, the table is out there. Have a seat."

Freyja and Nash moved into the next room where they found a long table elegantly set for three. Floor-to-ceiling windows offered a stunning view of the Pacific. The glistening ocean was warming as the sun crested over the eastern hills.

Whoa. The view left Freyja speechless.

Eduardo shortly entered with two steaming plates of fresh crepes and strawberry compote. "Would you like whipped cream?"

"Absolutely!" said Nash, who at the sight of delicious food had forgotten his earlier uneasiness.

Freyja had forgotten it, too. For in the dawning light that infused the kitchen air with a golden glow, Eduardo was even more handsome than the night before. His eyes were dark hazel with blue specks, like a swarthy prince from a far-off kingdom. Pulling out a chair nearest the end and extending his arm to indicate her seat, he was acting like one too. Freyja sat quickly, focusing on her plate and trying to suppress the wild knots in her stomach. How odd to feel so dirty, ugly, and out of place while everything around her was perfect. When she took a bite, the fluffy golden crepes melted in her mouth. Nash gobbled his portion down quickly.

Eduardo laughed. "I'm delighted you enjoy it. Please have as much as you like. I think I made enough for an army."

"How did you learn to cook so well?" asked Freyja.

"And how do you speak English so well?" asked Nash.

"Um, well, I don't know. I learned the first from my mother, one of the best cooks in the world. And I learned the latter in school. I've always attended English schools. Any more questions?" He smiled.

"Yes, do you always pick up strange Americans at the airport?" asked Freyja boldly.

"Well, no. Most of the encrypted messages I hack have to do with boring packages and intel gathering. Intercepted human targets was a first." He laughed. "Let's get you both a change of clothes, and then we can find your professor. No?"

Freyja shifted uncomfortably. How much should she tell him? Could she trust him?

"I need to find a Mr., er, uh Professor Darnell. He is at the University of Lima."

"Ah. Yes. University. Well, then, that should be easy." Eduardo pushed away from the table and picked up a phone from the buffet console along the wall. He spoke rapidly in Portuguese, probably to Carole, who had slipped off again. He hung up and turned to Freyja and Nash with a notecard.

"Give me your sizes and I'll have some new things sent up for you. You can shower, and we'll be on our way in an hour."

"Thank you," said Freyja. "I don't know what to say . . . You've been so kind."

"It is my pleasure. Don't worry." He winked and then returned to the phone.

Out of the corner of her eye, Freyja noticed that Nash gave a disgusted huff, though she needn't have seen, for she could sense it. "What's the matter?" she said. "Look, we got fed, didn't we? We're getting a ride, aren't we?" She tried to convince herself that there was every reason to be grateful rather than suspicious.

"Yeah, whatever," Nash said and walked out of the kitchen and back to his room. Freyja sighed and gazed out at the Pacific.

Later, as Nash showered in his room and Eduardo had gone to arrange fresh clothes for both, Freyja also got into the shower, letting the steam fill her pores and lungs. The remains of her black mascara and liner washed down her face in streaks. The black henna was slowly washing out of her ginger locks, making her hair appear more gray than black. Freyja's old life was passing away, moment by moment. She inspected her arms and wondered about the meaning of some of the symbols. Perhaps this professor would be able to tell her something more about them. She needed answers.

As she toweled herself down a few minutes later, there was a knock at the door. "Come in," she said.

No one answered. She peeked outside her door with a towel wrapped around her. A large box sat on the floor. She pulled it inside the room, placed it on the bed, and lifted the lid. Reaching inside, she drew from it a gorgeous midnight-blue tunic with modern ivory embroidery on the sleeves and along the neckline. It wasn't at all like anything she had ever seen before, but it would do. There were also silk brassiere and fresh underpants, a pair of jeans, and slip-on leather boots. She pulled it all on, and studied herself in the mirror—bad ass in a feminine kind of way. She was impressed by his elegant taste and apparent attempt to match her style.

Were all Portuguese men this thoughtful? she wondered.

She fastened her jewelry and pulled her hair back in a ponytail. It was refreshing to be clean again. For a moment, she forgot her reality. Not sure what to do with her dirty clothes, she folded them into her backpack.

CHAPTER TWENTY-FIVE

A HISTORY LESSON

The kids all converged on the elevator in style, Nash decked out in a dark polo and new jeans. Even with his hair still wet, Nash was refreshed and ready. Eduardo wore a light sweater over his black t-shirt and jeans. He smelled like a walking Armani ad.

"You look very nice," he said mostly to Freyja.

The elevator pinged open, and they all stepped inside.

"Thanks for the threads," said Nash to Eduardo awkwardly. He smiled at Freyja, nodding at her refreshed appearance.

They rode silently down until they reached the ground level, where the car parked in the garage. Freyja's mind was racing with what was going to happen next. She realized that Eduardo was staring at her.

"We found your Professor Darnell. He is at a private museum today. It's not far."

Freyja pinched Nash with excitement, and then reached into her backpack to make sure the map was there. The playing card that Sarana gave her was lying on top, so she drew it out. She wasn't sure what it meant—ace of spades—but she hoped it was good luck or something. She put it in her back pocket.

Carole was waiting in the garage, holding the door open for them. He made way for them back out through the underground tunnels. The highways were brisk and bustling in the morning, but Freyja's mind was too busy to notice any of the sights and details that Eduardo was pointing out along the route. What if this professor had the answers they needed? Would he know what happened to her parents? What if the pieces of the puzzle were finally coming together?

In no time, the black car pulled up in front of a building that appeared more like a residential home than a museum. Freyja tensed, scanning the street, eager to solve the mysterious connection that linked her past with her future. They were early. The roads were wet with morning dew. Freyja studied the sign on the side of the gated building near the large double doors.

Museo Larco

1926

"Is it open?" she asked Eduardo.

As soon as she asked, a man appeared. "Buenos dias," said the short man. He wore a crisp white shirt and scuffed black shoes. He stooped slightly and kept his gaze averted as he opened the gate and took something, perhaps a tip, from Eduardo.

"This way," said Eduardo smiling.

He walked briskly and purposefully up a wide ramp, past a towering wall of pink bougainvillea and lush gardens surrounding white stucco buildings. They turned towards what appeared to be the museum entrance. He spoke with the man who had let them in.

"We can wait here," he said, motioning to the benches just outside the arched wooden doorway.

Freyja did not want to sit any longer; the anticipation was building and making her fidget and bite her nails. After an eternally long moment, the doors finally opened. Behind a pair of thick-rimmed glasses peered a pale man with thinning hair. He tucked in his shirt and leaned on the doorway staring at the kids for a moment.

"Buenos dias. *¿En qué puedo servirle?*"

"Do you speak English?" asked Freyja.

"Yes, of course."

"We are here to see a Professor Darnell. My name is Freyja Wolfe."

"Ah. You look just like your mother," said the old man. He came out to shake her hand and then her curious companions. "And who are these young men?"

"Um, this is my friend Nash who came with me from America, and this is Eduardo."

The older man nodded, but something about his expression suggested he was nervous. "I only have a few minutes. Come with me quickly. But not you two. You two stay here," he said, pointing at Nash and Eduardo and then beckoning Freyja to follow him.

She did so, allowing the older man to lead her into the dimly lit museum halls. They walked past a room with large plaques so big they filled whole walls. These were dedicated to the Larco Hoyle family, distinguished private collectors of pre-Columbian art in Peru. An eighteenth-century mansion built over seventh-century Peruvian pyramids housed the most extensive collection of artifacts from several known pre-Columbian cultures. Freyja was dazzled but turned her eyes back to the professor as they continued along passages hung with golden masks and intricate tapestries, past rooms darkened and others lamp-lit, within which relics of old cultures sat gathering dust. Finally, the professor opened a door that led into a private office.

"Please," he said, waving her to the chairs arranged around a table full of papers and books. It was circular and grand, made of solid mahogany. He studied her intently. "How did you get here? Were you followed? Does anyone know you are here?"

"It's a long story. Um, I don't think so." Freyja clung to her backpack. Her head swam with all the questions she wanted to ask. She could not wait to share her mother's letter and the map and find out what he might know. Once they sat, she got right to the point. "I have something you gave my mother for safekeeping. I was hoping you could help me understand it." Freyja pulled out the map and laid it in front of the professor. Her ears began ringing.

The professor nodded and then lowered his eyes over the page. "Yes. It is very likely the last of its kind," he said, fiddling with his spectacles as he examined every inch of it. The focus of his study was the inscriptions. "Hmm. Yes. Caral, Moray, Ollantaytambo," he said. "These are very ancient and very important sites. Many would kill for this map. These instructions are only rumors. This area in Caral is fascinating. It is more than five thousand years old. Many areas yet to be uncovered, many pyramids that could well be part of the earth matrix. They have never discovered a single weapon here. A complex and sophisticated trading region, too. I would imagine that you will find a portal there. I've been there many times, but they have shut down much of the excavation work. Professor Shady has little means to do much beyond sell trinkets to fund research. Did she give you anything else?"

"Well, I have a key, a box with something inside it . . . Oh, and I have this," Freyja pulled out the star garnet she had found in the Columbia River.

"Let me see it," the professor said greedily, holding out his hands. Freyja handed the stone to him, and he proceeded to study it with a small hand-held microscope. "Star garnet. Where did you find this?"

"At the bottom of the Columbia River."

"Of course, of course," he muttered, more to himself than anyone else. "Yes, they would hide these there. Of course."

The professor then turned in his chair, hoisted himself up, and pulled a very ancient-looking book from a case. As he laid it down, clouds of dust lifted from it, causing Freyja to sneeze. When he opened the cover and started leafing through the delicate pages, the intricate text lines and exquisite little drawings came to life. "See, here. This key you have, I believe it holds—cradles—the three powers of life: Sun, Moon, stars, the trinity. These elements create life. Without them, we would die. Do you see it? Body, mind, spirit—life begins with one plus one, and then creates three. Do you see? It's the key." Professor Darnell laughed heartily at his statement. Then, he pointed to a page with several sketches and words in a language Freyja could not read.

"Um . . ." Freyja paused. How could he expect her to read that?

"Could you translate?" she asked meekly.

"Oh, I'm sorry. What am I thinking? Of course, of course. The language here is in Quechua, as translated by the Spanish when they conquered this land. They didn't get the whole story, though, but they got a lot. Much of this book is total hogwash, but the basics are here if you know what to look for."

The professor flipped through the pages and scanned for something. "The key . . . the key . . . this knowledge they have worked to destroy for thousands of years. The star garnet holds the stars' map, coordinates to celestial positions and frequencies, see? We are made of stardust. This is a map to where we come from, the first coordinates of creation. They say these calculations are so powerful they activate genome codes hidden away, hidden from all of us." He paused and surveyed the room, his wrinkled face aglow with joy.

Freyja didn't know what to say or if she understood anything he was saying.

Composing himself, the professor continued, "If you look into our cells, they look like solar systems. We *are* solar systems. The moonstone is clear, no? The moon is our unconscious self, the layers that speak in our dreams, those truths we hide, from others, yes, but mostly ourselves. And the sunstone—well, no one can agree on that one. Typically misrepresented as the father, or the conscious awareness, and often shown as a halo around the brain, consciousness. The sunstone is our eternal fire. They all believed it must be a stone from South America. But I don't think so."

Professor Darnell hobbled over to his desk and pulled out a key. He walked into a small room behind his office, and returned moments later with a small round polished piece of crystal.

"This is the Iceland spar, calcite. The Vikings and ancient sea peoples used it to navigate the seas for thousands of years. It can hold and refract the sun's energy. Some have tried to argue it was iolite, but this, I'm afraid I must disagree. This piece was found in an excavation in Northern Peru, in the Chachapoyas ruins. These people may have been ancient mariners, like the Vikings, who I strongly suspect used it for solar navigation as well as inner guidance. The iolite is the stone you need to reactivate your key. This is what I believe. Take it. Please."

Freyja held the small oval disc, and compared it to the key and the places carved out to hold precious stones. "It fits."

"Ha!" Darnell clapped his hands together enthusiastically.

"But I don't have the moonstone. Unless it's in this box."

"Yes, let's see this box. I'm glad to see it is safe." Professor Darnell studied it carefully with his magnifying glasses on. "These markings are . . . unique. We have studied this, but no real good translation exists, no known lingual relations, you see. I received it in secret years ago. How I would love to have a crack at it."

"I can't open it. I've tried."

"You will. Your mother did. Use your intuition. Don't fight it."

"My mother opened this. My aunt said I did when I was little, too. But I don't remember."

"Be patient. Everything has its time."

Freyja mused. That's what her mother had said, too.

"Where is your mother now?" asked the professor.

"I'm not sure. My aunt told me that she and my father were working in Utah and disappeared."

"Where in Utah?"

"Sego Canyon, I think."

"Ah." The professor stood up, grabbed another large book from his shelf, and put it on the table in front of them. Turning the pages, he showed her images of petroglyphs, drawings that depicted ghosts and giant floating bodies dancing on the walls. "Sego Canyon is a compelling place, too. I'm guessing your parents got too close."

"Too close?" she asked.

"You see, Freyja, the evidence is in plain sight. Human civilization, humanity as a species, is much older than they say, than mainstream archeology will allow us to know. We have found extraordinary evidence for a civilization far more advanced than our own. It makes the legends of Atlantis seem like the Stone Age." Darnell leaned back in his big swivel chair and pulled out a pipe. He lit it, pressed it between his lips, and took a big puff.

"In my work, which your parents supported, I believe I found proof that a matrix of powerful vortices, or nodes of universal energy, connects our earth. And if we can find them and repair the network, we would have rediscovered an infinite free power grid like nothing we can imagine. Free energy for all the world's people, renewable and sustainable. Can you imagine? Energy to bring irrigation to arid lands, plant crops, regrow the forests, filter, and clean land, water, and air, to heal and nourish all creatures, accessible by all. Only," he paused, and took another drag of his pipe and flinched, "these sacred sites with their ancient tech have been buried away, hidden from sight and memory. All efforts to uncover or understand them met with academic denial, ridicule, and even untimely ends for those who persist. For some reason, all efforts to finally reconnect them are not allowed."

Her head spun. Vortices? Free energy? "How is this possible?" she said.

The professor leaned forward, a crooked smile spreading across his face. It was clear that Freyja was indulging a passion that excited him more than anything in the world.

"Well, these vortices," he began, "conduct healing energy and free power to every continent. Positively charged electrons could flow thousands of miles uninterrupted, perhaps infinitely. These energies, it is said, had the power to transform everything on Earth. But those in power deemed it forbidden, as they would lose control over all the toxic systems they profit from, a toxic prison that no one realizes is shackling them. Your parents, and many others, knew the truth. There are more like me who glimpse the potential beyond this prison. It was your parents who were following the clues. They had been the most possessed explorers of this dark secret. But, as we have seen, those who get too close, who pose a threat, disappear. That is why the fact that you are here is, well, incredible." He reclined back in his chair and studied Freyja long and hard.

"So, that's what they were doing . . .?" Freyja whispered, more to herself than to the professor.

"Tell me, Freyja, what do you know of your lineage?"

"My what?"

"You have the markings, no?"

Freyja was stunned. "You . . ." She hesitated; how did he know? "You mean my lightning scars?"

"Yes. How old were you when it happened?"

"I was young. Maybe five."

"That was inevitable. You are a magnet for these forces. Some call them angel bites." He smiled and pinched his arm with his fingers.

Freyja rolled back her sleeve. With eager eyes, Professor Darnell leaned forward once more and studied her arm, adjusting his spectacles as he did so.

Finally, he nodded and said, "These are a combination of very ancient symbols. You have the genes of gods, like your namesake Freyja, the Norse goddess of love and war."

"The goddess of love and war?"

"Yes, Freyja is an archetype of sacred female energy, but more than that, she was a real being a very long time ago; what we mythologize as gods were not as distant and fictional as we now believe. Sometimes it's easier to tell the truth with myths and fairytales. They were instead just human beings, but beings with their potential fully realized. You know, before the gene tampering..."

"What do you mean? I'm a god?" she repeated, unable to stop the corners of her lips from spreading into an incredulous smile.

"No, you are a human, just an active, more fully realized human. Your genes also exist within everyone else; only yours switched on, and ours are not. Humans today are mutants. These ancient genes have been turned off or damaged by tampering, breeding, chemicals, injections. These genes simply grant access to a greater range of the celestial and earth energies all around us, like being able to hear more octaves or see farther away, or just move energy intentionally instead of tripping over it. You are awake to your living energy body. Few humans know anything about it. Your range of awareness is deeper and broader, which means that the system does not easily contain you. The system does not want cows that can jump the fence."

At these words, Freyja recalled the bump on her head. "They put something in my head too."

The professor nodded as if he expected that. "Yes, in that case, you may not have much time . . ." At that moment, Professor Darnell put his pipe on a plate and walked to the large bookshelf. He pulled out a skinny green book with a severely damaged cover.

"The most critical thing to know about your activated genes and your namesake is that she wore a coveted necklace called the *Brisingamen*. The myths are taken too literally in most cases. But you should know this: the Brisingamen does exist, but it was *not* a necklace."

Freyja recognized that word from when she had activated the black box back in Oregon. "I've heard that word. What is it?"

"Well, *Brisingr* means 'fire,' and *men* indicates a 'jewel.' The ancient goddess *wore*, or carried, the light of awareness in her heart. This is a very ancient practice, ancient wisdom, hidden in many traditions' myths and practices. The human heart brings light to the darkness or blindness of the mind. Freyja was mighty, and when the Christian missionaries came through the north, they could not allow this knowledge to undermine the influence of their new story of man, of human origins. Physics has now shown that the heart generates a hundred thousand times more electrical power than the brain. Freyja embodied this wisdom in all the symbols associated with her. If you study goddesses' various images, many of them held a hand to their hearts or wore a fabled necklace. All were referring to this lost knowledge, and all disgraced by half-truths and unfortunate lies." The professor gazed sadly at the papers on his desk.

"I don't understand," Freyja said, shaking her head. "So, she has this strong heart or whatever. How can this help anyone?" She was puzzled, not only at this but everything.

"Another significant myth offers us clues into humanity's greatest conspiracy. In the Nordic mythos, Odin, the ruler god, was supposedly jealous of Freyja's necklace—a symbol of her power—and accused her of gaining it illicitly from four dwarves. Dwarves are symbolic of our quest for self-knowledge. Freyja was willing to mine the depths of her psyche to understand herself, and, from that, she gained the illumination of a powerful being. Odin cursed the rest of humanity to battle as punishment. But he allowed Freyja to claim half the fallen souls to her domain. If this myth contains any kernel of truth, then to have the *Brisingamen* return to Earth could mean that all the sleeping souls that reside in *Sessrumnir*, her ancient dwelling place that I suspect simply means 'spaceship Earth,' could awaken. Humanity could rise and break the bonds of these unwelcome masters. Do you see?"

Freyja sat stunned, not sure what to think. "So, is that why I can see what I see and do what I do?"

The professor chuckled. "That is for you to discover. I do not know what the truth is and what isn't, but I do know that you are in danger the longer you stay here." The professor glanced over at the door. "We must leave immediately. Do you trust the two companions you are traveling with?"

"Nash, definitely," Freyja answered without hesitation. "But Eduardo . . .? I don't know. We only just met him. He has helped us in that time, but—"

Just then, Freyja's ears began to ring loudly. Then she gave a scream, and her hands shot up and clutched at her temples. Her head was pulsing. Energy surged through her chest, running down to her arms. The professor's eyes blazed with the reflections of Freyja's lightning scars. In that gloomy room, it was as if her arms were two flashing bolts cracking through an inky night sky.

"Freyja, may I?" He studied the illumination of her scars. "These may be runic. If so, then this one is for power. This one is for change. And this one is a kind of warning. Incredible." He grabbed a small booklet *of Ancient Ideographic Languages* off his bookshelf and put it in her hands. "Keep this. You may need it."

"It's happening," Freyja managed to say in between heavy breaths of pain. She put the booklet, the crystals, the box, and map back into her pack.

"Quick! There is no time; we must leave." The professor rushed over to the door to the museum and locked it. Then he raced over to the bookcase at the back of the room. He lifted a hidden panel and began punching a code into the buttons beneath. Suddenly, Freyja's eyes widened as the bookcase shifted forward in a cloud of dust, and then slid laterally, revealing a dark passageway behind.

Freyja's eyes darted between the gloom and the professor. "But what about Nash and Eduardo?"

The professor shook his head impatiently. "No time. We must get you safe first. I'll go back to get them after. Come!"

The two of them crept into the musty-smelling dimness of the passageway. It was wet, and the air was stale. After a few yards, the tunnel led into the basement of the museum. They inched towards it, and suddenly light and street sounds emerged. There was a large gate, and the professor worked quickly to unlatch the lock and open the door. Once he did this, they staggered out into a narrow alleyway that led onto the street. Halfway along this alley was a tall gate made of iron. Through the twisting ivy that clung to its lattice rails, the gate led into an enchanting garden. The white stucco home at the other end appeared modest and quiet.

Opening the gate, the professor led Freyja along a leaf-scattered lane and knocked on the side door.

After a few moments, a frail older woman answered the door. "Si?"

The professor rattled off something in Spanish as she nodded in reply. Then he turned to Freyja. "Go. She will keep you safe. If I am not back in fifteen minutes, you may be on your own. But do not go back to Museo or anywhere near the main streets or stations."

"But . . . what am I supposed to do?" Freyja asked, exasperated.

"Get to Caral. They overestimate their power. I will try to meet you there."

"And what about the box?"

"You carry the knowledge. Trust yourself."

CHAPTER TWENTY-SIX

A HUNTER HUNTS

The smooth titanium doors shut quietly behind Colonel Wayne as he slid into the mobile bunker's command seat where a small team of tactical experts awaited orders. They had left stateside within hours of Falcon Air's departure, but it took them longer than expected to narrow down which flights she may have taken. The tracking device was only giving them a hundred-mile radius. Fortunately, they could triangulate the signal from the air and figure out her heading.

Drake wanted her alive, and that was the colonel's intention. He was prepared for anything. This was not his first rodeo. Tracking Adepts for NuTech had begun ten years ago. So far, he had not lost one.

Arktik gave him new variables to consider, however. The mission debrief had been sobering. Dr. Mackay sent over some of the data, and he was very apprehensive. The Arktik device could do more than track implants. It could remotely take physical control of the nervous system, including a kill switch. However, the device had proved to be highly unstable inside Adepts. Their core temperatures fluctuated way too high. And, given what he'd seen them do, they could very well blow themselves and everyone else up just by overreacting. He did not want to risk losing highly trained men or triggering local collateral damage. Tracking a walking time bomb was not precisely a slam dunk.

The element of surprise was his best tactic. Freyja could not know they were on to her. Wayne liked to think containment was his superpower.

"Report," he said, staring at the data flowing across multiple screens on the far side of the van.

"She landed last night."

"How the hell did she get here?"

"We aren't sure. Stowed away, presumably."

"So much for the TSA."

"The Shaw boy is with her too. They have some local contacts."

The younger technician punched something on his panel, and images of Nash, Eduardo, and Professor Darnell appeared.

"We know the professor. He's been on our watch list for some time. Nathaniel Shaw, not active, but a liability. And Eduardo is the son of Maria doCeu Antonia, the trade minister. He picked them up last night at the airport."

"Anyone else know she's here?"

"Just the driver."

"Good. Get eyes on them now."

Colonel Wayne stepped outside the bunker, leaning against the wall to light his cigarette. He was a tall, broad well-built man, but age was slowly winning the battle against his prized vitality. He had hired muscle to send out, and he prided himself on the men and women whom he hand-selected. They were his alter egos now: fierce, smart, tireless. The trackers' program had been developed almost entirely under his discretion. They were the best in the world at locating and tracking these genetic misfits, as he liked to call them. He truly believed he was almost at one with the Adepts, understanding how they thought and why they would all eventually run.

He wondered if Freyja would be like her mother, Anya, in any way. She was a fighter. He was surprised how conflicted he felt taking her down like a beautiful lion who should stay wild. He never could understand poachers, even though he was a hunter of sorts. There was no prize in tracking these Adepts for him. He was more of a game warden or zookeeper, keeping the inmates under lock and key. Law and order were a virtue for him.

Inside the van, the team set up logistics to apprehend Freyja and the boys. Another technician received communication from the trackers surrounding Museo de Larco's premises.

"Base, we have visual on two of four. Target has not emerged. We have all exits in clear sight. Please advise. Over."

The message crackled over the communications system inside the van.

"What are the hours on this place?" asked Colonel Wayne.

"It opens to the public in twenty minutes."

Colonel Wayne reached over and touched the COM button. "Eagle, this is base. Secure the perimeter."

CHAPTER TWENTY-SEVEN

ADRIFT IN A NEW WORLD

Freyja sat quietly at the colorfully painted table in the center of the kitchen. The sweet older woman stumbling around it wore a green dress beautifully embroidered with flowers and birds. She had a bright blue apron tied around her as she clapped dough in her floured hands, making some pancake or tortilla. She hummed a sweet Spanish song as she worked and made a nice stack before she wiped her hands and turned with a big friendly smile towards Freyja. She pointed to a glass on the table and picked up a pitcher of water.

"Oh, yes, please," smiled Freyja.

After pouring a glass, Freyja drank it thirstily as the old lady left the kitchen for a few moments. She returned with a red and black woven bag, which she placed on the table. Still clutching it, she pulled out a feather. Then she dropped the bag and began waving the feather around Freyja's head and body. As she did so, she sang in a languid, rhythmic way, like an incantation. Sweetly and softly, she chanted as Freyja sat there awkward and puzzled.

Freyja's scars were still tingling and getting hotter whenever the old lady dusted the feather along her arm. It wasn't unpleasant, but more a visceral response to the sweeping of this gentlewoman with her intent. When the lady paused and placed the feather inside Freyja's hand, she took up the bag once more and drew from it a handful of leaves of some kind. With her fingers, she plucked one from the small pile and popped it into her mouth with a series of satisfying crunches. After swallowing, she gave one to Freyja, who studied the leaf, brow furrowed in confusion. Was it a bay leaf?

The woman nudged her and laughed, prodding her to eat it. "Cocoa, cocoa. *Es* okay! *Esta* bien!"

Freyja reluctantly put it in her mouth and began to chew the stiff chewy leaf. It tasted bland, but started to make her tongue a little bit numb. After a few moments, a wave of calm descended over her. Something colorful fluttered in her periphery. A vibrant blue hummingbird hovered in the window as if to say hello. The woman smiled and winked at Freyja.

"*Me llama Maria.*" She pointed to herself.

"My llama Freyja," Freyja replied, hoping that was close enough.

Wearing a happy smile, the gently weathered woman hummed a little song as she pointed at the leaf and nodded as if to say, "You like?"

"Mmm . . . It's good." She gulped in reply even though it tasted like you would imagine a leaf tasting: hard, earthy, and certainly not that satisfying.

The woman giggled, patted Freyja on the back, and then turned to the stove where she lifted a pan full of broth and placed it on a wooden board in the center of the table. Next to it was a plate of warm bread, and she gestured towards Freyja to take some.

"No, thank you. That's sweet, but I'm not hungry. It looks so good, though!" Freyja shook her head and furrowed her brow. The woman was having none of it. She pushed the bowl closer, insisting.

"Okay, just a taste. Really . . ."

Pouring a small portion from the pan into a porcelain bowl, Freyja placed the bowl to her lips and took a sip of the aromatic broth. It was spicy but delicious. She reached for one of the slices of bread and dipped it into the bowl. With every mouthful, her body strengthened. By the end of it, she felt restored, strong.

"Oh, wow. That was so good. Gracias, Maria."

Afterward, she thought of Nash and Eduardo and wondered when Professor Darnell would return. What had previously been a warm satisfaction was replaced abruptly with a knot in her stomach that grew larger with worry. She thanked the woman again and walked over to the door to gaze outside.

As she did this, a white van drove by the house. It was headed towards the front of Museo. She had come out of the backside of the museum with Professor Darnell. That van was not a good sign, and the knot in her stomach tightened in fear for Nash. She had less concern for Eduardo; he struck her like a dashing and resourceful hero who could find a way out of anything.

I need to go, Freyja thought and reached for the doorknob.

"No, no, no," came the raspy voice of the old woman suddenly. Her wrinkled hand fell on Freyja's. "*Estancia! Estancia!*"

"But I have to help my friends. They're in danger," said Freyja. With that, the older woman smiled somberly, and then removed her hand.

Freyja thanked her again, and then opened the door and raced out into the backyard. She came to the gate, opened it, and then walked briskly towards the Museo despite the professor's warning earlier not to do so. She scanned the streets, hopping in to hide next to bushes and gates as she went. In a moment, there were footsteps running along the pavement. She buried herself deeper inside the thorny bougainvillea bush, amongst the worms and snails feasting on its leaves. She glimpsed a figure on the other side, and her heart leaped. It was Nash!

Freyja yelled out his name, sprang out of the bougainvillea, and chased after him.

"Freyja!" he said, turning breathlessly. "We have to go . . . Darnell said to meet at the marina and look for Keyotay."

"Keyotay? What is that?"

"I don't know . . . That's all he said."

The pair ran back down the street towards the sound of the shore and waves crashing. Most of the neighborhoods of this area were just blocks away from the Pacific.

"Here it is!" said Nash. He pointed to a gate leading into the garage of a tall apartment building. Freyja followed him through the garage to an elevator. They took it down several levels where it led out to an entrance along the highway and close to the beach. There they ran across the road, dodging traffic, and came to a marina complex. There was an old restaurant surrounded by docks and boats, and they hurried down the main pier, glancing every which way to get their bearings.

"Now what?" Freyja said.

"Did you find it?" came a voice from behind them. It was Eduardo, who was panting and out of breath.

"No, we just got here. Where's the professor?" asked Nash.

"He had visitors. He said you might need my help. So, which boat is it?" said Eduardo.

"It's called *Keyotay*, I think . . ." Nash didn't sound sure.

"Or maybe, *Quixote*?" asked Eduardo, pointing to an old fishing boat at the end of the dock. It was dingy white with blue trim around the hull and a weathered empty cabin.

"That's our ride?" said Freyja cynically.

"I guess so," Nash shrugged.

They ran towards the boat, hoping for signs of life.

"Hello?" Freyja called out.

As Freyja approached the boat, she thought there must be some mistake. The shabby vessel, with exposed wood trim, knicks and marks all over the aged hull, barely appeared seaworthy. She knocked on the side of the boat. "Hello? Is anyone there?" Suddenly she was spooked. "Come on, let's go."

They quickly hopped onto the boat and sank below the bow staring at each other, unsure of what to do.

"So, uh, what's the plan?" Nash asked.

Then, a large rope whipped over their heads and landed with a thud on the deck beside them. The boat rocked hard as another rope flew over the bow and another dull thud echoed around them. This time the weight was heavier, followed by distinct human muttering. Someone had come aboard.

"¿A dónde vas?" A short dark man in blue overalls, with a perfectly round flush face from a life on the sea, stood smiling at them.

"Are you friends with Professor Darnell?" asked Freyja, hoping with all her heart that he was and that he wasn't an enemy about to snatch them.

"Si," he said sincerely, his grin revealing a glittering gold tooth.

Freyja nudged Eduardo to translate and asked, "Can you take us to Caral?"

As Eduardo spoke, the captain's face filled with alarm. Then he turned to see a white van pull up at the docks. Freyja saw it, too, and her heart thumped with fear.

"Freyja, we need to get out of here. You and Nash hide in the cabin, and I'll help navigate. Go."

As they climbed below into the lower cabin, the ominous sound of a helicopter wheeling in from the southern coastline hastened their departure. The captain rapidly pulled away from the docks, speeding out of the marina as quickly as possible. As the small fishing boat hit the waves hard, the sound of the helicopter grew louder under the roar and intensity of its blades. Overcome with curiosity, Freyja climbed up to the wind rush and ocean spray. The unimpressive little boat was speeding incredibly fast out to sea.

"How long is it to Caral?" she shouted.

There wasn't any time for an answer, for suddenly, a gunshot pierced the air and rang into the cabin wall near where Freyja and the captain stood. Freyja screamed and ducked, and then sank to the floor.

"*Cuidado!*" yelled the captain. He spun around, summoning his gun from somewhere Freyja hadn't seen. Then he pointed it aloft, aiming it at the helicopter and releasing a spray of bullets into the glittering sky.

"What the hell?" yelled Eduardo.

The helicopter backed off, but was still hovering nearby. There was a man with a very long rifle sight pointed at the boat. The captain was swearing under his breath and steering more determined than before. Blood was flowing from his shirt.

"Captain! Eduardo, look!" Freyja gasped.

Eduardo turned to the captain, who gave an anguished cry and then slumped to the floor, clutching at his wound as he fell. Eduardo grabbed the wheel of the boat, while Freyja knelt and held the captain in her lap.

"Stay with me! That's it," Freyja cooed, trying to remain calm.

"Nash, get the first aid," Eduardo yelled down to the cabin. "There's a white box with a red cross on it."

Freyja, her hands blood-soaked as she held them to the captain's wound, remembered something that Sarana had told her: "Call on power from the Great Spirit and Mother Earth whenever you are scared." She could also invite other spiritual teachers or anyone to her aid, like a prayer, but more inclusive.

Great Spirit, Pachamama, Jesus, Buddha, Mom and Dad, Anyone,

Be with me now, please.

Illuminate me, my heart, my, um, brain or mind or whatever.

Please help me. I have no clue what to do.

I'm scared.

Freyja turned towards the helicopter, suddenly fueled by anger. Her scars blazed with the build-up of heat blasting through her body like ten combustion engines. Head splitting, ears ringing—it was all so much louder and more painful than before. Instinctively, she threw her hands up towards the helicopter; every fiber in her body yearned for nothing more than to blast it right out of the sky. And just then, as if answering her call, an enormous beam of hot light shot out from her core, through her fingertips, into the air, and struck the helicopter square on the top propeller. It wasn't powerful, but it was enough to stall it out. The helicopter began to fall. A few men in black uniforms all jumped out, landing in the water, followed by the aircraft's hulking wreckage.

Nash poked his head out of the hatch. "Dude!" He had an armload of bandages and towels. "You just blew a helicopter out of the sky!"

"What . . . How did you do that?" Eduardo stammered in shock, steering the boat while starring at Freyja in disbelief.

Freyja sat next to the captain. His side was bleeding badly. Nash dumped a load of bandages and old rags next to them and handed Freyja a water bottle.

Freyja took it and poured some of the water over the wound. She had no idea if this was the right thing to do, but she had seen people do it in movies. The captain was going into shock. Eduardo tried to keep him alert by talking to him.

Then, he said, "He says we can't stop."

"He's bleeding too much!" said Nash.

Freyja piled on several of the bandages and applied pressure to them. She didn't know exactly what to do but followed her instinct. Perhaps she had seen that in the movies, too. As she did so, her scars tingled again. It was as if they were communicating with her somehow.

"Let me try something." She placed her hands over his wound and concentrated on an image of the captain's side healing.

As she held the wound, there was a cold and pointed pain. She realized the bullet was lodged in his side. She lifted his shirt to appraise the wound. It was a small hole, but blood was pouring out like maple syrup. She quickly pressed both hands around the hole as the tiny bullet slowly backed out, like a sliver from her thumb. She grabbed it and tossed it on the floor, and then piled his shirt along with a nearby towel over his wound to stop the blood flow. She was amused by her own ease and confidence, considering she had no idea what she was doing.

In a few moments, she could visualize his wound closing, and the bleeding stopped. Warmth flowed from her head and heart directly into his body. She checked the towel, but there was no more blood. He appeared to have passed out. Freyja slumped next to him, searching Nash's face and her mind for ideas about what to do next.

* * *

"*¿Qué hiciste?*" The captain slowly returned to consciousness.

"Hey, you need to stay still. I'm so sorry," said Freyja. She wasn't sure if she had helped him or not, as he was wincing.

The captain sat up and lifted his shirt. His side had stopped bleeding, and his wound now appeared to be a minor scratch.

"*Es cierto. Usted es un angel.*"

"He says you are an angel," Eduardo turned and told her.

"Wow, girl. You are an angel," cooed Nash.

Freyja sat stunned, staring at the captain whose wound was nearly closed. The bleeding had stopped. He was pale and ragged, but other than that full of health.

The captain spoke to Eduardo and hugged Freyja, showering her cheeks with kisses. His eyes were streaming with happiness and relief, and he kept touching the scratch where the bullet hole had been. He stroked it with his hand repeatedly. He couldn't believe it.

"Señor Darnell told him he would be saving an angel. He will get you to Caral safely. He will never doubt God again," said Eduardo, translating for a very excited captain.

The kids huddled on hard benches around a table attached to the hull of the old boat. Woolen blankets and life vests were scattered about. A tiny canteen with a large jug of water sat on the floor amidst loose ropes and a rusty toolbox. A Catholic rosary hung nailed to a post near the stairs up to the captain's cabin. It swung haphazardly in rhythm with the lurching boat.

"Well, that was interesting," said Eduardo. "Where did you learn to do that?"

Freyja was embarrassed. How could she explain this to him? Nash knew her. She trusted him. But Eduardo? He would surely think she was a freak. Maybe she *was* a monster. Emotions well up inside, and a tear dripped down her face. She turned away and rubbed her cheek on her shoulder. She wanted to stop somewhere and let him go home, let him remain the beautiful stranger who had smiled kindly at her at the airport, the stranger who had stirred such oddly exciting feelings within her.

"Hey, man. We're here on a kind of top-secret mission. You know, it's not something we can talk about. We can let you off at the next stop," said Nash.

"Oh, you mean like spies?"

"Yeah, something like that," answered Nash, who was in no mood to entertain the idea of having Eduardo as a companion any longer. "This is our quest and—"

But Eduardo wasn't listening. He was too excited about the idea of spies and cut Nash off. "Wow, that's so cool! Americans *and* spies. No wonder you came upon the encrypted line. It's like an action movie. Hey, I speak Spanish too, so maybe you could use some of my help?"

"Eduardo, there is a lot I can't explain. It's probably too dangerous to come with us," said Freyja.

Eduardo laughed. "I love danger, man!"

Freyja smiled. "Okay. What do you know about Caral? That will be a start."

"Uh, well," Eduardo began, lacing his fingers together, "I know it's like an ancient place or something, thousands of years old. Some archeologist has been digging there for a few years now."

"Okay, that makes sense. Is it nearby the ocean?"

"No, we'll need to find a car or something. It's a bit far inland," said Eduardo.

"I see." Freyja sighed. She needed some air. She climbed up top and found a bench facing the boat's rear. As the Lima skyline faded behind them, they cruised full throttle northwards along the coastline. Freyja pulled the stone box out of her backpack. She traced the carvings and tried to rattle her memory of the box. She recalled a math lesson with Aunt Lucy. What was she trying to teach her? Was it relevant to the puzzle of the box?

"Math is the language of beauty, and both are sacred. The natural expression of this beauty is phi or the golden ratio. If you take your sketch here, you will see that you intuitively understand this, Freyja, just as the most famous artists, builders, and scientists have." Aunt Lucy pointed to the circular face, pinching her fingers together to the space between her eyes and nose and mouth. "Even these swirls and symbols you've sketched across her face relate to each other with this proportion. They are everywhere in nature, too. Why don't you get a ruler and I'll show you?"

Freyja peered at the box's overall design. It had a perfect square inset with a wheel, or a circle. Inside the wheel were sections with symbols or letters, and inside the center of the ring was a kind of abstract flower made with overlapping circles. She turned the box over and studied the spiral dial that she dared not touch again. A row of similar symbols surrounded it. She flipped the box over to see if the bottom characters corresponded with the symbols on the front or sides. Some were the same. She pulled the map out and laid it on the bench. She studied them to try and find a pattern.

Aunt Lucy's words haunted Freyja. "Plato asked his students to break a stick unevenly. He wanted them to understand that the longer piece relates to the smaller in the same way the whole stick relates to the longer. The golden ratio can appear in a sequence of numbers that we call Fibonacci today, though he was not the first to identify them: 1, 1, 2, 3, 5, 8, 13, 21, etc. Every number is added to the last to create the next. The ratio between one number and the next becomes the perfect ratio of 1.618. Ancient cultures considered this the perfect number, and used it in all their art and architecture. It is the embodiment of the teaching 'one becomes many' as each part is related to the whole."

One becomes many. And many are one.

Freyja observed that each corner of the map had a different symbol, perhaps directions like north or south. The area the professor had indicated, Caral, had a series of symbols next to it as well—the same characters that were around the dial!

She started with the far left and turned the dial to the matching symbol, careful not to touch the spiral button in the center again. *Click.*

The next symbol, like a tree branch, was pointing upwards. *Click.*

The next symbol was a figure "8." *Click.*

And the last symbol was a circle with a dot in the middle. *Click.*

An inner latch released. Freyja's heart thumped with excitement and nervousness. The box hinged to the side, and the lid moved over enough for Freyja to peer at the crystal inside. It was a small worn luminous crystal stone icosahedra with twenty faces. She studied every speck of it, turning it this and that way in her hands. It was clear, like quartz.

Freyja put the new crystal in her pocket with the other two stones. Before closing the box, Freyja inspected the inside, scrutinizing the lid and every corner. Then she realized she couldn't tell how it latched. It was almost as though it had been carved out of one piece of stone or poured from a mold, for there were no hinges or prominent parts to it. It was dense like stone, though it was not as heavy as she would have expected. It was so light, but at the same time held in it a quality that made it as impenetrable as steel. She sat for a moment, staring deep into the corners, waiting for something. *There must be something else*, she told herself. There was more inside that box, whether she could see it or not.

The boat rocked now at a rhythmic lulling pace. Freyja sighed, slumped down, and allowed herself to just sit. Every muscle in her body ached with tiredness and tension. The shoreline shifted from town to desert, and the sun set slowly towards the Western Pacific.

She shivered and glanced down at her sleeve, just staring at her scars, at every line and curve. Her eyes traced the way they crossed each other and extended, the way they thickened and branched. She had studied her scars that way for numberless hours in her life, lost in thought. Now they lulled her into some sort of sleepy trance. But just then, as she did that, an insight struck her. These scars were shapes very similar to what she had studied on the box. Professor Darnell had a connection to runic and even older ideographic languages, many yet not decoded. Freyja studied her scars with fresh eyes: the delicate swirls, short arrows, and dotted lines, leading from her wrist up to her elbow. She pulled her sleeve back further, thoughts exploding like stars inside her mind. Could these scars, tattooed by lightning, be some encoded message, a cipher from the elements, from the gods of light, or whatever her aunt believed? Could these beings exist? Could there be a connection between her body and the box? Perhaps that was how she was able to open it.

Freyja climbed back down inside the hull. Eduardo and Nash, playing a game of cards, stopped and glanced up at her.

"Guys, check this out!" She pulled up her sleeve and showed them her arm, which she had managed to stimulate enough to glow a bit without it appearing to be a weapon charging.

Nash tried to diffuse the situation in front of Eduardo. "Looks like you got a killer tattoo," he said with a smile.

"It's *not* a tattoo, Nash," Freyja replied, annoyance clear in her tone.

"That is the sacred mark of an advanced Adept," said Eduardo as he pulled a card from the stack to his hand.

Freyja was puzzled. "How do you know that?"

"An Adept is a human with advanced abilities. It's rare, but it happens. You have the earth codes, the frequencies of nature, all turned on. Everyone has the same switches off. *You* are on."

He had said this all so casually Freyja was stumped into silence. She shook her head slightly and blinked. Then just as she was about to interrogate Eduardo about how he could know any of this, he leaned forward, rolled up his sleeve, and rested his elbow on his knee.

"Snap," he said, and then winked at Freyja.

Freyja's eyes pored over the strange markings that stretched over his forearm and continued up past his elbow. Then he straightened his back and lifted his shirt above his head. Nash shifted back uncomfortably as he did so, but Freyja, cast under a spell, was frozen still. She could only gaze at Eduardo's broad lightly muscled torso decorated almost entirely with scars. His were not illuminating the way hers did, she noted. His charred black scars appeared as though he had burned out his flesh.

"You?" Freyja gasped. "Why..." she hesitated. "Why didn't you say something sooner?"

Eduardo closed his eyes for a moment and focused intently at a mug on the table. It shook, and then slowly lifted, hovering for a moment, before gently lowering back down. "Psychokinesis," he said simply. "Yeah, I can move things with my mind. I just focus and imagine where I want to move it to and, guess what, it moves. It's just a muscle to train, not that big a deal. Most who have it just think they're clumsy because they're bad at it."

"Wha—wh...when did you find out? Why are your marks so dark?" Freyja stammered, realizing she wasn't alone. She had so many questions.

Nash sat there open-mouthed, a strange hostility in his eyes.

"I don't like to talk about it," said Eduardo.

"Have you met Sarana or Ursa?"

"Who?"

"Never mind. Eduardo, can you help us?"

"I can move some things around, but I haven't had much practice. My mother forbids me. It is not safe, you know. Though I can read minds . . ." he said, smiling at Freyja and winking.

Freyja blushed. She realized he might have overheard her thinking about him.

I have wondered if I can project my thoughts, too. Can you hear me?

Freyja's eyes widened. Eduardo's mouth had not moved. "Yes, I can."

"What was that?" asked Nash, visibly confused.

Can I do that?

"Yes, you can," answered Eduardo.

"Wait, what is going on? Can you guys hear that? That . . . that sound?" said Nash.

Freyja and Eduardo laughed.

"Nash, tell me what you hear," said Freyja.

Moonlight by the lake, she projected.

Nash waited a minute, and then said, "What do you mean?"

"Did you hear anything?" she asked again.

"Yeah, I heard a bunch of noisy static or low cymbals, like radio station out of tune. Why? Are you guys talking to each other? Like mentally or something?"

"It seems so," said Freyja.

Nash crossed his arms and scowled. "Great. That's just great. You two go on and talk about me behind my—ears. While I get nothing but broken instruments? Has anybody checked on our captain? I'll go."

Nash climbed up the ladder and disappeared. Freyja turned her attention to Eduardo. She was thrilled to know she might not be alone. Eduardo must understand all this better than anyone.

"When did you first find out you could move things?" asked Freyja.

"A few years ago, I started to knock all kinds of things over even though I wasn't standing anywhere near them. I have sort of a magnetic force that I can play with. It's on everything. I can change the polarity in my hands, depending on what I am around. It's bizarre, but I can turn it off now, so it's not a big deal." Eduardo shrugged.

"What do your parents think?" Freyja asked.

"Well, my dad is deceased, and my mom is often away. She worries about me. Carole knows, of course. But he protects me. For a while, it was a problem because I was breaking everything, but we could blame it on other things."

Eduardo's eyes sparkled. He was such a surprise—someone who understood her, even if just a little. Freyja reached across the table and touched his hand softly. She pretended to be checking his magnetic pulse. She giggled. He cracked a smile and laughed, too.

Powerful energy passed between them. A wave of joy and infatuation, humming and swimming through every cell in her body. She was suddenly much more than a girl. Her boundaries expanded out in his welcoming presence. The protective, intoxicating bubble around her grew to include him. The new spaciousness made her feel alive, more optimistic, more powerful, more creative, just more of whatever she was. She wanted to grab hold of his hands and pull herself into his chest. The force between them was truly overwhelming.

"Guys, the captain says it's going to be another couple of hours and then night. He said we should get some sleep," said Nash sternly, climbing down the hatch.

There was a large knot in her throat, as though she might be guilty even though nothing, technically, had happened. "Yeah, good idea," she said, noticing some floatation vests and a few wool blankets. "Here, anyone wants a pillow?"

The two of them stretched across the benches, while Nash propped himself over a pile of tarps between the ladder and the table. The boat sped forcefully along the undulating coastline. The rhythmic beat was like a steady drum that lulled them all to sleep, all expect Freyja, who could only gaze into the darkness and think about Eduardo, the Adept.

CHAPTER TWENTY-EIGHT

THE FASTEST WAY IS NOT ALWAYS A STRAIGHT LINE

"*Tierra!*" yelled the captain.

Freyja woke suddenly, nearly falling off her makeshift bed as the boat swerved into a slow reverse. The kids climbed up to the top deck, enveloped in a thick layer of fog. The captain maneuvered the boat into the dock, cloaked in darkness. They had reached the tiny port town of Huacho. Freyja gazed out at the nearby rooflines and smokestacks protruding out of the silky mist like submarine scopes.

"Where are we?" asked Freyja.

"Huacho," said the narrowly focused captain as he killed the engine.

He threw ropes onto the docks and jumped quickly over to secure the boat to tall posts. A figure appeared through the haze, walking with a noticeable limp. The two men greeted each other with enthusiasm, like old friends. They spoke rapidly for a moment, and the captain rushed back to help the kids out of the boat.

"*Este hombre es mi primo. Usted puede confiar en el.*"

"This is his cousin. He will take us to Caral," explained Eduardo.

"Thank you, sir. This is for getting us here," said Freyja stuffing all the nuevo sol she had left into the captain's palms.

"*No se ... el placer es mio, angel. Vamanos,*" the captain replied, hugging her, and insisting she put the money away.

220

Freyja thanked him humbly, and then gestured to the boys, "Let's go."

A thick bank of fog cloaked the distant hills and slumbering town, enclosing several miles offshore with an impenetrable ethereal silence. Simple wood huts dotted the shoreline, hosting a mirage of fishers pulling nets onto a misty beach. Seagulls faded into the seascape. Cars sat idle or lumbered along some distant highway. The old run-down stucco and ramshackle warehouses were long abandoned. Life paused in a cloud, but for a tiny trickle of anticipation.

As they reached an area of large dilapidated buildings scattered alongside railroad tracks, the fog line parted to bright skies and stark hillsides. Their guide stopped at a large blue van and motioned for the kids to get in.

Nash leaned into Freyja and asked, "What do you think?"

She touched her stomach and took a deep breath. "Yeah, I think so."

Nash heaved on the back door, rusty and jammed. He eventually swung it open, and they all piled in. The van was empty but for random tools and one window in the back door.

"*Como se llama?*" asked Eduardo.

"Miguel."

Eduardo struck up a conversation about Caral and where to go from there.

"*Si, si, si,*" said Miguel.

Eduardo turned to Freyja and Nash. "Miguel says it's about a half hour from here, but there is a lot of traffic on the main roads, so he is going to take some back roads; plus only locals know the way, so no one should be able to follow us."

"Great," said Freyja, lowering her backpack and stiff body to the floor of the old van. "I figured out the box. I have the crystals, the map, and the key. I am not sure what to do once we get to Caral, though."

"What's your best guess?" asked Nash. "I mean, this *is* pretty bizarre so far. It's like you're some superhero—"

"I am not a superhero," Freyja cut in, rolling her eyes.

"Okay," he admitted, "but in the movies, most ancient gods or goddesses reincarnated are superheroes . . . Anyway, you're being chased by some mad scientists who don't want us to reboot some old power station. It's like you're E.T. calling home!"

"You know, I saw some stuff one night," Freyja remembered. "It was a dream or vision, maybe. I saw some man, on top of a tower of some kind, holding her in a box."

"Your mom?"

"Yeah … Weird, I know," Freyja whispered. She had suppressed the longing for her mother for so long that even talking about her was difficult. "It was like she was a prisoner."

"Where?"

"I don't know. But maybe I can find her if she's alive. Is that crazy?"

"Not any crazier than anything else that's happening," Nash laughed.

"Freyja, what do *you* know about Caral?" asked Eduardo.

"Well, I know that it's on this map. I know that it's supposed to be a wild place, probably where there is a vortex or power station or something. I know that I have a key with these rocks that might unlock it and reboot it to generate some free energy that the earth needs. And I know that some guys want to stop us. The professor—" Freyja realized they had left him behind. "Oh my God, the professor. He knew about Caral, too."

"I'm sure he's fine," Eduardo said soothingly, as he watched where the van was heading. His eyes widened as it had suddenly sped up very quickly.

Miguel shouted, "*Aguantar!*"

The van swerved in all directions knocking everyone over in the back like bowling pins. Freyja tried desperately to hang on to something. Nash was splayed on the wall of one side and then rolled back to the other. The van swerved furiously down unpaved, potholed roads.

"Hang on!" shouted Eduardo, who had ducked into the front seat next to Miguel.

"What's going on?" yelled Freyja.

Eduardo shouted back, "We have visitors!"

"Who?" asked Nash.

"It's them," said Freyja. "The ones who put the implant in my head."

"How do you know?"

"I just know," she said.

Freyja became very quiet, holding on to a rope lassoed around a plank bolted to the van's inside panel. She hung on and tuned into her senses.

Base, advise.

"Neutralize target."

Copy that.

Freyja's scars blazed. Sarana had been able to shield the device and prevent tracking back in the United States, but now it must have worn off. The base of her skull throbbed with intense pressure.

The pain grew more substantial. She needed air. Grabbing the handles at the back of the van, she threw open the doors and hung onto a panel above her head.

"Freyja, what are you doing?" yelled Nash. But she couldn't hear him; the throbbing in her head was as loud as thunder cracks.

In a moment, air blew through her hair and over her face. Its effect was soothing, and she sighed with the pleasure of it, until she opened her eyes to the black military vehicle racing close behind. There were two men in the front. One leaned out the window and leveled a gun at her head. Freyja just froze, as if entranced by the moment. His face was cold and blank, and the weapon he held was strange, not like any pistol or rifle Freyja had ever seen before. Then the other driver leaned out of his window, too, and in his hand was a more typical gun, matte black and smooth.

This is it, she told herself.

Suddenly, there was a sharp yank at her shoulders. Her neck whipped back, and she landed on the floor of the van in a heap. A hiss of gunfire pinged off the van. They left little black holes in the bodywork as bullet met metal and rang loudly in their ears.

Suddenly the van turned another sharp corner and disappeared into a large alleyway. Miguel sped along furiously, making several sharp turns until they reached a tunnel. The black military van was no longer in sight. Freyja was crouched in one corner as the pain in her head eased.

"You saved me," she said to Nash.

Nash shrugged, and one corner of his mouth rose into a smile. "It was nothing."

"What happened?" came Eduardo's voice over the top of the headrest. "Are you okay?" The open doors were swinging wildly as the van still raced along with bullet holes riddling its roof.

"That gun . . ." she mumbled to Eduardo, holding her head and sitting up.

"What gun? Anyway, no time. We need to find a diversion." Eduardo gave directions to Miguel, and then scrambled into the back and helped Freyja up on her feet. "We need to jump."

"Out of a moving van?" Nash scoffed. "Look at her. She can barely stand."

"Got any better ideas?"

"I'll be fine, honest," Freyja said weakly. Nash glared at Eduardo.

On the next right turn, the van slowed enough for them to leap out. The black car had fallen back now, but it would only be a matter of time until it returned. The three kids lined themselves side by side at the doors.

"Ready . . . Now!"

The trio tumbled out of the van. Freyja didn't scream even though she wanted to. Knees buckling, they all rolled along the dusty road until coming to a stop. Eduardo was the first to hoist himself up, as Miguel took off in the van, driving wildly through the industrial park alleyways.

"Come, this way!" he commanded, and ran towards a nearby building and slipped underneath a loading dock. Nash picked himself up more gingerly, hobbling over to Freyja and helping her to her feet. She had a few scrapes on her elbows and palms, and some blood was dropping from below her chin.

"I've suffered worse," she said, raising a hand to wipe the blood from her chin. "Let's go!"

They ran over, and joined Eduardo in hiding beneath the loading dock and peered out as the black car sped around the corner past them in pursuit of the van.

"Now what?" asked Nash.

"I don't know, but if we stayed in that van a second longer—" Eduardo began to say as if making a point to Nash. But before he could utter another word, there was an explosion. And then, silence.

"What was that?" Nash whispered. Keen-eyed, they all scanned the distant horizon, and then there it was, a tall plume of black smoke rising half a mile away.

"Oh no," said Eduardo.

"Miguel?" Freyja said.

Tears welled as her heart broke. Was that man's death her cause? First her aunt, then the boat captain who was shot during the helicopter chase, and now this. How many people might die trying to protect her? As these thoughts began to torment her, Nash reminded them that they needed to get out of there, and fast.

"Once they pick through the rubble, they'll know you're not there," he said. "Then they'll backtrack and search the area."

"Yeah, we can't stay here," Eduardo agreed. "Let's go."

They crawled out from under the dock. Ahead lay a path through bushes towards the mountains and away from the sea.

They jogged through an area of woodland just outside Huacho for about a mile, and then came upon a group of vaqueros, or cowboys, with a pack of horses.

"Can we borrow a couple of your horses?" asked Eduardo.

"*Si, pero son mis unicos caballos.* How much you pay?"

Eduardo negotiated with the amount of nuevo sol he had remaining, and then asked the man a few questions.

"He says Caral is exactly due east up into that valley." Eduardo pointed straight ahead into a grove of trees.

Freyja and Nash tried to give Eduardo all the cash they had, but he shook his head, "This is on me."

In a few moments, they were climbing onto the backs of the horses with nothing but wool blankets tied around their stomachs with rope and rope halters.

"What should I name her?" Freyja said, grinning as the pain in her head had stopped.

"How about Smelly?" laughed Nash.

Freyja had to crack a smile. She realized how tense her entire body was. "I was thinking Calista. I've always loved that name."

"Well, his name will be Hard Ass because that's what he has!" Nash frowned as Hard Ass started to trot down the path on his own. "Whoaaaaaa!"

Eduardo laughed and gave his black horse an expert kick and cantered after Nash. He turned to Freyja. "Let's go help him out, shall we?"

Freyja patted Calista on the neck. She was hopeful, about the quest, about her destiny. She even wondered if maybe Miguel had escaped the van, too. Perhaps he had rolled out before it exploded. Or what if it wasn't the van that exploded at all, but the pursuing vehicle? She held hope in her heart, and it warmed her whole body.

"Thank you, Calista. Can you get me to Caral?" she whispered, leaning forward and cooing into the horse's ear.

Calista flicked her tail in response and trotted along after the boys and their horses.

CHAPTER TWENTY-NINE:

NOT EVERYTHING IS A NAIL

"**G**oddammit. These kids!" yelled Colonel Wayne. He paced around a control panel in the Lima command center.

"One helicopter down. You lost them in the fog? You lost them in the van? Perhaps I should lose you."

"Sir, this is highly unusual," replied an agent with a thick Spanish accent. "We won't lose her now. We know where she's going."

"Christ, what the hell am I going to tell Drake?" Colonel Wayne grumbled to himself as his phone rang. "Yes?" Wayne bowed his head, and sighed. He listened patiently to the voice on the phone, scratched his head, and nodded. "Yes, sir." He ripped off his headset and sat his bulky frame into a large swivel chair next to the console.

He studied the maps on the console and enlarged the map around Caral. Three small dots were moving slowly up the valley nearby: one green, one blue, and one violet. He touched the area to zoom in closer. Wayne never expected he would use tactical and strategic training to hunt for young children and adults running from their fates. He didn't fully understand what was so special about them, but he had seen enough over the years to know that they could do things no one else could, and that made them targets. His job was to keep them away from the competition. And while they were generally easy to subdue, he had lost far too many men to take any of it lightly.

The kids were special; no one could deny that. They had some genetic predisposition, and there was no way to predict who was affected. All he knew was that they didn't think or act the way everyone else did. They were wild, destructive, unpredictable, and dangerous. Early on in his missions, he would try reasoning with them to come quietly and submit. They never did. They would often have unsuspecting allies like parents or neighbors who would get in the way. Through trial and error, he learned that the best way was always stealth when the target least expected it.

"Agent Serrano, can you get me Director Drake on the line."

"*Si, un momento.*" The local agent picked up a headset and dialed a number on a pad nearby. He then handed the headset back to Colonel Wayne.

"Director Drake's office," said a woman's voice.

"This is Wayne."

"Oh, colonel, he's already in Lima."

"What?"

"Yes, he left right after you did. Did you want me to patch you into him?"

"Yes, thanks."

Colonel Wayne prepared for nearly everything, but *that* he did not see coming. Before he could assemble an answer to why Drake was in Lima, there was his friend's familiar voice.

"Status," asked Drake, walking into the center.

Wayne spun around, shocked. "What the hell are you doing here?"

"I needed to get out," he said, smiling wryly.

"I see." Wayne sized up a weary but sharply dressed Drake. "I suppose this means you want to call the shots?"

"Ha. No, this is your show. I wouldn't want to interfere. Plus, I have dearly missed my pisco sours." Drake shook Wayne's hand vigorously and patted him on the back. "So, status?" he asked again.

They had met early in the program, both selected to train for the NuTech Special Operations division. Wayne came out of the Marines; Drake was a private industry in bioengineering.

"We tracked them to Huacho. We think they're headed to Caral. We've got reinforcements headed there now," Wayne answered.

Drake nodded and placed his hands together. "We need to be careful with this. I want her alive."

"Sir, Arktik is not responding. I've been advised that, if she does not power down, we are to hit the kill switch."

"No!" Drake snapped.

Colonel Wayne stepped back to analyze the situation. Drake shifted uncomfortably, alarmed by his own reaction. He knew that attachment to outcomes would undermine his position and control. "I mean, not yet. Give me a shot at her first."

"Sir, I . . . understand how you may feel. But I have my orders."

Drake paused. "Have you made contact with the asset?"

"Yes, sir. He is online."

CHAPTER THIRTY

WHERE THERE ARE RUINS, THERE IS HOPE FOR TREASURE

The dry dunes folded into ragged cliffs rising higher and higher as the kids rode farther away from the sea. They crossed into a cobbled path that stretched alongside a shallow river. They stuck to the trail's rocky areas to avoid making tracks, continuing upriver towards a fantastic gorge of blue mountains shrouded by the verdant valley. Farms lined every inch of ground from north to south along the river basin.

"Are you sure we're going the right way?" asked Freyja.

"This is the only valley I can see. These horses know this path, so I am guessing this is the place," answered Eduardo.

"Can we stop for a minute? My ass is killing me," said Nash.

Eduardo nodded and said, "Sure, the horses probably need it, too." He hopped off his horse and helped Freyja down from hers, smiling chivalrously.

"Thanks," she said, cheeks blushing.

Nash could only scowl as he rather ungainly tumbled down from his horse.

The kids led the animals to the river's edge, and tied them to some long branches that hung down over the river. Nash excused himself to find a place to pee.

As Nash disappeared into a thicket, Freyja walked over to Eduardo, who was stroking the mane of his horse. "Where did you learn to ride like that?"

"Me? Well, I have been riding in hunter and dressage for years," Eduardo answered casually.

"Dress what?" said Freyja.

"Dressage. It is French for exercise or training. It's a form of riding, originally used to train French battle horses."

"Ah, I get it."

Eduardo patted his horse and refastened the ropes around the makeshift saddle blanket. He knew how to position it correctly and keep it taut. Everything about how he moved, to the way he methodically handled situations, Freyja found smooth and oiled to perfection. His posture was tall, noble, athletic. He stood like a young man bred to lead the pack, a young man who belonged on a horse at another time. What different lives they had led, she thought. And yet, there they were, sharing this strange genetic anomaly that brought them closer together than anyone else on earth.

Suddenly, Nash called out, "Hey, Freyja! Over here."

Freyja smiled at Eduardo, and then climbed over the rocky beach to a path through some trees to the other side of the riverbank.

Nash stood on a large rock positioned over the river and skipped some smaller stones across the surface, trying to hit a cluster of large rocks on its way. Nash blushed when she came around the bend, but he paused to calm himself and collect his thoughts. His hair was a tousled mess. His clothes were dusty and filthy. And yet, he appeared vibrant, more determined than she had seen him before.

"Freyja, I, er . . . Well, I just wanted to tell you. Even though, hmm, I know I don't have any special powers or anything, or I'm not that smart or even that strong, but what I'm trying to say is . . . I will do my very best to protect you!"

His cheeks blazed redder than she had ever seen, like two apples. But his eyes were steady, not darting, or nervous, just steady like a bear hunting fish, calculating its next move. He left these heartfelt words in the space between them with a fire she hadn't expected.

Tongue-tied and hesitant, she knew his incredibly tender declaration deserved a response. "You do have . . . powers," she stammered. "You are starting to hear and know things, in a new way. You have traveled all this way with me, to my home, the river and cave, stowed away on an airplane! You are the bravest person I know."

She searched his face for some cues on what was happening here, between them. Nash turned towards her, gazing deeply into her eyes. She understood more than his words. He reached out for her hand and wrapped his arms around her, pulling her into his chest. He leaned in and kissed her. Freyja soaked up his courage and conviction, her whole body flushing with warm affection and gratitude.

Then she was hit with a sudden flashback to reality. "Oh my God, Nash. Your parents! They must be so worried!"

Nash just shrugged. "Nah, I texted them before we left the country. They know I'm alive. I'll call them as soon as we get to a safe place," he assured her.

Freyja smiled, and he pulled her in close again. She squeezed her arms around him and then, loosening, softly whispered, "Now it's my turn to pee."

He smiled and kissed her forehead. Freyja excused herself while Nash stayed, exhaling deeply after sharing his heart. She needed to get some space to process all the strangeness. Why was she so triggered? Clearly, there was an incredible level of uncertainty and mystery before her. This journey had begun so suddenly just a few days earlier. A surreal world had opened that both terrified her and was utterly vital to her existence.

These strange affections and attractions to her longtime friend and ally and this new stranger were very confusing. She hadn't ever been in love, technically, so she couldn't even say if this *was* love. But she clung to these people, sharing the arduous journey into something unfathomable. How could she not? They were entwined and reliant upon each other for survival, but even more for witnessing the magic and wonder of all that they were discovering. It was like uncovering a vast kingdom of treasures and delight, wrapped in a cloak of unimaginable danger. She couldn't imagine this experience without either of them at this point.

Once she finished in the bushes, she headed towards Calista, sizing up her ropes and wondering if she ought to tighten them as well.

"I know how you feel," said Eduardo, coming out of the brush nearby.

"You do?" said Freyja, wondering if he had seen the kiss. She did not want to have any of these confusing emotions or experiences discussed out in the open. There was just too much at stake, too much unfolding at lightning speed to consider or inject meaning into it.

"Yeah, I mean, it's strange to see things, hear things that others can't. Everything about us is special, but there is a price to pay for being different, no?"

"I guess so," said Freyja. "Different is normal for me. I don't want to be alone anymore."

She kicked herself for saying that out loud. She was far too familiar with lonely. It was there in a crowd of a million or just standing next to only one other. And most of all, she didn't want Eduardo's pity. She wasn't interested in going into that level of depth, certainly not at this exact moment.

Eduardo walked over to Freyja and reached for her hands. It was a strange reflex to give her hands to him automatically. Wasn't it rude otherwise? Her impulse was to pull away, but she didn't want to embarrass him or call attention to the conflict. She wondered what his intentions were.

He stared deeply into her eyes. "Different is wonderful. Maybe different should be the new normal."

Freyja's heart thumped with excitement. She thought of Nash, and the kiss they had shared by the river only moments ago, but somehow, she was powerless to steal her hands away from Eduardo. She cringed at the whole exchange.

"Why, er . . . Why don't you show me some of your moves?" she blurted out, hoping to distract him from whatever it was that was going on.

Eduardo smiled, undaunted. "Sure."

He let go of her hands and turned to face the river. He breathed deeply, closed his eyes very slowly, and then lifted one hand over the water, and with the other, he stirred the air in a circular pattern. A small funnel of water began to build into a large towering whip-like snake. He lifted the funnel higher and higher, and then whipped it in a powerful blast towards the opposite shore. It ripped into the trees and bushes like an angry fire hose, sending birds and branches darting in all directions.

"Dude, that's serious," said Nash arriving from the trail behind them.

"Can you teach me?" asked Freyja.

"I don't know," answered Eduardo. "Here . . ." He stood behind Freyja and lifted her hand as he had done.

A powerful surge of energy collected in her body, coming in from all angles: head, feet, arms, and spine. Her hands were hot and tingly. She focused on the water and visualized it coming to her. Nothing moved. She kept trying to focus. Eduardo nudged her hand around a few more times. The magnetism was powerful. All she could think about was how she was attracted to him and disloyal to Nash.

"I know you feel it, too," Eduardo telegraphed to Freyja's mind with his own.

Freyja stepped away from him, annoyed. "It's no use. I can't do that."

"Well, you can't have it all, I guess," said Nash, walking over to scoop up some water. As he touched the water, he shook awkwardly and fell backward onto the ground.

Freyja dashed over to him. "Nash! What happened?"

"Electric shock is what happened." Eduardo laughed. "You charged the water with electricity. I guess something happened after all."

Nash opened his eyes and started laughing. Freyja sighed with relief. Luckily, he was not hurt.

"It felt like when you touch the light switch after running around the house in wool socks, only a thousand times stronger." He gazed up wearily at Freyja. "But please, next time, warn me when you are going to super-charge the water."

Freyja squeezed him tight, grateful he was okay.

A few minutes later, as they all sat beside the river recovering, a rumbling sensation stirred deep in Freyja's core. Nash cocked an ear to the wind and listened for what sounded like a distant but growing drumline. Dark clouds rolled in over the hillside. A few large wet drops landed on their shoulders.

"Rain," she noted.

"I predict there will be a lot more wet stuff shortly," Nash complained, flipping up his hoodie over his head.

Out from the thunderous heavy mountain of clouds, there was a faint trembling that rolled quickly into galloping hoofbeats. It was an insistent whipping of metal through the air like a dragon's tail pounding through slabs of rock. Something big was coming. She turned in alarm towards Eduardo and Nash.

"Yes, I feel it, too," said Eduardo.

Nash jolted to his feet. "We have to get out of here."

Freyja grabbed Calista's rope and hopped up onto her back. Eduardo was off on his horse close behind Freyja, racing up the riverbed. Nash had thrown one leg over his horse as it started to chase after the others.

"Whoa, whoa!" he yelled, hanging on for dear life, barely getting his hands around her neck.

The horses moved urgently, carrying their lean stocky frames stealthily over the uneven terrain. In a few miles, the river became shallower, and the trio splashed through the many splintered streams fanning out from the main river on to a sandy trail through stretches of farmland. The rain pelted and saturated their clothes, dripping down the horses' manes. They passed quickly through a small village of huts, and over a sandy hill ahead of them. An ancient valley of excavated mounds and pyramids stood beckoning on the horizon.

This is it. Freyja started to vibrate powerfully like a tuning fork ringing in unison with others. *Come on, Calista.*

Freyja clung to her mane with an urgency to reach the pyramids. Then that distant roar chopped through the clouds. A fleet of black military helicopters hammered up the riverbed, closing in behind them. Still galloping, Freyja whipped her head around to make sure they were there, her hair blowing back like a storm.

"Go! Go! Go!" she screamed.

But it was too late. They couldn't outrun the choppers and were soon surrounded by pounding propellers on all sides. One had sped ahead, turned, and landed in front of them. Two on either side were descending, too, while the fourth continued to hover above them. Military men in black fatigues rappelled down from the descending choppers like spiders hanging from a web. When they landed, they unclipped from the ropes and set their sights straight at Freyja, Nash, and Eduardo.

"Stop!" boomed a male voice from a microphone in the hovering helicopter.

Freyja hesitated a moment, peering around in a cloud of dust to find where they could escape. The storm whipped them sideways and across the nose so fiercely that visibility was nearly impossible. Although she was nearly blinded, her horse Calista led the other horses, galloping away through an unseen gap between the helicopters. Eduardo raced out on his horse, pushing through the rain barrier and moving quickly towards the pyramids.

Then the shots—her ears rang with the familiar rattle of gunfire. Nash fell from his horse, and her heart froze in terror.

"Nash!" she screamed. Freyja slowed and started to turn back.

"No! Freyja, don't stop," Eduardo insisted, pressing his commands into her mind. *"You can't save him."*

Her heart burst into a million shards of agony. There wasn't anything she could do to help Nash. Tears flowing down her face, she leaned down and put her arms around Calista, who was in a dead gallop over the rocky dunes. She was taking Freyja straight to the center of the ruins. Eduardo was right beside her. They slowed at the foot of the most extensive ruins. She hopped off hugged Calista tightly.

"You must go."

Caught off guard, Freyja asked, "Are you talking to me?"

Calista flipped her tail and trotted to a nearby grove of trees for shelter.

Freyja wasn't sure which way to go, despite the impulse and intense adrenaline. Her body tingled confirmation and her scars illuminated as though she was in the right place. The scars lit up brighter as she swiveled her body around. The markings directed her up to the top of the pyramid, like a compass arrow. She stood facing the steps and platforms leading up at least one hundred feet. She immediately recognized everything. This was the place from the vision when she was with Ursa in the lab. This was the place where her mom was in a box, and she saw the buried man.

"Freyja, I'll hold them off. You do what you came here to do," Eduardo roared, slapping his horse on the rear and sending it off to safety.

"But Nash!" she screamed, for fear of abandoning him, tearing her heart to pieces.

"We can't help him now. Let me try to hold them off as long as I can!" he shouted again. He glanced around the rain-drenched ruins and at the streams of water running across the sands. He pulled off his sweatshirt and wrapped it around his head to shield his eyes, revealing his bare torso covered in black scars. Then he ran and crouched behind a collapsing stonewall.

Freyja sprinted up the crumbling steps, climbing her way around, higher, and higher. When she reached the top of the crumbling pyramid structure, she found a semi-circular stone platform. It was like a turret, encircled by a four-foot-high wall. Most of the stone surface was submerged in sand, quickly storing a pool of water.

This is it.

She bent down and scooped a pile of wet sand off the stone in front of her. There was a clear spiral symbol etched into the sandstone, at least a foot in diameter. A similarly shaped swirl on her arm lit up immediately. She traced the spiral with her fingers. It had a strange soothing vibration. She didn't just feel it; she could hear it. The pulse was a melody. It was haunting the way something reminded her of a lost place or loved one, a time when she was safe at home and drenched in love.

That song.

Freyja's back felt beaten by pounding fists of air as the thundering helicopters landed on the sands below. They swiftly emptied of men and guns, racing to tactile positions around the base.

"Ms. Wolfe," boomed a loud voice, "Ms. Wolfe, come down. We will not hurt you."

Freyja, rain-slicked, hid behind a wall peering out. She gazed down towards the clearing in front of the pyramid. They had Nash, his hands bound behind his back. She couldn't tell if he was hurt, but he was not okay. He was kneeling, and his head was hanging as though he was not fully conscious. There was another man on the ground next to him, but she couldn't tell who it was. Miguel from the boat—did he survive the crash? Did they have the professor? And Eduardo—he stood there unbound. Why was Eduardo with them?

Freyja projected to Eduardo. *"What's going on?"*

He stood calmly defiant, wet hair clinging to his face.

"We can't fight this, Freyja."

"What do you mean?"

"There's a lot you don't know."

"You are with them?"

"We have to survive. Don't be a fool."

Freyja noted the dozen or so men, all pointing their guns up at her. Betrayal, confusion, and terror all fought deep within her bosom. Her heart pounded, deafening in her ears. A terrible chill crept into her bones as the storm cracked open and flooded the desert valley in a blackening haze.

Freyja couldn't process what was happening. She returned to Sarana, her training.

"What do I do?" she begged. "Ursa . . . please! I need you! Can you hear me?"

Freyja waited a moment, eyes scanning the sky. She curled up into a ball as the rains collected and pooled around her ankles. Panicking, she tried to remember all the things she had learned.

Ground yourself from the earth.

Pull in energy from above.

Gather it in your heart.

Create a vision or target.

Channel it with intention.

"I can do this," she whispered.

Freyja closed her eyes and connected to the earth below her: the stone layers all stacked one on top of the other, drawing up the minerals, crystals, and molten strength. It became a channel straight into her body; the earth that supported all life flooded into her flesh, bolstering her bones with the sensation of iron and steel.

She reinforced, reinvigorated, and rebuilt her body with the primal forces of terra firma.

She reached her arms high over her head, hands broad to receive the animating fire of the cosmos, the free energy that enlivened all matter. Luminous starlight and moonbeams trickled down into her fingertips, flowing into her bloodstream, infusing her cells with life and spirit. The electricity of the universe was super-charging her like a lightning rod. The sacred symbols etched on her flesh pulled her conscious awareness into a quantum body, stretched out beyond the constraints of time and space. The downpour of rain amplified the energies, giving her a hyper boost unlike anything before.

She mentally envisioned this power swirling into her heart, a ball of light charging into a weapon of nuclear force, ready to be unleashed. In her mind's eye, she conjured a vision. In this vision, all the threatening men below were disarmed and bound, allowing her to proceed to find the portal, unlock the mysterious energy of these ruins, free Nash, and restore power to this sacred place.

She cocked her arm like a pitcher at the World Series, stood up just a bit, and lobbed a fiery strike at the men below. A luminous ball of fire roared down and struck the sand like a fifty-ton boulder. The force of the impact threw several of the soldiers off their feet. They rolled away, taking cover under anything they could find.

"This is your last warning. Come down now," hollered the man on the bullhorn.

Freya gathered another ball of energy, giving it more power than before. The round sphere shapeshifted into a bolt that she threw like a javelin. She missed a helicopter by inches, but it hit the front hood of an off-road truck that had joined the standoff, flipping it over onto its side.

"Fire!" yelled the man with the bullhorn.

A rapid succession of shots pelted at the stonewall around Freyja. She ducked for cover, gasping at the barrage. She expected bullets, but when she opened her eyes, there was a dart near her head, buried in stone. She pulled it out and studied it. A dart? She started laughing hysterically. "I'm not afraid of sleeping darts!" she yelled down at them.

"They will kill you if they can't get you to cooperate," said Eduardo.

"Go away, you traitor!" Freyja fumed.

"No. I'm a survivor. You should be, too," he said.

"Go to hell!"

Freyja launched a fiery lightning spear straight at Eduardo. He threw up a magnetic shield to deflect it into the side of the pyramid, rocking the foundations where she stood.

"Please, Freyja. It doesn't have to be like this."

"Yes. It. Does."

Freyja launched another dozen lightning bolts, blowing up a helicopter and creating a narrow channel between the pyramid and the men. Like the one in the military van that had chased them, a man with a menacing super gun set up position near the jeep. An excruciating jolt zapped the base of her skull vigorously.

"Ms. Wolfe, last chance," boomed the voice in the bullhorn.

Freyja groaned in agony, clutching at her head. The pain was piercing and unyielding. She fell on her knees in the rising pool of rainwater, burying her face in her backpack as tears streamed down her cheeks.

Oh, God. Help me.

She pulled the stones out of her pocket and held the key in her trembling hands. The melody was coming from them. The star garnet, moonstone, and Iceland sunstone were all singing an otherworldly harmony. She sat crying, rain-drenched, kneeling in a pool of water. In her hands, she held the treasures that her incredible journey had yielded so far: the three stones and the old key little Sammy had given to her in the garden of the Rahumans' house back in Oregon. Now, somewhere in Peru, amongst pyramids and rainstorms, soldiers were aiming guns at her head—death was certain.

With that thought, she sent one last desperate cry into the universe: "Mom. Where are you?"

CHAPTER THIRTY-ONE

PERCEPTION IS EVERYTHING

"Freyja," the man's voice was low and calm, a quality that startled her.

His tall and lean silhouette stood out against the dark cloud bank behind him. He wore a broad hat, spilling rainwater off the brim. He appeared more like an archeologist than a military commander, a kindlier shadow figure and somehow familiar.

"Who are you?" she asked.

"Someone who is here to help you," he said. "You can call me Drake."

Freyja peered over the ruins where the helicopters and Jeeps were stationed below, all full of guns still pointed up at her. Adrenaline pumped through her body as she studied this man standing now just feet away. She tried to see if he carried any weapons. Her head was throbbing in constant beats. She could scarcely parse the pain in her head from the rain hitting her face.

"What do you want from me?" she yelled over the breaking cracks of thunder.

"Relax, Freyja," he said, trying to soothe her. "This has all been a huge misunderstanding. If we had known how strong you were, we could have brought you in sooner."

"What are you talking about? Who the *hell* are you?" she demanded.

"Freyja," he paused, "you are not paying attention. I wanted you to have more time. I . . . didn't think you were ready. I tried to protect you. I was wrong. Please, allow me to help you."

"Help me? You are trying to kill me!"

"No one has to die," he said. "That's the last thing I want. But you are a danger to yourself and others. With great power comes great responsibility. We want to help you."

"Help me? By putting things in my head? Did you help my aunt, too?"

"That's . . . complicated . . . But I can certainly help you understand if you agree to work with us."

"Who is *us?*"

The man dropped his head and placed a palm to his chest. "Let's start over. I am part of a network of future thinkers and scientists. We are developing ways to enhance human potential, to improve the lives of all humans. It's a global network, and one that you can be a part of, too."

"You help by locking people up and killing them, huh? Is that what you do? Not my kind of help. No thanks." Freyja winced in pain as the vice-like grip on her skull tightened.

"Freyja, I can offer you sanctuary and training. With your abilities, we can help you find the answers. Don't you want to know more about your gifts and yourself? We will chalk this up to your first training session. I can stop that pain you're experiencing right now, just as soon as you say the word."

Freyja peered at him, struggling to think through his words and what she should do. A dark web appeared around him. It was thick and heavy. He was not only covered with the web; it was coming *from* him.

"Let me tell you a story, Freyja," Drake said, moving around the perimeter of the tower, but remaining in the shadows. "Humanity and spiders have much in common. In Japan, they have a sport called *Kumo Gassen*. Do you know this story?"

"No." Freyja tried to steady herself.

Drake continued, "Kumo Gassen is an annual sumo spider fighting event held in Kajiki, Japan, although it is practiced in a similar form in other countries throughout Asia, too. Japanese spider owners find female black and yellow Argiope and raise them to fight. There is a great deal of skill to picking the winning spiders.

The sheltered and docile spiders that live peacefully in the forests are easily killed. The aggressive spiders, those that receive training to fight, are the ones that survive and win. You see, Freyja, if we are to survive, we must not reject this natural law, but embrace it. You know what law I am talking about, don't you? It is the law of evolution. I want *you* to learn to survive. Most of humanity are docile and belong in the forest. They will not survive. But you, you must embrace this opportunity we offer you."

"Opportunity?" Freyja scoffed. "You call all this an opportunity? I think I know how to survive. I've been doing it all the while you and your comrades have been scrambling after me. And I'm not dead yet, am I?" she scoffed. Drake shook his head.

Disgusted, she turned towards the crystals, now glowing in a melodic pattern calling to her. She knelt to pick them up.

The man laughed. "Freyja, do you think a bunch of rocks make any difference?"

Ignoring his words, Freyja gathered them into her hands. These sparkling stones sang in unison; their different tones and frequencies were like a cricket symphony in the field. They were sending a secret, or rather, an unknown message of some sort.

What are you trying to tell me? she thought.

"You know, you are just like your mother."

"What do you know about my mother?" she demanded.

"I know her very well. I know that she managed to hide her abilities until we had you . . ."

"What . . . what did you say?"

"Freyja, your mother was an incredible woman . . . but . . ." Every word stung and seduced at the same time. He was talking about her mother, the woman she had ached to see for so long, her flesh and blood, the woman who brought her into this world and then promptly disappeared from it.

The man continued, "But, she resisted reality. This moment in history is far bigger than you or me. Your place is with me. The time is now."

Drake moved out of the shadows and showed her his face. He was very different from her memories, but there was no mistaking who he was. His icy blue eyes and peppered hair . . . Why hadn't she realized it earlier? Malcolm Wolfe, Malcolm Drake Wolfe—her father.

She cried. "I don't understand. I thought you were dead!" She was flooded with memories long buried. She remembered his strong hands lifting her into a tree to pick apples; reading bedtimes stories in the library, his feet up in the big wing chair as he finished his evening bourbon; the little robotic figures he would bring home from his work and let her play within her dollhouse; and his eyes, always piercing in her memory, a distant love, a stranger to her now.

"I can explain all of that. I promise. But for now, we need to leave this place, together."

Furious, betrayed, and confused, she looked around as her heart pounded in bold death march beats. Her entire world had turned upside down in an instant. She felt a delirious rage rising and erupting from her core.

She sobbed. "Why did you leave us? What happened to Mommy?"

Drake sighed. "Your mother didn't want you in the program. But I knew it was the best way to protect you. Do you remember the lightning?"

"Yes, how could I forget that?"

"That's when we knew—you were stronger than the others. Your activation would be difficult to hide. We left you with Lucy and arranged for an implant to slow down the process."

"But why not just tell me?"

"Because humans are sheep, and you are a wolf. The only way to keep you hidden was to hide you from yourself."

"What does that mean? Where is Mommy?"

"She's gone."

Something in Drake's voice did not sit right. Freyja studied his face. She remembered his cavernous gaze. It wasn't empty, but deeper than the seas and impossible depths. He was always quietly thinking impenetrable thoughts. Her mother always said he had the best poker face.

"Here. Remember?" He handed her a card. "You are my ace of spades, the card of the Magi."

He wanted her to take it. She did remember. He used to play some games with cards, spreading them out and flipping them over one by one. She once asked him to teach her. He showed her how they represented each day of the year. He said everyone had a card for the day they were born and the day they would die. She asked him which cards were his. His was ace of diamonds.

"What does it mean?"

"It just means that we are a team, you and me. And now, we need to get to work."

She wanted to reach out and bring him back into her life and never let go. And yet, she felt certain he was lying to her. Everything he had told her so far, he could have learned somewhere. For all she had seen—Ursa, the star being; Sarana and her brother Tommy, the shapeshifter; Seamus, the merman—he could be anyone.

"Who are you? Really?" she asked.

"Freyja, you know who I am. Stop the games."

"You are not my father. My father is dead. My father would never hurt people."

Freyja reached out and touched a spiral etched in the stone in front of her. The ground began to quiver below where they both stood. This was the way. The key she brought, somehow it would open where she needed to go. More determined than ever to complete her mission, to listen to her own calling, she waved him off and searched for a way to open the vortex or portal, whatever this matrix thing was.

Drake's expression grew dark. It became clear that he was not going to persuade her. He had made a vow. The Adepts could either become part of the future, or die with the rest of them. Even his own child was expendable. He had made peace with that risk long ago. The secrets of latent human power were just being harvested, and there was no room for error. Her rebellion would threaten the safety of the scientists and organizations working to decode the matrix. He thought about Anya and how impossible it had been to convince her to come with him. He realized that Freyja was more like her than him. Anger rose in his fist as he lashed Freyja with a powerful bolt of lightning. She stiffened from head to toe, falling to her knees. Drake began wrapping her energetically with a thick black webbing, like a spider lassoing its meal caught in a web. Dizzy and achy, as if some poison was spreading around her body, Freyja crumpled. The water from the torrential rains began to rise over her mouth and nose, drowning her by the second. She gasped for breath as the pool rose higher, and her body froze in its trap.

"You did this. We would have welcomed you."

Freyja's life and those she loved flashed before her eyes: Keyo, Lucy, Nash. Her life force shrank into her chest, getting smaller and smaller.

Drake took a last look at his child. "Sleep well. I'm sorry."

CHAPTER THIRTY-TWO

THE GREATEST POWER IS WITHIN

Freyja lay frozen on the stone platform; her shoulder leaned into the etched spiral on the stone beneath her. She was groggy and barely conscious. But then her senses detected the faintest whiff of rose, a phantosmia of her mother, a perfume she always wore. Freyja began to come around and then . . .

"Jump."

Freyja's mind was a blur of pain and distortion. Her body and the energy field around her were collapsing into a chaotic static. She rolled back and forth, on and off the spiral stone underneath her. The great relief her body felt when it touched it was like the soothing sensation from stepping onto a cool patch of sand over a scorching hot beach. But when she rolled off and away from the spiral, her entire body became wracked with the most intense pain. It shot down her limbs and held her chest in a vice-like grip. She writhed repeatedly, and when she rocked her shoulder back to the spiral, then came that voice again.

"Jump."

"What?" she groaned. She wasn't sure what she was hearing. Was it in her mind? She was too groggy to know.

Jump? she thought. *Jump where?*

She rolled one last time to touch the spiral, clutching the crystals that hummed in her hand. She imagined herself flowing into the ring, like rainwater swirling into a drain. It wasn't jumping so much as succumbing—surrender.

Her consciousness slipped away from the bounds of her body. It happened quickly and softly like a hand passing through the smoke. Freyja began falling forward and into the blackness of space like she had in the river in Oregon, and when she had triggered the small spiral on the black box back at the lake. Paralysis gripped her physical body, though her spirit floated like a parachute in the sky. Had she crossed over? Was this death? As she became lucid in this state, she realized she could slow her descent, too, as though she were rappelling on a sheer cliff, just flowing along, down, and down. She commanded herself to stop and hover. And she did. She floated in complete darkness, sensing the faintest boundary between her larger self and everything else. Like a drop in the ocean, she was aware of being both a part and apart.

After a few more blissful moments like this, Freyja came to land softly on the boughs of an illuminated tree. It was solitary, with nothing but mist surrounding it and a giant root ball at its base fixed only to air.

Suddenly, a voice said, "Hey, you made it." A boy was sitting on one of the boughs close to where she had landed. His legs swung freely, and he wore the most contented smile she had ever seen.

It was Ben, or at least, it looked a lot like Ben, the boy from Room 101 at Roosevelt High.

"But … What?" Freyja hesitated; Ben was so *different*. "What are you doing here?"

"I thought I would help you out." He smiled. "You know since I got to help you break out of jail, so to speak."

"What do you mean?"

"Well, the reality is hilarious. Don't you think?"

"I don't know what to think …" said Freyja.

"Well, let me help you understand. There are many more dimensions than people realize. Because my soul in the real world is trapped in a swollen brain, I come here a lot. It's cool. This astral realm is where I found out about you. And I wanted to help you, so I bit you—sorry about that, by the way. I wanted to get that contraption out so that you could grow." He started to laugh as though that was obviously funny.

"Ben, that hurt," Freyja said, shaking her hand at the memory. "But I guess I forgive you."

"Yeah, I figured you would, eventually."

"So, what is this place?" she asked.

"Oh, this is the Between Place, between worlds. Anyone can come here. But it's not for beginners. It can be a bit dangerous should you lose your way. I call it the astral treehouse."

"Astral treehouse?"

"Yeah. I call it that because we are in between dimensions. The neat thing, though, is that it has a kind of structure that you can climb or descend like a tree. It's like the backstage of a theater. Like anything you can imagine would be born here and then constructed out there." He pointed out into the darkness somewhere. "This is like where the 3D printer instructions come in, and then get sent to the right coordinates. Or a dressing room for the big stage production, I guess. Make sense?"

"Uh... this feels more like a psychotic dream," said Freyja

"Well, interestingly, this is where you are awake, and out there, that is where you are dreaming. The treehouse is the creative workshop where your soul conspires with destiny and fate."

"So, my soul is here right now? Like a ghost?" Freyja said.

"No... like you are floating in a space between your body and nobody. We all come here when our brains are dreaming, but we're awake. Sorry, that isn't very clear, I know. Let me show you around."

Ben hopped up the main trunk of the tree, as agile as anyone she'd ever seen. He could hardly hold a coherent conversation in Room 101, and yet here he was, like a regular Olympic gymnast.

They climbed up the trunk, touching and swinging on limbs and leaves, which responded with their responsive light show. Every branch and every leaf grew out of the other in a grand spiral as they climbed. The tree kept growing and growing until she realized she was but a speck in a massive infinitely spiraling tree that had no beginning and no end. She climbed and climbed, never tiring.

"The way of life was infinite in all directions," Ben yelled down at her.

She remembered the lessons of the golden ratio and how that reflected in every turn of every branch. The branches were related to each other in proportion to the trunk and the leaves' tiniest veins.

Ben plucked a nut from one of the branches and handed it to Freyja. It unfolded into a tiny sapling. Everything had a heart in the beginning, and then extended to create more hearts and more beginnings—a repeating spiral.

"Every organism on earth is blossoming into mind-blowing mosaics of interconnection. The smallest spinning atoms swung into galaxies that exploded into cells that multiply into tiny beings. These small creatures morphed into bats and dolphins and little animal babies. From one touch, many creations, all the way and including attractions and symbols, a language adopted and adapted continuously throughout time."

Ben laughed and pulled her onto a branch with a chorus of birds lined up in the boughs before them.

For the first time, she understood what they were saying:

"One is becoming all. All is becoming one. All are one."

The bow where she sat bent slowly, sliding her onto a cool obsidian floor. It was familiar.

"Well, I have to go now," Ben smiled at Freyja. "They'll be thinking I'm having another seizure soon. It's hard on my body when I leave. It wasn't random, the seizures. It was my soul needing to be here."

Freyja realized that maybe her seizures had been like that. She didn't remember ever coming here, but she recognized the space between held something. She always suspected there was something there. It wasn't just empty. It was never just a blank.

"Remember, nothing is as it appears. Don't get trapped." Ben smiled and kissed Freyja on the cheek before he evaporated before her eyes.

Freyja now found herself sitting upon the glassy obsidian floor, the same one from the lake. She twitched, remembering the sinister darkness. She groped around for an edge or object or anything to hold onto. She took a deep intentional breath to attempt to relax.

Suddenly, something very alien washed over her. It was icy, colder than anything she had felt before, and it moved. It slithered and squirmed, and greedily stalked her. As it drew in, it feasted on her scent like a ravenous hyena studying its prey. It was so close now, its breath tracing long icy fingertips over Freyja's etheric body. The terror was electrifying. Finally, it was close enough to make out a form. Freyja steeled herself with courage as she beheld a scaled and fetid body of earthly underworld, a black savage in female form. Her eyes were piercing and terrifying. Freyja could scarcely move.

"Do you know the riddle?"

"Uh . . . no . . . I don't," Freyja stammered, gulping hard. Something about this creature spelled out only one thing: death.

"What has no eyes but sees in the dark?" it whispered.

Freyja paused. She wrestled with different thoughts in her head. It was no use; fear filled her mind. So instead, she tried to think about everything she had learned so far: about energy, the body, lightning, channeling power, the *Brisingamen*. The Brisingamen! That was it—the power of the heart to bring light into the darkness. The heart was the most powerful organ in the body! The heart's electromagnetic energy was more significant than any other organ in the body, including the brain. She had experienced this power all along her journey, in her craziest moments, when she was training with Sarana, working with Seamus, trusting her instincts that whole time. Her heart had been her compass. She found clarity and sight in her heart in a way she had never experienced with anything else.

"The heart! The heart sees in the dark!" she yelled out.

The scuttling creature slowed her pace around Freyja. She locked her black godless eyes onto Freyja's. The gaze was penetrating and deadly.

"Who are you?" Freyja asked. "What do you want?"

The creature did not answer. It slithered around and around, stalking Freyja in the darkness. And then, as Freyja struggled to come upon any response, the beast was no longer aggressive. It was suddenly curious. Freyja felt a little relief, but still quite terrified. The dark mistress of the underworld stood between Freyja and something she desperately needed—hope.

"What can I do for you?" asked Freyja, trying to intuit the tension and what the creature was after.

The creature rattled, or shifted, wryly. It swerved back and exhaled a dank and toxic cloud around Freyja. "Are you the Guardian?" she asked intently.

Freyja's heart pounded feverishly, as though she had been caught sneaking into the wizard's room without permission. Then, she realized the markings on her arm were glowing as light flowed up and around her arms and into her heart. Freyja wondered how long she had to live.

"Are you the Guardian?" The voice was forceful and final.

Freyja was afraid to say anything because she wasn't sure what to say. What was the right answer? She was just a girl. Who was she to guard anything? What was she to protect? She had been a bystander, a passenger, a child, a victim, all her life. She had no power, nothing to offer. Freyja's mind swam with possible answers, all cast away as soon as she thought of them. Her heart ached for Nash and the professor. She didn't want to return to that world, but she didn't want to leave it either.

She remembered the story of Goddess Freyja. She helped people wake up and guide them into the battle *for* life. Freyja was the Guardian of heroes and heroines in love and war. Freyja Wolfe's journey had shown her strength of heart and purpose. She had found her way here, against all odds, discovering a world of magic she scarcely could have imagined before. It was incredible that there were so many dimensions at work, but she was awake, and perhaps this was *her* destiny, to help others, to step into her own as a powerful human, a powerful woman.

As Freyja realized her mission, her chest, arm, and shoulders crackled with a fiery affirmation to help others wake up. She stretched taller and bigger than ever before. The stones shimmered in her palm, and then slowly liquefied and melted into her veins, infusing her with their strength and power. Every cell in her body responded, urging her to step forward, to claim her birthright.

"Yes, I am Freyja Wolfe. I am the Guardian."

A chorus of harmonious voices were speaking as one:

"Hail Freyja. Human Be-ing magic. The Guardian helps others remember who they are. Powerful Be-ings here to heal. Humanity belongs to the Uni-verse, the song of One life. Free-dom is the kingdom. Great Spirit flows freely to every heart, animating all with one and one with all. Welcome to the lineage—keepers of the Light of Life. Thank you. We honor your life and your light. God speed on your path."

The dark priestess bowed at Freyja's feet and slowly backed away.

Before her stood a vast arena of smiling beings, all illuminated, famous faces with famous names, and other names long forgotten, all linked throughout time and space by their devotion to humanity and Earth. A chorus of grateful humming and singing enveloped her. She was overwhelmed by their embrace.

"Thank you," she said, tears streaming down her soul face.

"Thank you."

Humbled and awed, Freyja finally understood she was not alone. She felt intricately connected to all life, here and throughout the cosmos.

The void withdrew its cloak around her.

Freyja slowly emerged from the otherworld as though from a deep dream. The rain pelted the pool that rose around her face. It had risen to cover nearly all her mouth and soon would envelop her nose and drown her. Freyja bolted awake as though her life was in danger, which it was.

CHAPTER THIRTY-THREE:

ENERGY SHIFT

Freyja gasped violently. The water was in her nose, mouth, and ears. She spat it out, taking long and lusty wheezes so loud and hard they shook her ribcage. But she was still somehow bound and could barely move. The water had risen quickly over her head. Then she remembered the necklace that she wore. Seamus, the merman, had given her a necklace to breathe underwater. She relaxed into the watery pool and verified that she could indeed breathe. She glimpsed dark energetic webs Drake had wrapped around her, which were beginning to cut into her flesh, but their power was failing.

Drake's eyes darted left and right as he struggled to understand what was happening. Freyja had returned to her body, stronger and more potent than he expected. He slowly backed away and moved swiftly down the steps.

"Get back here!" she growled in an unearthly voice.

Drake scrambled down and away to join the commander. Freyja stood up to shake off the water, and then slowly fixed her eyes on Drake. He and his regiment of soldiers in black boots and khakis had rolled in some tent on a trailer. It splashed through the mud and sand and came to a stop next to them. With a nod from Drake, one of these men pulled down the tarpaulin from the top and threw it on the ground. It was a contamination unit probably, as there were some men in total containment suits hopping down and running wires to another device.

While crumbling under thousands of years of neglect and sand, the stone tower walls still towered over them. The spiral carving was part of a large mosaic of symbols on the floor. She crouched and crawled through the sandy muck and cleared as many symbols as she could. Her eyes widened as she recognized that they were the same symbols as those that scarred her body and decorated the box.

"Now what?" she asked herself. "What do I do?"

Below, Drake stood next to Commander Wayne. He was staring up at Freyja, shaking his conflicted head. He turned and nodded at the man holding the strange weapon, its crosshairs fixed directly on the girl. He fired the weapon.

Above, Freyja's knees buckled as the implant screamed inside her head.

Nash writhed against his wrist bindings. A pulsing beat echoed in his head. He tried to interrupt the pattern mentally, like he remembered from Sarana's teachings. The powerful feed to the weapons had a rhythmic pattern. He could hear it. What if he could disrupt it, interrupt it? At first, he struggled to will it to stop. But what if the power derived from a specific frequency? Nash intended to pound on the keys like a monkey and sabotage it somehow. He had nothing to lose. He strained his mind, and then instinctively, he started to hum. He played with his tone, to make it flat and then sharp. He hummed louder and louder, feeling his whole body vibrate in unison with the weapon, and then going sharper into the stream of sound. Then, the weapon's tone faltered, just a half tone. It was likely imperceptible to others, but Nash heard it and felt it!

Drake turned and shouted at the man with the gun. Why was it not working? "Fire again!"

Another bolt grazed through Freyja's head.

"Dad! Stop!" Freyja screamed in agony.

"Freyja, please. Surrender. We need you," came the sudden telegraphic voice of Eduardo.

Freyja narrowed her eyes viciously. *"I won't surrender to tyranny and fear!"*

"Look, Freyja, they have put a kill switch in your brain. They will take you out and everything here if you don't cooperate. You can do more by surviving."

Another sickening jolt of that weapon's fury coursed through Freyja's head, jarring every bone in her body. She fell to the ground, silent.

Nash lowered his head in defeat.

Down below, the gunman staggered in confusion. His gun hadn't fired at full power. He rapidly readjusted the wires and fixed his sights back to the precipice where Freyja had now fallen. Drake appeared annoyed, but raised a hand to the man with the gun, telling him to lower the weapon. He took a few tentative steps forward, eyes fixed on his lifeless daughter. Nobody moved.

But Freyja wasn't lifeless, only motionless.

"You're right," she whispered. "I can do more. I intend to survive."

Suddenly, with the power of a jaguar, Freyja sprang up to her feet to gasps from those down below. Her body outstretched as far as she could, she reached into the heavens. The highest star overhead beamed towards her, offering a bright pulse of energy, which Freyja now drew into her heart.

"What is she doing?" Drake shouted at his men. "Watch out! Disable her now!"

Some of them were distracted by the skies. They lit up like fireworks. Bolts of lightning rained down around them, crashing against the valley floor.

Meanwhile, Freyja started laughing, despite the daunting, painful situation. Her body and luminous field were almost alive with a thrilling power flow. As the implant's heat increased, Freyja focused her mind and thoughts on removing it and neutralizing it entirely.

Great Spirit, Mother Earth, Elements of Life, I ask for your assistance. Please help me to dissolve this harmful object in my body and be free from its control.

A massive bolt of lightning shot out of the sky, striking Freyja at her crown, rushing down through her spine. The charge threw her off her feet, and for a moment or two, she lay dazed but alive. Freyja touched the side of her head. There was a spot of black soot where the implant had been stung out of her skull. Rattled but determined, Freyja stood up and smiled at the men below.

"Take that!" she hooted and laughed. "Electric surgery! I'm free! I'm free!" she started to chant and dance around in euphoria, staggering to catch herself on the tower wall, aware of the immense power that had just shot through her flesh and bone. Her body was free of their control!

Freyja was ecstatic and yet still marveling at the reality of what she could do. She felt truly brave and powerful for the first time in her life. Freyja realized that she was the key. She could open this portal and restore this point on the grid of planet earth. Here is where change would begin with her and in Caral. She stood on top of the spiral and held her arms out. She focused her mind on her heart, where the *Brisingamen* was now beaming brightly out of her heart. A warm field of energy was building underneath of her. The spiral began to vibrate and glow.

Undeterred by all the lightning and failure of the Arktik implant, Drake sent orders to the commander on the ground. A laser cannon, a menacing final response, was moved into place.

"Shut her down!" his voice was shaky but determined. "Do it!"

A bright beam exploded from the weapon and blasted the side of the pyramid, sending hundreds of loose boulders and cracked pieces of stone, laid thousands of years before, crashing down around her. Freyja ducked for cover, but it was too late. Several chunks had already fallen. One sent her sprawling, while another crushed down on her leg, pinning her to the ground. She screamed in pain, and then cast her tear-dashed eyes down to Eduardo. He huffed and paced, his fists balling in anger.

"Again!" Drake cried out, turning to the commander who ordered the soldier to control the laser cannon to fire once more.

As he did so, it reached full capacity and fired. Eduardo sprang out from nowhere and threw himself in front of the laser beam. The noise was deafening. A giant burst of light erupted into the night sky as it collided with the boy's magnetic shield. Eduardo flew a hundred yards away, landing in a crumpled heap on the ground. He was motionless.

"What the hell are you doing, boy?" cried Drake. The explosion evaporated into space, and he and some of the soldiers rushed over to where Eduardo lay, his face and arms covered in cuts and bruises. To their amazement, Eduardo stirred and groaned. Then he pulled himself up and raised his hands as if ready for battle.

Drake gritted his teeth like a dog. "Stand down," he said.

"No. I won't let you hurt her. That wasn't part of the deal!"

"She made her choice."

Freyja realized that her leg was pinned under a heavy rock. It was crushing and searing into her flesh. She quivered, summoning the power to kick the rock off with her free foot. The boulder pressed deep into her bone as it crushed the rest of her leg and tumbled off.

Freyja grimaced. She attempted to block out any thought of her now crippled leg or the blood flowing from the gash in her thigh. She drew herself up onto the wall, staggering and wincing at the daggers of pain shooting through her damaged leg. She balanced her hip on the wall and stood, grimacing, but determined for some sign of what she must do.

Intuitively, she reached her arms out and called to the energies around the pyramid, in the cosmos, within herself, to gather and to energize this portal, power station, whatever the heck it was.

"Let's go! Start already!" she yelled into the ether.

Freyja gasped as a giant beam of light shot into the sky, from the center of the platform where she stood. The earth shook violently, knocking everyone to the ground. Freyja recoiled from the beam at first, but was quickly in awe as it arced into space and over the planet. It was the most beautiful rainbow of light she had ever seen. The waves resonated like beautiful chords of music through her body, the frequency of pure love. It was the melody again. She reached her hand into the flow of the beam and closed her eyes.

Mission complete.

In her mind, Sarana and Tommy stood beaming at her. Ursa descended, and urged Freyja to lie down and rest. She wrapped her leg in an energy band-aid, humming around brightly until the pain was gone.

"Thank you," said Freyja.

Freyja scooted herself over an opening in the wall and spied on the men below. The mercenaries were all standing around stunned. Dark webs lay shriveling at their feet. Many of the military men were dazed and confused, and then slowly overcome by joy. They started to laugh and dance together.

Eduardo was helping Nash and Professor Darnell to get up. The laser weapon was crushed. Drake was escaping in one of the helicopters.

A large group of curious people stood at the base as well. They were short in stature with giant smiles, colorful cloaks, and hats. They had a few smaller horses with them, as well.

"Who is that?" asked Freyja.

"These are the keepers of knowledge. They will teach you the ways and show you the path of a true warrior. They have kept and passed down the teachings from the beginning, from before the forgetting. This is your destiny, Freyja. You were made for this."

Ursa shimmered brightly next to Freyja, warming her with this understanding.

Calista sauntered up next to the base of the pyramid and waited for Freyja to join her. Ursa's surface reflected joy. For the first time, Freyja recognized her path, her purpose in life.

CHAPTER THIRTY-FOUR

THE HEART WAY

Freyja ran down the steps to hug Nash tightly.

"Are you okay?"

He smiled. "Yeah, a little bruised, but no big deal. I'll survive." He didn't want to let her go.

Professor Darnell grinned proudly. "Freyja, I cannot tell you how incredible this moment is for all of us. Your mother was right about you."

"What was she right about?" asked Freyja, eager to discover anything she could about her mother.

"She said you would never give up."

"I won't. Do you think my mom is still alive?" Freyja asked him.

"I'm sure of it. The question is where . . ."

Freyja pondered that and hugged him tightly. "I'm glad that you're okay. Thank you for helping us." She glared at Eduardo. "You can go away."

Eduardo, hands held out, took a few steps forward. "You don't understand. There are others. You have nowhere to go."

"I'll be fine," growled Freyja, turning away from him.

"Yes, we won the first inning. Congratulations. Let's all clap ourselves on the back . . ." Eduardo said sarcastically. "But don't think for a second the Nine will let this stand. You have no idea who you are dealing with here."

Meanwhile, on the battlefield, the soldiers had changed, transformed. One was shedding tears of joy. Another was singing a song with crazed delight. A couple of others were dancing and hugging each other.

"It appears there is a lot more happening here. Hope is alive," she said, staring at Eduardo forcefully.

An older Peruvian man suddenly approached and took Freyja by the hand. He had a delightfully warm smile, and he spoke an unfamiliar language. Somehow, his message felt clear to her anyway.

Eduardo nodded and relayed it to Freyja. "He says they wish to be of service on your mission."

"My mission? It's not over?" asked Freyja.

"Oh no, Freyja. You have no idea who you face. Cleaning up one pond does not fix the ocean. They'll send a mining operation in now. Or then there will be a natural disaster, what with their weather modification programs. War is the most efficient means of burying these sites," Eduardo said.

"Well, you can keep those stories. You are not welcome on this journey."

"Freyja, I wanted to stand up to them, but they threatened my mother. I do know of others who are resisting. I can take you there."

"You do?" she asked.

"Yes . . . Some were able to avoid being tracked, and others escaped as you have. But they must constantly move locations. It's not easy to find them."

"How do I know I can trust you, Eduardo?"

"How can you not?" He held her gaze and never flinched, not even for a moment.

She hated him for lying to her. Could she ever trust him again? Yet, he *was* her only connection to the others, whoever and wherever they were. He understood so much more about what was going on than she did.

The pyramid complex glowed in the light of cascading energy like a beacon of hope on the earth. Something in that energy stirred a tremendous sense of peace and faith. The serene and peaceful faces of the Indians standing before her warmed her heart. They waved and beckoned her to follow them. Freyja swung herself onto Calista, patting her side.

"I'm coming with you," said Nash, hopping onto Hard Ass.

Freyja studied Nash's face. "Are you sure?"

"Heck, yeah! I want to unlock my human potential." He laughed. "What are you going to do, professor?"

Professor Darnell appeared to be evaluating his options. Eduardo stood holding the rope of his black horse, waiting for Freyja's decision.

"You can come with us, but if I ever—and I mean *ever*—suspect you are withholding something or working against me, I will make you regret it," Freyja said sternly.

Eduardo laughed at Freyja's attempt to sound harsh. "I would never be so foolish again."

The professor said, "I wonder if you might need someone versed in the mythologies and esoteric concepts of the pre-Columbian civilizations to come along for the ride? I mean, I probably cannot return to my post at the university at this point anyway. So, if you will have me . . .?" he sighed with a wry smile.

"I would be honored if you would join us." Freyja reached out her hand to him. He swung his leg around and climbed on the back of Calista with her.

Freyja turned to take a final mental picture of the pyramid, with the powerful luminous beam flowing out into the atmosphere. A sea of clouds flushed the dusky skies with vivid watercolors and a serene mist. This fantastic journey had utterly changed her forever. Destiny and fate had conspired to set her on this path, and she had responded with a heart compass that she had no idea she possessed. The seeds her parents and aunt had planted had grown into the faith and determination she needed. The journey ahead was uncertain, but no more so than it had always been.

Freyja had so many questions, but this new boldness and confidence to face whatever might come was enough for now. Absorbing the reality that one of her most significant obstacles may be her own father gave her a terrible ache. She refused to relent to whatever belief system had hijacked his mind. She believed in his soul. And though she feared he might no longer be the man she once knew, that was not something she would dwell on.

Nor would she fall into the abyss of despair over her mother and imprisoned Aunt Lucy. Her mother was out there, somewhere. That she may be alive, this gave her hope. And she prayed for Aunt Lucy, that she would remain safely tucked away until she could get to her as well. She would not abandon them.

Freyja smiled, thinking about all the fantastic new friends she had met: Seamus, the merman, the tragic hybrid; Tommy, the wise elder; Eir, the Valkyrie. How many others were there? Where did they hide? Oh, the mysterious Ursa—an enigmatic spirit or perhaps an alien? Who or what was she that arrived out of the ether to transmit incredible knowledge? She shuddered, thinking of the dark mistress in the void. She hoped not to have to answer her riddles again. And then Sarana, her lynx Keyo forever shifted into a magical teacher. Despite the uncertainty before her, there was deep comfort in knowing they were all somehow by her side.

A jewel-colored hummingbird buzzed near Freyja as she adjusted herself to Calista. She laughed, as Nash bounced helter-skelter on Hard Ass ahead of her. This was not just her journey, after all. It was for all of them.